CARNIVAL WOLVES

ANCHOR BOOKS

DOUBLEDAY

NEW YORK LONDON

TORONTO SYDNEY AUCKLAND

CARNIVAL WOLVES

PETER ROCK

AN ANCHOR BOOK
PUBLISHED BY DOUBLEDAY
a division of Bantam Doubleday Dell Publishing Group, Inc.
1540 Broadway, New York, New York 10036

ANCHOR BOOKS, DOUBLEDAY, and the portrayal of an anchor are
trademarks of Doubleday, a division of Bantam Doubleday Dell
Publishing Group, Inc.

"Convalescence" has appeared previously in *Fourteen Hills*.
"Beware My Friend" has appeared previously in *Epoch*.
"Death's Door" has appeared previously in *Columbia*.
"The Submariners" has appeared previously in *Weber Studies*.
"Wilderness" has appeared previously in *American Short Fiction*.

BOOK DESIGN BY DANA LEIGH TREGLIA

Library of Congress Cataloging-in-Publication Data
Rock, Peter, 1967–
Carnival wolves / Peter Rock.
p.   cm.
I. Title.
PS3568.O327C37   1998
813'.54—dc21   97-44208
CIP

ISBN 0-385-49209-X

BVG 01

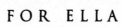
FOR ELLA

CARNIVAL WOLVES

THE EMPIRE STATE

DALMATIAN

Polyester is not one of those fabrics that breathes. On the hot days I walk back through the bottom of the gorge, where the air is cooler. Stone steps descend, over a hundred feet, and as flowers hang on for dear life along the cliffs, as trees reach down and stretch upward, the sound of the creek rises to meet me. The creek has run here for millions of years, wearing down shallows and digging pools beneath its falls. High above, the bridge spans the gorge. The bridge is metal, with holes in the bottom. Cars shake and echo as they pass; looking up, you can guess their make and model from their shadowy underbellies.

This is something that happened to me. I want to say it all, to see how it sounds.

The flagstones along the creek fit together, cracked by frost. I had been on my feet all day, walking. The college girls lay like sleeping mermaids along the stones. Their clothes folded and piled to one side, they held books frozen open in their hands, never turning a page, and the clear, cold water licked at them, pulled at their bathing suits as it reluctantly slid away. I would like to take off my shoes and sneak close, to run a finger along their throats. They are perfect, languid. I doubt if they have belly buttons, if they could unwind umbilical cords from inside themselves. I would like to take off my clothes and rest myself alongside them, our bare shoulders touching, our skin dulled by water. I would pull leeches from the backs of their smooth thighs, I would rub until sensation returned, I would ease snails from between their toes.

They did not look up until I was past them. I went around a bend, leaving the girls behind, my mind still turning them over. The gorge narrowed and I walked through the shadows, the walls closing in. The creek ran slower, deeper.

At first, looking up at the sound, I thought it was squirrels or maybe a raccoon—yet they are always certain of their holds, they do not lose their balance. The tree was collapsing in sections, top to bottom, the branches slashing down and then slapping back, loosening again. Birds escaped upward. I stopped walking to make sense of it. Flashes of white were coming down, hidden as the branches gathered, separated, and cracked. Spots of black stretched into lines. It was no mistake that I was there.

The dog came out headfirst with its legs swimming in the air; its eyes seemed to watch me as I stood motionless. It fell frantically, inevitably, all at once. I heard the splintering and the solid collision; the dog's body recoiled from the flagstones before it settled. Then, miraculously, it stood, took ten steps toward me, and collapsed again.

There was no time to doubt that this was happening. Branches and leaves were still coming down in its wake, and the dog was whining, crying. I leapt off the path, cupped my hands, brought water to where she lay. Her snout was caved in and thick blood ran out, and from her ears, and from her anus. I ran my hands over her skin and there did not seem to be any cuts— as if everything had been broken inside and held there.

A bird's nest lay on the flagstones; I could not see any eggs, cracked or otherwise. Flies were everywhere, as if they had followed the dog down through the sky. She was a dalmatian.

You're fine, I believe I was saying. Everything is perfectly fine. I could see the bridge from where I was kneeling, cars passing. Many students jump from that bridge each year—some say it's the stress, others say the damp clouds—and I've heard that sometimes the bodies roll along the bottom, held under the falls and beneath the rolling creeks, and don't surface until the runoff eases.

A small crowd had gathered. Someone had been shouting. The dog still lay on her side, bleeding, wheezing desperately as she tried to breathe through her broken face. It sounded as if teeth were lodged in her throat. I brought her more water. I said someone should go for help.

Aren't you a policeman? a man said.

I didn't know if I should pick the dog up myself, or if that might be exactly the wrong thing to do. People moved on once they'd lost interest. Others pushed their way past on the narrow path, breathing hard under backpacks, muttering to themselves. The blood was tracked all around, footprints growing fainter from where she lay.

A girl in a bikini top with a towel around her waist came barefoot down the path.

What did you do to your dog? she said.

All I could do was keep on with the water, with the words. I did not know what else to do and I could not sit still. Her eyes spun in their sockets. Her breath rasped and whistled. Then I saw the ambulance on the bridge, its red lights silently revolving. People were gathering on the bridge, looking over, hoping for disaster. In a few minutes the paramedics came down the path with their tackle boxes and their oxygen tanks.

Where are they? the one said.

Here, I said.

You all right?

It's the dog, I said.

Wait a minute, he said.

I heard the other one talking into his radio: It's a fucking dog. Yes, that's right. D-O-G.

What are you waiting for? I said. You already brought all that stuff down here.

Exactly, they said. Someone's going to have to pay for it.

The owner's name's on the tag, I said.

They turned away from me, whispered to each other, and then turned back. They told me this really wasn't their job.

Listen, I said. This dog is dying.

This went on for a while. When they finally took her, they

didn't even run with the stretcher. The dog whined when they hit the steps. I could not tell if she looked back at me.

I did not go with them. I had done my part. I slid my feet along the flagstones, trying to scrape the blood from my shoes as I continued on down the gorge. I followed the path to the bottom, where it let out onto the streets downtown, and I passed through all the shops that sell crystals and pottery, holographs, designer clothing.

Above the Chanticleer, the neon rooster was not yet turned on. A man wearing baseball cleats sat beneath it, bending wire hangers and adding them to a giant cage attached to the handlebars and seat of his bicycle. Keychains hung everywhere in the mesh, stuffed animals imprisoned here and there. The man looked up, past me, into the sky.

Inside, the felt of the pool table was worn down, stained and torn. Quarters lined the rail like silver eyes. I stood next to the skee-ball game and had a shot of Wild Turkey, sticky and sweet.

This area secure? the bartender said.

Enough, I said.

Outside, though, the man in the cleats was throwing an x-acto knife at a tree and talking about how it wouldn't stick. I could only agree as I passed him, as I kept on into my neighborhood. Down there, there are brick houses where the bricks are peeling away; they're just sheets of shingles, made to look like bricks. My house is like that. All the black guys laugh as I pass them, pointing at my uniform. It's ninety degrees and they're wearing sweatshirts with the hoods pulled up. They double over, just behind my back, and I keep going. At my house, I look back through the trees, all the way up to where the museum sits like a giant coffeemaker on the hill.

———†———

So-called indigenous peoples—from the rainforests or wherever they live—say we never look into the sky. They wonder how we can see what's coming. The fifth floor of the museum has windows all around and, looking down, I can vouch that this is true. I can see the small people below, their eyes on the ground in front of them.

From the windows I see the town below, the treetops, the lake deeper than anything, its bed cut by glaciers. Inside the museum, old people without their bifocals make me anxious. Children tangle my nerves. All the once-verdigris breasts of the bronzes have been burnished; all the genitals shine. We have two life-size Zorach bronzes, wrestlers, facing each other, and I've seen children stand between them, arms outstretched, with a hand around each penis. I've caught men pretending to sodomize them, joking with their friends, and I let them know that the moisture from a fingerprint can, over time, wear a hole in the metal. It's my job to tell them this, whether or not I believe it.

The other guards and I play a hand of poker at seven-thirty every morning; that tells us where we start, which floor, and then we switch at intervals, whoever's on break going up to the fifth and everyone moving down one. We do this all day, not speaking, just waving, nodding, descending. They all have children, trailers, problems we don't talk about. On the radios we refer to each other not by name, but by number, and even these numbers are not our own, but those on whichever radio we've been given that day.

They say I have done my job well if nothing changes. I watch the lush green jungles of Rousseau, lions and tigers with soft whiskers, their jaws almost smiling; they look too gentle and bewildered to trust. I ask you to step back from the Kandinsky full of stick horses, steeples, sharks in the waves. I'm not allowed to lay a hand on anyone, and to touch a mother's child is to invite untold wrath, curses upon your person and home. The paintings need constant temperature, constant humidity, and the machines never work. Polyester is not a natural fiber, it never kept anyone warm, animals don't grow it. I can whip off my clip-on tie in one motion, use it as a weapon. I am not allowed to touch anything or to touch anyone. I circle, turn a corner to meet the Giacometti who cannot escape me despite his long legs.

People get close. They want to touch the paintings, and this has made me a psychic of movements—I can tell what comes next, if someone will get closer or retreat out of my concerns. I myself go inside the paintings, hidden behind the flat slabs of the Léger, blindfolded in the Chirico but still looking out, watching you all pass, seeing myself—I know the creak of every floorboard, I have walked them all—listening as girls follow me, all long hair and unraveled sweaters, corduroys singing between their thighs, yawning and trailing perfume as I follow, as they hide behind sculptures. They watch me close.

When I am up on the fifth floor, early in the mornings, I catch flies against the huge windows and throw them back against the panes. I collect their dead bodies in my pockets. All the Asian art is on the fifth, but mostly people turn their backs to it. We have all sorts of Buddhas, ceramics from before time began, snuff bottles painted on the inside with paintbrushes of three horsehairs; we have landscapes on rice paper whose vertical symbols make children kick and karate-chop each other. People come up here for the panoramic view. They miss the delicate screens, the mahogany furniture, the sculpture of bone. When there is a fire in town, the people come here to watch it, to second-guess the firemen, and when someone jumps from the bridge they come to watch the rescue, the winches and ladders and trucks, frogmen in wetsuits, the stretcher spinning like a fat propeller at the end of its line. Standing there, at those windows, I could see the jagged white of broken branches, the very trees that slowed the dalmatian's fall, the edge she had failed to recognize.

If I could entice you to step back from the windows, if I could guide you by the shoulder, your hip, the small of your back, I could show you art that will straighten your hairs. All in gold leaf, men wearing turbans smile as they work themselves deep into women with rings on their toes, contortionists with their legs around the man's neck, jewels on their throats and arms, one hand down behind her, tearing at flowers—they are in a garden somewhere, on a bench—and the other deep in his beard, her ankles at his ears as beautiful birds and a sky full of insects pass overhead, watching it all.

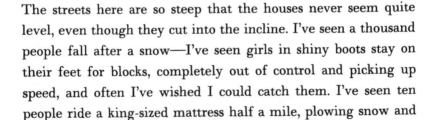

The streets here are so steep that the houses never seem quite level, even though they cut into the incline. I've seen a thousand people fall after a snow—I've seen girls in shiny boots stay on their feet for blocks, completely out of control and picking up speed, and often I've wished I could catch them. I've seen ten people ride a king-sized mattress half a mile, plowing snow and bouncing off cars, using nothing but gravity and screaming all the way down.

Now the snow is long melted and the cold has been replaced by damp heat that burns in your throat and boils in your lungs. All the insects are slow. The air is too heavy for them. I was looking for an address and I didn't know if I remembered it right. The number was odd, that was certain. I stayed on one side of the street, climbing up and down. Then she was there, the dalmatian, framed in a window, her tail slapping the pane. I turned onto the walk, waving to her.

The man opened the door before I even got to the porch. He was completely bald, standing there, waiting.

You some kind of policeman? he said.

Security guard.

Carry a gun?

If I did, I said, they'd have to pay me real money.

Small potatoes, he said, satisfied, and I was certain he knew I was the one.

I saw your dog fall, I said. Wanted to check on it.

He stood aside, opening the door. I was prepared to accept his thanks, to resist only to the point that I still got whatever reward he offered. Yet I did want to see her, I do admit that, that's why I was there. She looked fine, shying away from me. She stayed against the walls, far from where I stood. I really don't know why I expected or wanted her to show some gratitude, to remember me.

Second dalmatian I've had, he was saying, and the first one was stupid, too. Don't know what that says about me.

Right, I said.

They say she probably went after a squirrel or something and just went over the edge, you know, didn't see it.

Hypothetically, I said.

It looked like it was just the two of them. Cardboard boxes were stacked along the walls and I wondered what they held, if he would hang cheap prints of ballerinas or some such thing. Now there was only a calendar hanging there, a hashmark of days under a photograph of a dalmatian sitting next to a sand-castle. August.

I searched for eyebrows, I wondered if he was one of those people who's allergic to their own hair. He was saying she'd cracked a few ribs, but didn't break a single bone. What happened was her teeth got knocked into her nasal cavity, and then they just pulled them back down and she could breathe all right. She looked fine, shying away from me. I really wanted her to open her mouth. I wanted her to come close so I could see her teeth, so I could listen to her breathe. The skin around her lips seemed too pink.

Well, he said. Now you've seen her.

You putting up a fence? I said.

No, he said. If she didn't learn her lesson, well, that would serve her right.

If I said he was not much bigger than I am, that would be a lie. He stood with his arms crossed, the wings of his nostrils flaring, shifting his weight from leg to leg.

Do you know, he said, how much an ambulance costs? What with just moving here, I have enough to worry about. If I got my hands on whatever fool called that ambulance.

I think there was some misunderstanding about the ambulance, I said. I pointed at the dog, nodded, slapped my hands together, and went for the door.

About the only thing worse than having a dog stupid enough to fall off a cliff, he said, is having to pay for it. I can tell you that.

I believe it, I said.

Once the door closed behind me, I went around to the side of the house, walking atop flattened cardboard boxes, and tried to see into the backyard. Through a window I saw the man's broad back as he crossed a day off the calendar. At the chain-link gate I saw how the yard ended abruptly, no fence, straight into the treetops. I wanted to go all the way back, to look over that edge, but just then the dog began barking at me through the glass. As I was thinking that she must remember me, that she connected me with the fall—that explained it, her fear—the man turned and crossed the room, looking down through the glass at me, neither smiling nor frowning. He put his hand on the dog's head and she was quiet. I turned and walked away.

The break room is far underground and there are no windows. Twice a day I sit for fifteen minutes, half an hour at lunch, my feet up on the table, resting my legs, drinking chocolate milk and eating potato chips, cheese crackers with peanut butter, whatever the machines offer. There's a dictionary down there, for people struggling over crosswords, and that's where I learned a little about dalmatians.

If other employees come in I don't have conversations with them; I am not used to talking in the museum. They think that I'm quiet, dependable, a self-starter, and I let them, for I know I'm overpaid. I clip my tie back on, stand, and take the elevator up to the fifth floor. I do my job, though I'm not even qualified to straighten a crooked painting—there are men who are, who wear white gloves, who get health insurance and paid vacations.

I watch how the museum wears people out. Their minds are not used to it, the attention the paintings demand. We have triptychs of heaven and hell that torturers could learn from; fold in the hinges and the paintings would press their colors together—angels would make love to the tormented souls, become one with those whose parts are mixed with animals'. People have to sit down after something like that.

Don't you get bored? they ask me, and I say, Absolutely not.

True, this would be an easy place to steal from; you wait until the guard is out of view, wait until I am in another gallery, and simply take a painting off the wall, put it under your arm, and run out the front door. That's it. Even if you agree it would be easy, I know you won't do it. I don't even bother to follow you, not unless you are the girl who held the smooth bronze belly of a Moore and told me she couldn't help herself. I wondered, slowly shaking my head, how far would that excuse get me with you? My hands would follow that curve, over the sharpness of hips, the skin so warm and lazy. Baby, I want to say, I know about irony, I can tell you've noticed how my hair is working today, that you want me to practice one-handed with the buckle of your belt.

This started as a true story and now, looking back, I want to clarify a few things, to admit some others. These young women, for instance, don't even notice me, that's the truth—they are not alarmed to be alone on a floor of this whole huge building with me, even when it's just the two of us surrounded by all that art. They don't meet my eyes because they don't recognize the possibility.

I have never been caught. I will never be caught. My fingertips tickle canvases. I lick paintings. I taste the colors. And yes, I suppose my hands are dry when I do it, when I run my fingers along the cold metal, stroking arms, cupping breasts, rubbing the ancient wooden belly of the Buddha. Hardly anyone visits the museum, after all, and I unzip my fly and press myself against polished verdigris torsos, finding their navels. On the fifth floor I move silently, behind the tall windows, and hold myself against

Shiva, against those cold thighs, as the many arms close around me—long nails sharp at my neck, my back, my legs. Held there, I read the card on the wall. Shiva is the destroyer and restorer of worlds.

My truck does not like the hills. My emergency brake is broken and so I park with my front tires cut sharp into the curb. I try to walk like a meter reader, all business—I am, after all, wearing a uniform.

There are no neighbors in the windows. I go through the gate, past her empty dish. In the middle of the yard is a picnic table, paint chewed from its crossed legs.

She does not run from me. I walk a slow circle around her, to cut off the cliff. I hear the creek below me, the voices of mermaids. She stands her ground as I back her up against the house, and then she leaps out and she has my hand in her mouth. She is quick, ferocious, but I am prepared; I just hold her there, onto her lower jaw. Her teeth cut me even though they are still healing, still loose. I try not to hurt her, not to let her hurt herself as I wrestle her around and get the rope in a slipknot around her neck. I do not cry out and give us away. Her front legs are off the ground, raking the air, and her whole hind end is lashing back and forth like an alligator's.

I get her turned and I almost fall over; she gasps, lets go of my hand, is pinned between my knees. I try to drag her. Her shoulders and haunches bunch up, her nails line the cement, her collar pulls folds of skin around her head. Finally I pick her up, keeping her head as far away from my face as possible.

Out on the street, two men slow down, looking at us.

She knows we're going to the vet, I say. She hates it. I get the door with one hand and force her into the truck.

Driving is easier than I had feared. She sits pressed against the passenger door, growling from time to time. I almost hope for sirens, yearn for some pursuit; I'd welcome the chance to account for my actions, yet no one pays us any attention.

We head out of town and it doesn't matter which way. Carefully, I open her window enough so she can get her head out, but not enough so she can jump. We climb onto the flat lands, past dairies and gravel pits. It won't rain. It will only turn darker, hotter. The clouds are heavy; if they came unbalanced, if the cables snapped, they'd crush buildings, leave craters. The dampness collapses houses here. Roofs sag and the sides rot away so there's nothing but beams and studs, walls starting again five feet off the ground. Houses under construction seem abandoned half finished—mold climbs up new plywood.

We pull off the highway, into a rest area, pointed roofs over tables, maps behind plexiglas. I let the truck idle, the engine jerking its belts in circles. I stare through the windshield. I try to think.

A woman comes around one of the structures. Middle-aged, in terrycloth shorts and a baseball cap, she leads a puppy at the end of a leash. The puppy chews at her sandals, trips over its own paws. The woman bends down, smiling, and lets the puppy lick her face. For some reason, then, I believe this woman would provide a better home. She seems caring, attentive, kind. I look sideways at the dalmatian; she's not even paying attention. I turn off the ignition, roll down my window.

Hey, I say. The woman does not look up. I'm talking to you, I say.

She steps in our direction, wary.

Your dog must be lonely, I say, pointing.

Why's that?

Come closer, I say, but she will not.

There's something wrong with your dog, she says.

That's my blood on her, I say. She's a good dog.

The dalmatian is pressed against the other door, breathing hard. There's blood on her coat, where I held her. Her spit is smeared along the window. She came down out of the sky and survived the fall, showed me how gradually I have fallen—how I never touch, never really talk to another person. My fingers tremble with anticipations, I am full of words. I am hardly a person at all.

What you have there is a problem dog, the woman says.

She's not a problem dog, I say. You can't have her.

What? she says.

I'm the one who saved her, I start to say, but then I stop. Of course I should have known that consequences stick and tangle, that good deeds find their punishments. I stare at the woman as if we'd had no conversation at all.

My husband's just around the other side, she says. He has two friends. You try anything and they'll be here in a second.

I can't believe this, I say, and turn the ignition.

Back on the highway, we keep moving, away, further from where we started, away from the museum, where I will never return. There's blood on the steering wheel, sticky between my fingers, the road stretching out.

Your life just took a turn for the better, I say to the dog, trying to convince us both.

Truth is, I could abandon her right here; I could leave her with some firemen somewhere. I tell her what I've learned. Dalmatians are inbred, skittish, flat-out dimwits, can't be trusted with children, always land on their feet. Sometimes they're called coach dogs, carriage dogs. They come from some part of Yugoslavia, or whatever it is now, and I look out the window and can't imagine it's all that different. Driving, I stare straight ahead; I can hardly look at her. When I do, my dog is watching me with dull eyes, curling her upper lip to show me her teeth. It's all I can do to return her smile.

TRAMPOLINE

Paul had spent hours watching wrecking balls, bulldozers moving debris, but he had never seen a building taken all at once, folded in on itself. He imagined they left the top stories full of things not worth saving—it made no sense to carry them all the way down when gravity would do it. Tomorrow he could go and see what remained. Today he stood on a rooftop, across the East River from the building that would be demolished. An overpass ran fifty feet away, below him, cars weaving around each other. Barges moved slowly up the river, waves slapping along their sides; somewhere beneath the surface, the Midtown Tunnel snaked full of cars and people, all breathing underwater; farther up, by 60th, helicopters nearly collided between Manhattan and Roosevelt Island.

A friend had lent Paul a key to the building where he stood now. The rooftop was bare, covered in gravel. Unfolding the legs of his tripod, he looked over the edge, down onto the roof of the next building over—an empty pigeon cage, a tall antenna, a round black circle that could be some kind of vent or even a garden, full of fertile soil. He screwed the telescope onto the tripod and squinted through it.

Paul worked for a company that insured such demolitions; this was how he knew when buildings would be taken. The building to be demolished today was in Queens, all the way across the river. He followed the shoreline, focusing in tight until he found it. Long abandoned, its lower windows were boarded up; in some, chalk people had been drawn, looking out, women in dresses or naked, breasts like fried eggs, arms of chalk lines stretching off the plywood and along the bricks. The upper windows were empty, framed in broken glass.

Closer, beneath him, cars moved in both directions, the lanes of the overpass separated by ten or fifteen feet. Through that space, Paul saw a man standing on the riverbank, facing Queens. The man turned toward Paul, then away again. Paul lifted the telescope and trained it down. The man was heavy, wearing a baggy blue sweatsuit and basketball shoes. He was black, bald, his beard white; turning again, he seemed to point something at Paul. Paul squinted, frustrated. The telescope would not focus so close. Again, the man turned and pointed at him.

Paul stepped back and checked his watch. He shielded his eyes from the sun, trying to figure what the man wanted. With two hours until the demolition, Paul slapped his pocket to be certain he had the key, then crossed the rooftop and went down one flight of stairs. He hit the button and waited, but the elevator did not come. To his right, a door was marked STAIRS. Ten stories, twenty flights, cutting back and forth. Windows ran along the stairwell, one every other flight. Paul paused, uncertain of a motion in his peripheral vision.

A girl was flying. She rose and fell, her joy apparent; she flew above the rooftop of the next building over. Only the span of the alley, the pane of glass, separated them. Paul realized that what he had mistaken for a vent or garden was actually a trampoline.

Outside, on the street, the air was thick, hard to breathe. Paul walked under the overpass, the cars above; graffiti gave way to dirt, chain-link fences held trash as if they'd been dragged like nets through the streets. The man was not far away, standing perfectly still, facing the water. He turned, a fishing pole in his hand, then cast his bait farther out.

It should have been clear to Paul from above—it was just that fishing in the East River never would have occurred to him. Three fish lay pale on the gravel, not even gulping at the air, clearly dead.

"Plan on eating them?" Paul said.

"Hell, no." The man turned, a pole in his hands. "Think I'm insane? I just line them up there so every fool that walks by doesn't say 'caught anything?' "

"Seems like a waste," Paul said.

"Instead," the fisherman said, "what I get is people acting like these things do some good out there. They were biting better earlier. Damn heat."

Slabs of concrete slanted up along the river, cracked and tilting away from each other. Plastic bags and other flotsam jerked by. The fisherman cursed as seagulls hovered and settled, trying to move in on the fish. The sun did not ease. Cars honked overhead. Paul tried to stand in the shadow of a girder.

"Good morning," the fisherman said, looking past him.

Paul turned to look at the skinny man who had come up behind him. The man wore a baseball cap that said CAP'N above the brim; his pants were dark blue polyester and his shirt bore a patch in the shape of a badge. SECURITY, it said. A knotted rope, a piece of clothesline, stretched from his hand. At the other end, a dalmatian strained its nose toward the fish, then wagged its tail as the fisherman scratched behind its ears.

"How you doing?" the man said to Paul. Setting the rope down, he stood on top of it, then eased a pack from his back and took off his shirt.

"I'm all right," Paul said.

"This looks like a pedigreed dog," the fisherman said.

The other man did not answer. He folded his shirt and put it in his pack. A few dark hairs circled his nipples, making them look like spiders. His pants rode low, revealing the sharp bones of his hips.

"Catch these fish," he finally said, "or just buy them from some fishmonger?"

"What?" the fisherman said. "Let's talk about this dog. What would you say she's worth?"

"These fish," the other man said, pulling the dog away, "they look freshwater, not even from around here. Even if the dog was for sale, I'm not so certain I'd trust you with her."

"What?" the fisherman said.

"Just based on what I've seen here."

Paul checked his watch, stepping backward. The two men were paying him no attention; their voices did not falter as he turned away. He hurried back under the overpass, in through an open doorway, onto the stairs. This stairwell had no windows, and still he climbed, taking two steps at a time.

At the top, a door was propped open with a piece of cinderblock. Paul stepped into the sun. Along one side of the rooftop, cars churned past, closer now. The shapes of tools—a hammer, pliers, a circle that must have been the bottom of a bucket— were pressed into the tar. Broken glass and bottlecaps were held fast.

Paul went around the long cage, feathers in the wire, and then he saw her. Her skirt kicked around her waist, her long hair straight up before crashing down to hide her face. The trampoline's legs dug into the tar, scarring it. He moved closer.

"My name's Alicia," she said, spacing it out so she said every word in midair.

"Paul," he said.

"Guess what?" she said.

He could hardly see her dark eyes as she squinted into the sun. She was no more than eleven, twelve years old. There were runs in her black tights, snakes of flesh up her legs, red polish where her toes poked through.

"I pretended to be sick so I didn't have to go to school," she said. "Come closer." Not bouncing now, she slid her feet along the black trampoline; she reached out her finger and shocked his nose. He leapt back. She laughed.

"Want to jump?" she said.

"No."

"What are you afraid of?" she said. "I'm not afraid of anything at all."

"I believe it," he said.

"Think I'm afraid of you?"

"Why would you be?"

"You're a stranger," she said.

"I told you my name."

"Still," she said. "Come on."

"No."

"How did you know I was up here?" she said.

"I didn't."

"Then why did you come?"

"I don't know," Paul said, looking up at her. "I used to do this," he said.

"All right, then," she said.

"I could do a back flip."

"Couldn't," she said.

Paul untied his shoes and set them next to hers. He pulled himself up, across the springs, and stood next to the girl, his hands out for balance. The top of her head just reached the middle of his chest.

"Jump," she said.

"Alicia," he said, testing it out, remembering. The trampoline was ten feet from the edge of the building, and to be airborne made him anxious, as if a sudden breeze or a shift in gravity might pull him sideways and down. He kept jumping.

"Nice bracelet," she said. "Bracelets are for girls."

"Nice necklace," he said, watching as the cheap chain bounced along her chest, twisting and untwisting, circling her smooth neck.

"Closer," she said. "Bounce right before me, so I can steal your bounce."

"Like this?"

He was rising as she fell, falling as she rose; it was difficult to see her face, all her hair slashing around. Her mouth open, white teeth, eyes wide, her perfect ears. The rooftop next door stretched higher. He could just see his telescope, angling down from the tripod.

"I saw all the way past the cars, out to the river!" she said. "Again! Closer to me."

The hem of her skirt snapped against his legs; they rose and fell, faces only two feet apart, just out of sync.

"Closer," she said, bending her knees to time it right, not to waste the bounce. He smelled the shampoo, sweet apples, in her hair as he watched their feet against the black fabric of the trampoline. She landed right after him and he felt his rebound dampened.

At an angle, she wheeled past him, sideways. Her head just missed his, her hair in his face, her feet twisting over them both. Upside down, in midair, she screamed, and he felt the shrillness in his bones. Still wheeling, she came down, one of her arms straight through the springs. Her head rang on the metal pipe. Her body wrapped around the pipe, then disappeared beneath the trampoline.

Paul hit his own head on the bar, trying to go under, after her. He pulled her out, into the sunlight. She was not moving, but she was breathing. His head on her ribs, the bones of her chest, he listened. He stared low, the heat shivering the air, strands of her hair hanging from the thick springs. His knees burned, the tar through his pants. Searching her dress, he found a pocket, then a key. A square of masking tape bore the number 502.

He shuffled across the rooftop, toward the door. Her feet brushed the wall and she whimpered, alive; he shifted her body so her waist bent over his shoulder, her head hanging down his back. He took the stairs slowly; he could not see his feet. Voices rose from a floor below and he struggled with the key, trying to hurry, not wanting to be discovered.

When he set her on the couch in the front room, he felt the blood on his back. She was still breathing. The key bounced and settled on the floor where he dropped it.

Paul left her there. In the bathroom, his hands were steady, calm. He pulled the mirror right off the wall, mistaking it for the door of a cabinet, then kicked it out of the way. Under the sink, he found a bottle of rubbing alcohol.

She had gotten up from the couch.

"Alicia," he said. "Alicia."

He found her standing in the kitchen. She did not seem to hear his voice. She moved half balanced, like a sleepwalker, her face turning like a flower to light, nothing more. He was not sure if he should touch her, try to wake her. She started down the hallway, bouncing gently from wall to wall, and he followed. She went through a doorway, into a room, and collapsed onto the bed. Paul sat next to her.

She would need stitches, at least. Perhaps she had a concussion, though he was not sure how to tell. The right thing to do would be to call the paramedics, and he was going to get to that. Uncapping the alcohol now, he poured some into his cupped hand, spilling cold between his fingers, and then he splashed it onto her head, where the blood was thickest in her hair.

A person could not scream like that and not be all right, he told himself. He held her down because she would only hurt herself, thrashing around, and there was nowhere to run. He circled her thin arms with his own.

Finally she was quiet again, resting. Paul saw where the hot tar had burned her arms. He smoothed her dress. The window opened into the alley. A nightgown lay twisted on the floor; the

short bed was unmade. Through the window he saw the building across the alley, someone going up the stairs. He held Alicia
still, smoothing the folds of her dress. She might have fallen
asleep; he held on to her, stroking her leg.

She whimpered, then went silent again. He looked into her
ear, its folds, uncertain if blood had gathered there or was rising
from inside. All he could hear was her breathing and his own; he
could not tell if there was something else. Standing, he stepped
into the hall. He heard footsteps.

The doorknob turned by itself, as if by a ghost. The front
door opened, and a man stepped into the hallway. He stood
looking at Paul; his face was angry, his mouth twisted down.
Blood marked the wall between them—handprints, the brushing
of her hair. The man wore a suit. He was a head shorter than
Paul. Paul wanted to say he didn't know where to begin, yet he
could not even get those words out.

"Where is she?" The man stepped closer, forcing Paul back
into the room. He went right around Paul and then he had
Alicia in his arms and had spun around, past him again.

Paul sat down on the bed, trying not to make any noise,
waiting for the man to leave, to forget him. Suddenly the door
slammed shut. Paul heard another door slam, and then it was
silent. The man had not even touched him, but Paul felt as if
he had.

A report card rested on the windowsill, Alicia's whole name
printed across the front. On the bulletin board, a series of photographs showed her getting older a year at a time. Crayon draw-
ings of animals—elephants and giraffes, tigers and apes—circled
the walls; they chased each other, high up by the ceiling. Paul
sat on the bed and still it was silent, still no one came.

His watch said three o'clock. He went to the window, but

could see nothing beyond the tightness of the alley. He knew the building across the river would fold in on itself. Its upper two-thirds, twenty-five or thirty stories, would remain intact at first, falling straight down as if dropped from above, piercing the earth and now heading for its liquid core. Dynamite or plastic explosives, precise calculations made by engineers and physicists that would limit collateral damage. All stress would be relieved at once. Years of strain gone like that. At the window, he could not even be certain the light had changed, if dust filtered the sun.

"Wait," he said, just to hear his own voice.

Two glass jars full of pennies stood atop the dresser. He opened a drawer and touched the soft balls of her socks, the puckers of elastic in her panties. A tiny tree held earrings; all different colored ribbons hung over the top of the mirror, multiplying themselves. He pulled a few loose, bunched them up, and put them in his pocket.

The door would not open. The lock was on the other side, and so were the hinges. He stepped back and threw his body against it, then gave that up. The window was open, but it was a long way down. Sirens came closer, passed by, faded again.

The jar of pennies weighed at least fifteen pounds. He held it in both hands, carrying it across the room; first he looked down into the alley, then he threw the jar out the window. It shattered below, spilling copper in a perfect circle. Paul could barely hear it. He waited. No one came. The second jar was already in the air when the man stepped into the alley.

"Watch out!" Paul shouted.

Hands over his head, the man ran in the wrong direction— the jar missed him by five feet, coins exploding around his ankles.

"Jesus Christ!" he said, turning his baseball cap backward to look up. It was the shirtless man; his dalmatian was nowhere in sight.

"I'm locked in!" Paul said. "Fifth floor!"

"What number?" the man said.

"I don't remember!" Paul pulled the key from his pocket, but it was the wrong key. He leaned out the window. "This side!" He watched as the man disappeared from the alley. Two seagulls hovered above the coins, settled near them, then moved on. He turned away from the window. He pulled the bracelet from his wrist, opened Alicia's drawer, and hid the bracelet in her clothes, where she would find it.

He could hear the man coming, crashing noises from farther inside the building.

"Yes!" a voice said.

Paul listened to footsteps in the hall, the lock snap back, and then the door swung open. The man just stood there, gasping, sweat on his skinny chest.

"Put down the ax," Paul said. "Easy there."

The man looked at the long ax in his hands and smiled. He rested its head on the floor, but did not let go of the handle. He reached out his other hand for Paul to shake.

"Call me Alan," he said. "Now let's not just stand around here."

Paul followed Alan out of the apartment. He saw that the doorknob had been taken cleanly off the front door, that now it rolled along the floor.

"Wild," Alan said, hanging the ax in its place on the wall. "How they leave this where anyone can get hold of it." Cloth firehose looped like intestines at their feet; Alan picked it up in both arms, then dropped it again.

"Hey!" a woman said. She stood a little farther down the hall, in front of her scarred door, a loose doorknob in her hand.

"Can't wait," Alan said. He took hold of Paul's arm and they ran down the stairs, back and forth until they were out on the street.

They walked away from the building, toward the river. Paul looked back once and saw the two piles of pennies shining in the alley. Ahead, the dalmatian sat next to the fisherman, looking out at the river. Paul followed Alan; the noise of the traffic covered the sound of their approach. When Alan picked up the loose end of the leash, the dog saw him and cringed.

"Thought you'd abandoned her," the fisherman said.

"I didn't," Alan said.

"I have money," the fisherman said. "And the dog likes me. Look at her, now that you're here."

The dalmatian shivered, her eyes glancing sideways, her nails scrabbling along the concrete.

"Freshwater," Alan said. "You don't know about her, everything that's happened." He turned to Paul. "Let's go," he said.

"I caught these fish," the man was saying behind them. "I have no idea what you're talking about."

Paul walked along next to Alan, the dog trailing. It was then he realized he was in stocking feet, that he'd left his shoes up on the rooftop. Black tar had dried along the heels of his socks, under the balls of his feet. The street was warm.

"You should take off your shirt," Alan said.

"That's all right," Paul said. "I'm fine."

"No, you're not fine. You got blood all over your back." Alan pulled his shirt from his pack and handed it to Paul.

The shirt was tight around his shoulders; the bottom did not reach his belt, and the SECURITY patch scratched his chest.

"I think I'll get going," Paul said.

"What?" Alan said. "Where?"

"Thanks."

"Wait," Alan said. "Just a little time. Company. You owe me that."

"I don't know," Paul said.

"Of course," Alan said, "it's nice to believe there are selfless acts. I'd like to believe that. It's not really like you owe me anything."

"All right, then. Whatever." Paul looked out across the river. A cloud lingered there, coloring the sunlight, dust still settling. He had missed it.

"That girl," Alan said. "She was in pretty bad shape."

"Who?"

"I saw them come out. Who was that with her, her old man?"

"I don't know."

"And here you are, walking around wearing a bloody shirt!"

"I didn't do anything," Paul said. "There was an accident." He did not like the sound of his voice.

"Don't get me started on accidents," Alan said. "People are never, ever understood when they're trying to do something good. I've sure learned that one. You're always misunderstood because no one expects your actions, everyone doubts your motives. It's real cynical."

"A trampoline," Paul said.

"Whatever," Alan said. "Let's go down here."

The steps led under a building; the bar was half hidden, below ground level. Paul followed Alan down, the dog trailing behind—no one said anything about bringing her inside.

"Let's sit at the bar," Alan said. He brought out another shirt, just like the first, and put it on, so the two of them looked like twins.

The ceiling was low. A few people sat at tables behind them. Paul felt the cold rail under his feet. In front of him, painted on the bar, was the number 11; Alan had 12, and all the seats were marked like this. Alan pointed at a kind of roulette wheel behind the bar.

"Every odd hour they spin that thing," he said, "and if it lights on you the house covers your drinks. We got ninety minutes."

The bartender set down two beers; Alan looked at Paul before paying for them.

"Should have brought those pennies," he said. "You almost hit me with that second one."

"Listen," Paul said. In the mirror behind the bar he saw himself, and Alan, in their shirts. The mirror was close, so it seemed there were four of them sitting there. Quadruplets.

"You live here a long time?" Alan said, cutting him off. "Ever think of moving?"

"Not really. I've worked for the same company over ten years now—insurance—so I'm pretty well set."

"Here we are!" Alan said. "Security and insurance. I can't remember ever feeling so comfortable and relaxed." He smiled ironically at Paul, one eyebrow raised.

"I'm used to living here," Paul said. "That's all."

"Exactly," Alan said. "I've been upstate for a while, but it's not much better than the city ever was. People. You and your little girl, for instance."

"What?"

"West," Alan said. "I'm moving on. I've worked as a security guard, a waiter, a mechanic, whatever—I got all number of irons in the fire and they're all stone cold."

"It was an accident," Paul said.

"I don't believe in accidents," Alan said. "Coincidences, neither."

"It was a mistake I was there at all."

"You think it was a mistake," Alan said. "More like a subconscious premonition, you know, nothing overboard—you didn't know why you went up there until now, later, when it's clear why you were there."

"I don't know about that."

"Well, you had your fun, anyway."

"Wait a minute," Paul said.

"Dalmatians," a man said. "They're real high-strung."

"Now that," Alan said, turning away from Paul. "That varies dog to dog."

Paul counted the bottles behind the bar. He felt like he'd done something wrong. Ashamed, and he was not sure why. The windows by the door, up by the ceiling, were at street level. Feet walked past. He asked the bartender for a phone book, then wrote the numbers on his hand with a ballpoint pen. He palmed a few coins from the bar and no one noticed.

"Have to make a call," he said to Alan, but Alan was talking to the other man, bending down over the dog.

The phone was in the back of the bar, a kind of booth built into the wall. Paul closed his eyes and remembered Alicia's last name, from the report card. Even with the glass door closed he could still hear Alan's voice. Paul felt the bump on his forehead, from the metal frame of the trampoline. He opened his eyes and saw them jerking back and forth in the door's reflection.

He called three hospitals, and each one told him the same thing—that they could not identify patients over the phone. They could neither confirm or deny; that was the policy.

"This is her father," he told the last one.

"You're not her father," the woman said.

"He's there, isn't he?" Paul said. "Is the girl all right? Alicia?"

The line went dead. Paul opened the door and stepped back into the bar. Alan had the dog on his lap and was pulling back its lip to show its teeth. The other man wasn't even looking at the dog. Ducking so his head wouldn't show in the mirror's reflection, Paul went for the door.

As soon as he was outside, he began to run, straight down the sidewalk, his bare feet making no sound. He'd gone four blocks in the wrong direction before he realized where he was, and then he slowed, went two blocks over, and headed back the way he'd come. Between buildings, he saw the lights of boats in the dusk. The wind cooled. People shouted for cabs, asked for money, walked with downturned eyes and then tried to sneak glances, to learn something from his face.

At first the key wouldn't fit, then it did. He waited for the elevator and rode it up, the button alight under his finger. He leapt onto the stairs, up the last flight and onto the dark rooftop. Cursing, he thought his telescope had been stolen; then he saw the tripod had fallen over. He picked it all up, careful of his footing, then looked out over the cars' headlights, to the boats on the river and the buildings that remained across it, their windows lighted in random patterns.

Walking to the side of the rooftop, he looked down onto the building next door. The round trampoline was darker than the night; it sat like a round hole bored through the building's center. Turning, Paul went back through the door, into the stairwell, counting the flights as he descended. He stopped halfway down and looked through the window.

Headlights cut high up in the alley, slid away, and were replaced by new ones. Alicia's window was less than twenty feet away, dark. Paul thought about what Alan had said, about the premonition; he wondered if he had touched Alicia, if he had wanted to, and what the difference might be.

He stood a long time in the darkness, staring across the alley. A light went on. He circled his bare left wrist with the thumb and forefinger of his right hand. Alicia wore her nightgown; a white bandage covered one side of her head. Beautiful, she winced as a yawn pulled her skin. Her hand went up to touch the side of her head, but she did not touch it. Paul tapped on the glass; he found a light switch and flicked it on, then off, shocked by his reflection, the numbers on his hands, the ink smeared on the white metal of the telescope. Alicia did not notice him. She did not yet miss her jars of pennies. Paul felt the tangle of ribbons in his pocket. He tried to guess their colors without looking.

CONVALESCENCE

Neville could no longer read a book without his glasses, and he had not even been compensated with the ability to see great distances. He sat at the table, looking out the window. This is what he thought he saw: a duck, attempting to take off from the river, caught the bottom strand of a fence stretched across the shallows. The duck splashed down, then limped off, doomed, into the tall grass.

Three hours he'd been awake, and Alicia had not yet risen. Something had happened to the girl, down in the city, something no one seemed clear about—he was inclined to take her word and leave it at that. He was composing a letter to Ronald that would ease this imposition. It had never been a good idea and he wasn't certain how he'd agreed to it.

The words he wrote would not straighten on the page. They trembled. His ears were so good he could hear the hands of his watch now, if it weren't for the scratching of the pen. He turned, but there was no sound, nothing there except the room, the clear plastic breathing in the doorways. Winters, he sealed off half the house, so he wouldn't have to heat the rooms he didn't use. He never broke the seal; things were lost for months. None of the drawers in the house matched their dressers—Alicia had noticed that—but over the years they had been forced to fit. He did not know how that had started. Now the drawers would not fit the dressers they'd been made for.

"What do you do when I'm not here?" she said.

"Think that's your business?" he said. "Why don't you get dressed?" Yet when he turned she was dressed, smiling at him, hands behind her back.

"I've been up for a long time," she said. "You just haven't noticed. I ate toast and honey. I walked right in behind you and saw what you were writing to my dad."

It wasn't as if his blood was wrapped up in this, as if they were relations. Her father said she had changed, but this appraisal did not impress him. Young girls changed, after all—anything else would be a cause for concern. And Neville had never believed that children were better off in the country than in the city. That was a sentimental notion caught up in memories people pretended to have.

"I can write better than this," she said, holding out a sheet of paper. "Found it."

He took it from her. The sheet was covered in rows of numbers, the alphabet, simple words, facts. He had been practicing his handwriting to keep it from falling apart. My name is Neville Miller, it said. I live where my family has always lived, upstate, and that's how I like it. The girl was laughing at him. In the window now the clouds scraped down, giving themselves away only through motion. They were the same color as the sky.

Folding the paper, he faced her again. Alicia's hair was shaved all along one side and there were stitches in her scalp. If she shaved the other side she'd have a perfect Mohawk—he was saving that joke in case he needed to put her in her place. The skin along her jaw was rough and pink, where she'd peeled scabs.

"Why did they bring me here?" she said.

"I told you. I was a friend of your grandfather's."

"Who died."

"He's no longer with us, that's right."

"Dead," she said.

"Yes. And I knew your father when he was a boy."

Ronald had set him up, saying, Believe me, I'm doing it as much for you as for her. Christ, you're fifty and you act like an old man. Neville had told him people aged differently, that not everyone craved new sensations.

"You want me to leave," she said. "I saw what you wrote."

"That's neither here nor there," he said. "Get your coat. Let's get out of here, if you've already eaten."

Outside, he sat on the porch, lacing his boots. His cane was only for snakes, not for walking. She waited, a braid of hair on one side, the part cutting back and forth, failing on the other side. If things got desperate he'd take her up to Niagara, but for now he was saving the falls in case he needed them.

"Did you have any nightmares?" he said.

"No," she said. She'd found a stick of her own and she ran ahead, slashing at the bushes. There were some suspicions about what the man had done to her, though the medical examinations were inconclusive. What she had to say was so uninteresting that everyone agreed she had to be hiding something. Neville tried to catch up. The sun wasn't visible, but the air was already warm and thick. The week before, pollen had dropped out of the sky, soft and white, eager to choke him.

"Did you have nightmares?" she said.

"Last night?"

"Tell me."

"I wouldn't want to frighten you," he said. "You might never sleep again." He pointed out an eagle to distract her. It circled and climbed above the river. "They're not so smart," he said. "Probably dropped a fish and now he's searching for it."

At the highway, she took his hand. The thruway covered the route of the old canal; now semi trailers rolled where barges had once floated. The canal was filled from here all the way west to Buffalo, though locks and canals still connected the Great Lakes to the Atlantic. Cars came and went, appearing all at once and moving so fast. It surprised him, how he liked the feeling of Alicia's hand in his. On the other side, though, he felt how eager she was to pull away.

Mosquitoes thickened. Trees had tipped over, both into and away from the river, their roots loosened and the earth washed away. Water slid around the snags as if the land were pulling itself around the river and not the river through the land.

Down on the bank, Alicia found a styrofoam cooler, half hidden in the reeds. She took off the lid; the cooler held three cans of soda and a stick of salami, crackers in a plastic bag.

"Leave that alone," Neville said, and then he noticed the Indian. He hadn't seen him at first because the Indian was standing perfectly still, fifty feet out in the river. He was spearfishing.

Neville stepped right to the edge of the river. The Indian was younger than he was, but they all looked young—they only betrayed their age once they were ancient, and then they collapsed into something new and entirely different. Wizened. Wise.

"Hey," Neville said.

The man's moccasins were tied around his neck. He wore a baseball cap turned backward with feathers sticking up in front. He didn't move.

Neville threw a stone. "Leave the fish in peace!" he said. "Thought you all were rich from that casino of yours!" He looked sideways for Alicia's reaction.

The Indian was wearing rubber boots, up to his knees. He did not take his eyes from the water, the spear held over his head, its point facing down.

"Go home and eat some lobster!" Neville said, throwing another stone. It landed much closer than the first.

"Why don't you fuck off?" the Indian said, hardly turning his head.

"Watch your mouth," Neville said. "Can't you see I have a child here?"

"That's all the more reason for you to fuck off."

"If that's how you want it," Neville said. He put his hand on Alicia's back and turned her around. They began walking away from the river. She looked over her shoulder one time.

"Those Indians," he said. "They think it's funny if you treat everything like a joke. Makes them think you're stupid or that you think they are. Or both."

"I don't think he was joking with you," Alicia said.

"They have a different way of talking," he said. "You wouldn't understand."

They walked until they came to the abandoned canal, running twenty feet deep, bone dry. Alicia kicked an aluminum can and it rattled all the way to the bottom. She led him along the edge.

"Used to be this was the tow path," Neville said. "The mules used to walk along here, pulling the barges. They wore collars to do it, and the collars wore sores in their shoulders, so I had to carry salve along with me."

"You did not," she said.

"There were always dogs and snakes on the path, too," he said, "so I was always having to calm the mules. I sang to them." He kept talking as he led her down an escape hole—ramps cut in the banks in case mules fell in—and into the canal. The bottom was littered with old tires, steel belts showing through. Neville kept talking. He really wanted to describe it right, and the fact that he'd never seen it did not seem like any impediment at all. All that was before his time—it was his father who had led the mules, rode the barges, who cooked in lumber camps each winter when the canal was closed.

"Tell me one of your nightmares," she said. "I'm not afraid of anything."

"Nightmares are only scary to the person having them," he said.

"I don't care if it's not scary."

"All right," Neville said. "I dreamed that the mules went over the edge and I was tangled in the harnesses and went down with them, wrapped tighter and tighter. I couldn't get loose, couldn't get to the surface." Their sharp hairs burned his skin, the leather straps cut his blood, their hooves were hardly slowed by the dirty water.

"What about the escape holes?" she said.

"Well, they weren't always enough, especially if there were tangles, and there aren't any escape holes in nightmares."

"Did you get out?"

"I woke up."

He talked about taking lumber to the Steinway piano company in Brooklyn, how a sunken wreck could block the canal, about snapping turtles and how barges rode higher when unloaded. They scraped the bottom of bridges. Now she was staying close to him, listening. Now she was not straying. He told her how gardeners would throw their produce onto the barge and you'd stick coins in a potato and throw it back to pay for everything.

As he talked, he trailed his cane along the dry wall of the canal, cutting a thin line in the dirt. Happy amid her attention, he almost wanted to sing out, to awaken and calm everything. It came as no surprise that this was the moment—it was as if someone had gently taken his breath, tapped suddenly at the backs of his knees. He smelled the dirt, tasted it, even before he was all the way down, and he knew then that he was dying. His eyes rolled back, away from the world, and he would not let them light on Alicia because he did not want to be tempted to blame her.

She saw him fall.

"Hey," she said. "Stop that." She stepped closer. She reached out and touched him, then jumped back, unsure if he had moved. She put her fingertip on his eyelid, but did not pull the lid back. Then she turned and ran up the canal, out the escape hole and straight into the fields.

The grass and bushes were so tall she could not see over them. They were so thick she could not see through them. Shouting seemed pointless, but she did it anyway. Over her breathing she heard the cars on the highway—she could not see them or even guess the direction. She tried to go back the way she'd come, afraid she might not be able to find the way back to him. She ran wildly, so fast down the escape hole that she almost fell.

The Indian was already there. He laid his head flat on Neville's chest, then a finger along his throat.

"What are you going to do with him?" she said, kneeling close.

He looked down his straight nose at her. His spear lay next to him; it was just a broomstick with a knife duct-taped to the end. Beneath his loincloth, she saw, he was wearing red shorts with white stripes running up the sides. A leather belt went around his waist, holding nothing up, just for the knife's scabbard. The knife was long and serrated, for scaling fish. He saw her staring at it.

"What do you think?" he said. "Scalp him? Jesus."

Alicia took a step backward. The Indian was skinny, not too tall; he struggled, hiking Neville's body over his shoulder, the spear in his other hand. He turned and started walking away, down the canal, without looking back. Blood ran from Neville's mouth, down the Indian's shoulder. Alicia picked up the cane. When they disappeared around a bend she hurried to catch up. The Indian staggered and weaved beneath the weight.

She followed ten feet behind, up another escape hole and down the path, through a stand of trees and then onto a road where an old pickup was parked. The Indian threw his spear into the bed and she tossed the cane after it. He eased Neville's body in the driver's side of the truck and then pushed it into the middle. When Alicia climbed into the other side she had to grab hold of Neville's dead leg to pull herself up.

They started driving, bouncing through ruts and then onto blacktop. Fishing lures hung from the visors above the windshield: tiny smiling fish with staring eyes and bellies full of hooks.

The Indian was gasping, still catching his breath. Alicia looked at him as he drove. The beads on his vest were sewn into the shapes of cowboys and Indians, a straight line, a cactus between each one. The speedometer said fifty, as if there were no rush at all, no emergency. When he shifted gears, he touched Neville's knee and then Neville's whole body slumped over, like he was taking a nap with his head in the Indian's lap.

"Are we going to bury him?" Alicia said.

The Indian pushed Neville's body so it was sitting upright again. The spear and cane rolled back and forth, over each other in the back of the truck, clattering and settling together. She realized he had left his cooler behind. Maybe it had not been his, after all.

"Where's all your fish?" she said. She tried not to look at Neville or think about him. He was dead, she thought, he could not feel his head knocking against the back window of the truck, he could not hear anything or see where they were going.

The Indian looked over at her, holding the wheel straight, then out the windshield again.

Alicia couldn't stand to think he was laughing at her. Now he would take her wherever he lived and she might never escape. She might never again eat in a restaurant or ride the train or jump on her trampoline. She shifted so Neville's foot would not touch hers.

"I'm not afraid of you," she said.

This time he almost laughed, but he choked it back.

"Don't touch me," she said.

"Am I touching you?" he said.

"You know what I mean."

"Up here," he said, pointing through the window, to a rise in the land. "Used to be giants lived there."

"You're trying something," she said.

"We're driving with a body," he said. "I'm passing the time."

"Is he dead?" she said.

"Anyway," he said, "the Oneida Indians used to fight with the giants—they were called the Stone Coats—and finally the giants were trapped in a cave. A boy, a frightened young boy about your age, found that cave, and they whispered their secrets to him, through the cracks, so the secrets wouldn't be lost. That's why the Indians started making those masks, the big ones—you ever see those?—so they could speak the giants' words in those false face shows."

"You do that?"

"No."

"Why not?"

"For one thing, because I'm not an Indian."

"Sure," she said.

They drove in silence, hardly breaking the speed limit. Neville's body rolled a little, so their thighs touched. Alicia pressed herself against the door, watched the fences and telephone poles, the smiling fish hanging from their hooks.

"What are you afraid of?" she said.

The Indian didn't answer or look her way.

They came into a town and every red light caught them. He did not run the lights—he just waited, watching the people in the other cars—but then he did pull up to the emergency entrance at the hospital, right next to the ambulance.

Alicia pushed Neville's body as the Indian pulled, then she climbed out the same door. She followed them inside.

The nurse at the desk looked up as they passed.

"Wait," she said. "Hold on, there," but the Indian kept on down the hall. He set Neville on a stretcher and grabbed a passing orderly by the arm.

"Easy," the man said. "What did you do to him, Chief?"

"He's not breathing," the nurse said, and all at once they wheeled the stretcher away. Alicia watched the soles of Neville's shoes disappear through the swinging doors.

No one stayed behind to ask them any questions. The Indian sat down in a chair and she sat down in another, across the hall.

"Why don't you leave?" she said.

"I might do that," he said, but he didn't move.

The clocks in the hallway ran five minutes apart. The Indian's feathers were dyed a fake blue and the beads at his wrists and neck looked plastic. Another stretcher went by, one wheel jammed and spinning like a coin. Alicia stared at the Indian and he didn't seem to notice. He looked like he was almost asleep, in a kind of trance. She had no idea what was happening, but she knew better than to let anyone know she was afraid.

The last time she was in a hospital was after she'd been jumping on the trampoline. The trampoline was on the roof of her apartment building, in the city, and a man had come up and asked if he could jump with her. She had never seen the man before. With both of them on the trampoline she went higher and higher, until she could see the whole river, cars on the bridge, and then, trying to see it all, she'd gone sideways and her head caught the frame and her face went into the metal springs.

The man had been helping her when her father found them, but after that no one believed what she said had happened and they asked her again and again and again.

"She's just come in so we can see how it's healing," the one doctor was saying to the other. He touched her head. "I have to admit I'm pretty proud of the job I did, though of course the hair will cover it."

"I'm just waiting," Alicia said.

"I know that," the doctor said. "Of course you are."

"She's not a patient here," the Indian said. Suddenly he was standing. "It's her grandfather."

"He's not my grandfather," she said.

"Something with his heart," the Indian said. "She's waiting with me."

"Is that true?" the doctor said.

"I guess so," she said. "I'm not from here."

The Indian sat down again, closer to her.

"Strangest thing," the one doctor said, leading the other away.

William watched them go. Fools, he thought.

The air was full of medicine, static from the radios and fluorescent lights, beepers calling and answering each other. People passed, their eyes skipping around him. He'd been back a full month now, here to where he was born and raised. In the city, nothing he'd done had ever mattered—like plowing furrows in the water or whatever the good book said. Now he saw it was foolish to think it would be simpler here, to believe he wouldn't be drawn into some stupid drama. Any small number of people could tangle and muddy any amount of space.

The friends of his youth still lived here, though they would not join him like they used to. Nor were they eager to tell him much about what they were doing now. True Indians, he found them dealing blackjack, oiling the cogs and wheels of their friends the one-armed bandits; their girlfriends carried cocktails, wore buckskin minidresses and feathered headbands. So much had changed since he'd been gone—it was not just that he'd gotten older. His friends wondered why he'd returned, why he wanted to play at the games they'd given up so long before. These were fair enough questions.

William didn't even want to guess what was wrong with the girl's head. The stitches along her skull, over her ear, made him think something had been taken out or put in, or that perhaps her brain had been switched with that of another. What was he afraid of? He was afraid of everything—could he tell her that? Heights, the dark, animals, loud noises, other people. And maybe she was right and he should just leave, yet he had found himself there, right after the man had fallen; he had known the man would survive, had felt assured it would turn out all right.

William felt the girl watching him. He turned to face her.

"I threw them all back," he said. "Got a freezer full of fish at home."

"You threw them back after you put spears through them?" she said. She stood and sat down again, next to him.

He looked at the threads in her skin, where the ends had frayed, the raw abrasions on her ears. No doubt in the old days the fish had run thicker; you could hit one with your eyes closed, couldn't miss, could walk across the river on their backs. Those salmon had been learning how to evade spears for thousands of years and during that whole time people had been forgetting how to throw them. He wasn't even sure he'd seen a fish all morning, but he'd thrown the spear a few times, for practice and just in case.

"It's not easy," he said. "You try it sometime."

"Your costume is fake," she said.

"True," he said. How could it be otherwise? There was some integrity in that, after all, some honesty. He wasn't trying to trick anyone. He spun the cheap beads on his wrist, then unclipped the bracelet and handed it to her.

"He's conscious," the nurse said. "He wants to see you."

"Go ahead," William said.

"No," said the nurse. "It's you he wants to see. Saved his life, we told him."

He stood slowly, turned, and went through the door. The curtains were drawn. One fluorescent light shone overhead. The doctor and nurse stood off to one side, out of the way.

Neville sat up in the bed. The backless hospital shift sagged forward to show his pale chest. His bare feet stuck out, his hooked toes and hairless ankles close to William's hands.

"I don't even know you," Neville said.

"You saw me this morning," William said. "Threw stones at me."

"So," Neville said. "Now what do you have to say for yourself?"

"If it wasn't for the girl," William said, "I would have left you to drown."

"Drown?" Neville bent farther forward. "You think you know something?"

"No."

"Don't try that mystical bullshit on me. You're no Indian."

"Never said I was," William said.

"What's wrong with the girl?" the doctor said.

William turned and saw that she had followed him in.

"Nothing," he said. "She's fine. Could you leave us alone in here?" He waited for a moment, then turned back to Neville. "This has nothing to do with me."

"That's where you're wrong," Neville said. "No one asked you to get involved, meddle with me."

"I thought you were dead," Alicia said, moving closer to the bed.

"My sweet girl." Neville held up his hand as if he were too tired to say anything more. He closed his eyes.

William sat on the couch next to the bed, waiting. The girl sat down next to him, the cheap bracelet around her wrist. He watched the bottles empty themselves one drip at a time, the tube that snaked down through the air, taped into Neville's arm, straight into his vein.

"Well," Neville said, suddenly awake. "I thought that was it, that I was done and it was all better that way, but now I'm not so sure. There's still plenty—"

"Is that a thank you?" William said.

The sky behind the curtains had gone dark. Neville was asleep again—he would not answer the question. The girl was sleeping also, leaning against William's arm. He did not like the feel of her scratchy head against his skin, but he could not move without waking her. He closed his eyes, and through the darkness he knew when he opened them next it would be morning; the morning, he knew, would find the three of them like this. Like this, only ready to begin.

THE BADGER STATE

WEAPONS OF THE ARCTIC

Every year, Ursula walked to the island; first with her parents, then with friends or boys, and now alone. Her feet made almost no sound on the ice, which was frozen in ridges not quite reminiscent of water. She breathed in cold air and crystals formed and melted in her throat, in her lungs. Summers she would stand on the shore in her bathing suit and try to imagine someone walking out here. It was always impossible to believe that the ice would come again. She would wade in up to her knees and squint over the waves, trying to see the island.

Now, looking back, she could barely make out the steeples of
the churches in town, the fine houses along the shore, empty
nine months of every year. Finally even the trees were folded
away by the cold; the air was too thin to hold colors. Bending
down, she took off her mitten and held her hand an inch above
the ice. She felt the cold rising up, casting itself outward, climbing through the soles of her boots.

Half a mile out, she saw a fishing hut between her and the
island, a truck off to one side. The lake was solid now, but in a
few months the waves would throw great plates of ice into the
trees. Ursula moved west, toward the island. Tears welled in her
eyes when she lifted her glasses, the ice multiplying the cold sun.
South, she saw the cliffs, the bluff of the state park, the lookout
tower atop it. When she was a girl there had been a wishing
tree, a branch that hung out over the road. She wished as they
passed underneath. That branch was a hazard, it was later decided; when it was cut down she feared none of her wishes
remained binding. The park still held the totem pole, though—
every face an accusation, mouths full of teeth, wings for ears.

She walked. If she turned north she could follow the peninsula all the way to her five-year-old son, where he lived with his
grandfather. She could follow the ice past Sister Bay, through
the Little Sister islands, around Ellison Bay and to Gills Rock at
the tip of the peninsula, twenty miles away; she could cross the
stones of the shore, through woods thick with icicles and abandoned boats, across the fields to Edvar's house, where she could
look through the windows to see them drinking hot chocolate,
the old man repeating a ridiculous story as her son chewed the
pieces of a jigsaw puzzle. Now, as she walked west, her shadow
followed, fifty feet tall, sliding thin and dark, slung over her
right shoulder.

"Hey!" the man called out. "What are you doing?"

Without noticing, she had walked close by where the man was ice fishing. She saw that what she had taken for a truck was actually a tractor with a trailer attached.

"What are you doing?" he said, coming closer.

"Nothing," she said. "Walking."

"I know who you are," he said. "I knew your folks, you know."

Ursula saw the round holes cut in the ice, lines attached to flags that tipped up when fish took the bait. The man was wearing a parka with fur around the hood, closed down like an Eskimo's. She could not tell if he was drunk or merely old.

"Call me Eddie," he said. "Eddie Polenka. What's your name?"

"Thought you knew me."

"I know who you are, which is a different thing from knowing your name. Forget it."

There were seven holes in the ice, in a semicircle around the shack. Five fish, four bass and a perch, were laid out in a line, their colors pale in the cold. The fish nearest Ursula gulped air through its gills. Its fins jerked once, its eye staring at her.

"I put red pepper in my socks," Eddie Polenka was saying. "In my gloves. This here's farther out than most go, but what I got is a map. It's a map of the lake's bottom, you know—there's a stretch of shallows here with a trench running the whole length."

She heard other voices, then realized it was a radio in the shack. Eddie noticed her listening.

"Packers are getting killed," he said. "By the Vikings, no less."

"I better keep moving," she said.

"Where you going? You have plenty of time."

A flag went up at a hole behind him and she pointed to it.

"You work at the cherry factory," he said. "Now I remember. Hold on, now. Don't go anywhere."

The canning season only lasted two months. At the plant, smaller conveyor belts circled out from the one in the center, carrying cherries past each worker—farmer's wives and the stout women of fishermen, girls who had been up hours before, to milk, and who would return, at the end of the day, to the same cows. These women's fingers were stained red and pink and they picked out the bad cherries and the ones the pitter missed, any stems that had gotten past. Ursula managed the plant; she knew the idiosyncracies of the simple motors that ran the conveyors, knew how the belts liked to loosen. She sat reading the manuals, biographies of Henry Ford, *Playgirl*, Jack London and whatever else. She wasted time. She went outside and ran through the meadows as soon as the sun burned away the dew.

"You have a boy," Eddie said. "Don't you? I believe I saw him out with Edvar Christiansen."

"He's the boy's grandfather," she said. "On the other side."

"I know that," Eddie said. "It'd be nice to have a boy like that."

"I'll see you," she said.

"Hold on, hold on. Got something to show you." He headed toward the tractor.

Ursula knelt down, close to a hole in the ice, next to the augur that had cut it. She shook off her mitten and spun her engagement ring, her thumb on the diamond; next she forced the wedding band ahead and over her knuckles. She watched them slide into the dark water, then looked at her bare finger, the pinched skin that had been held down around the bone. The rings were gone and that surprised her; this was not something she had expected to do.

Eddie came back with his hands in the pockets of his coat. Now his hood was thrown back and he was wearing a ragged coonskin cap, the tail off to one side.

"See something down there?"

"No," she said. When she looked up she saw he was holding a pistol in his hand.

"Come over here." He took hold of her arm and led her farther from the shack. He opened the gun and showed her the round silver ends of the bullets in the cylinder, then slapped it shut again.

Holding the pistol out from his body, he fired it straight down into the ice. The sound was small, pathetic, stolen by the space and cold. Eddie showed her where the bullet was lodged, embedded in the ice, a dark smudge almost impossible to see.

"That's how I do it," he said. "If the bullet goes through, then I don't drive my tractor out here."

"That's it," she said. "Goodbye."

"Wait," he said as she turned away. "Just fifteen more minutes. Just stay and visit."

The sky was the exact white of the lake and there was no horizon. The island was a dark line, rising up unbounded, floating weightless. As she walked, she thought of the breathing holes whales made in the ocean; she remembered the end of *The Call of the Wild,* where the sled tipped up and went down through the ice. She took off her jacket and tied it around her waist. When she looked back she saw Eddie Polenka was no longer watching her.

She wondered if the rings were still sinking, slicing down, cutting long cold cylinders. Perhaps the water was more viscous and the rings moved more slowly than they would have on a summer's day. They went down into the darkness, cutting the gnarled lips of fish and spat out again. The yes and I do and the no, never, settling along the bottom.

She was closer to the park now, the tower high above, its accordion of stairs cutting all the way to the top, names and initials carved everywhere, weakening the whole structure. Once, when she was a girl, she had taken a boy up there, at night. Now she could not even remember his name. In the darkness they had chased each other up the stairs, back and forth, and had reached the top dizzy in the cold wind, fighting out of their clothes, losing pieces over the railing, wrestling all gooseflesh across the names and letters. As she rose above him she saw his face, and in his expression she saw that he was not the one, that he took risks to impress her, not because he wanted to. She still waited for someone to understand, to say the same to her, that they could not accept anything they'd seen, that it would not do. She looked past the boy's face, his head all the way over the edge, and saw the lights of the police car revolving, a hundred and fifty feet below.

The glare of the ice hid things, swallowed them up in the cold opposite of a mirage. Looking back, she could not see Eddie and she was relieved to think that he could not see her. She walked faster. It started turning dark around two, these days, and by four-thirty night had fallen all the way. She wondered about the migration of animals, from the peninsula to the island, back and forth. There were no snakes in New Zealand, she'd read that—or perhaps that was Tasmania. It was too cold for them, in any case, to get across the ice; cold-blooded, they took the temperature with their tongues, and they could not overcome their torpor to attempt the crossing she was making now.

The island descended as she came closer. The harbor slowly opened, revealing itself. The island was shaped like a horseshoe, which was its name. Snow had drifted high along the shore. Ursula made her way into the harbor, a place where she had swum in the heat of summers, when thin green tentacles of seaweed wrapped around her ankles and threatened to pull her down. Now she saw the ends of these underwater trees, the topmost branches frozen in the ice. The harbor was deep; in the summer, boats would anchor here, weathering storms. Ursula had a friend who had spent four months with a man on a sailboat. His dog had run circles around the deck, barking, whenever they got down to business in the cabin, close to the slap of the water.

Ursula stopped on the beach. She saw a few old snowmobile tracks, but no footprints, no signs of deer or even seagulls. The snow was not so deep under the trees, and the ground was frozen. She followed the path past picnic tables, toward the center of the island. A squirrel ran across a branch overhead and snow sifted down. In the shadows she saw the tiny footprints of mice. The white sky was torn and splintered by the bare branches above. She had made it again, and she would always make it. It did not matter if memories thickened or if people tried to slow her. She did not care what happened during the year, when the lake turned fluid—she had done it before, she was doing it now, she would always make it to the island. When she was a girl she'd come with her class from school, in boats, and they had held hands and walked all the way across the island, fingers slipping loose only to pass trees and then joined again. The deer crashed ahead, finally turning in the shallows to face the line, then swimming arcs along the shore, waiting for the children to leave. The deer swam close enough that she remembered the black lines of flies on their backs, trying to stay out of the water.

There had once been a large house on the island, right in the center. She came to the rubble of the foundation, the scattered logs. A family had lived here once, parents and children, listening to the waves and trees, back when these walls stood against the weather. The logs that hadn't rotted away had begun to petrify, their notched ends sticking up through the snow and ice. Ursula took off her sunglasses and stepped into the middle of the ruin, through a doorway and into a room. She kicked at cans, broken bottles. Then there was a voice behind her.

"Was this your house?"

The man was about her age, shorter than she was, wearing a red and black plaid cap with earflaps and a pom-pom on top. His jean jacket had fake wool at the collar. He was wearing basketball shoes.

"Think it was Indians?" he said. "Cigarette?"

"No," she said. "It was the stock market."

"What?"

"In the twenties," she said.

The man blew his nose on a red bandanna, then jammed it into the back pocket of his jeans. The tips were missing from the fingers of his gloves. He held a flask out and she waved it away.

"So boring in the winter," he said. "Have to figure out things to do. Man. I've just been walking from island to island, all day long. Started out with my dog, but it was too cold for her feet."

"I see," Ursula said.

"Have to get her some of those dog boots, like they got for sled dogs."

"Is she a husky?" Ursula said.

"She's just a dalmatian." He paused, squinting at her. "Have any pets?"

"Have to be going," she said.

"But you just got here," he said. "I watched you coming across the ice."

"I heard voices," Ursula said. "Other people out here."

"Don't you want to know my name?" He held out the flask again, until she took it. "Relax," he said. "What are you afraid of? It's good for you. Trust me."

She did not want to know his name, to invite familiarity. He seemed familiar, but so many people did. As they stood looking at each other, the light was gradually giving out. Shadows spread from beneath the trees. A couple times the man breathed out quickly through his nostrils, a kind of laughter, but he did not speak.

"I have a knife," she said.

"So do I," he said. "It's a good thing to carry."

"Yes, it is."

"Person could freeze to death out here," he said.

"I'm on my way back in."

"Alone?" he said. "If we started a fire—"

"I have to be home," she said. "I'm expected home."

"Well, I'm not freezing to death." He turned his back to her and stepped into the trees. The gaps between the trees were barely visible, and it wasn't long before he disappeared. Ursula could not hear him. She could not tell if he doubled back or continued on, onto the ice and away, maybe south to Fish Creek, or if he was gathering firewood, or if he had circled the island to wait for her.

The edges of her footprints on the path were already frozen.

She followed them back through the trees. In the harbor she felt surrounded and, shivering, she tried to breathe silently as she hurried for the open water.

The stars were out, tilting into constellations. She could not tell if she was being followed, and on the ice it was too slippery to run without falling. After a few minutes she saw lights moving toward her, headlights; she heard the two cars coming closer, out of control, spinning in circles, pulled around by the weight of their engines, lights wheeling, and then she heard girls screaming from within. She felt the ice shift a little, felt the heat of the cars pass by. If they hit her, if they ran her over, that was what would happen, they would take her down. Those were her thoughts. She walked a straight line toward the pale lights on shore as the cars spun obliviously past her, returning. She listened to the boys' howling and the girls' protestations.

The silence was anxious to close down again, once the cars were gone. Ursula knew she would make it. Next year she would bring her son along. Now he was already in bed, no doubt, warm under the blankets with his grandfather, listening to the stories that would bore anyone over ten years old. Children were reassured by repetition. When she got home, Ursula would have tea, some soup. She'd find bread or crackers to hold honey, or she'd eat it straight from the jar. Teaspoons full. She would take a hot bath.

Close to shore, almost there, she heard a skittering like claws going sideways, close in the darkness and then gone again, like a dog running across a wind that was too strong or a wolverine unable to control its ferocity, lost in a cold frenzy. She listened. The lake was so silent in the winter, especially at night, that the trees cracked against each other, rattling the bare sticks of their branches.

BEWARE MY FRIEND

Around five in the morning, the raccoons came through the cat door, into the kitchen of Eddie Polenka. They leapt onto the counters and got into the cabinets. Breaking glasses surprised them, as did the clatter of pans. They pulled open the door of the refrigerator and pulled out all the food; they sucked eggs dry and spilled milk across the floor, whipped each other with strips of bacon. The raccoons ran back and forth in the mess they'd made, sliding into walls, tangled in electrical cords, bringing the toaster and blender down to the floor.

Eddie lay in bed, listening to them. He lived alone in the house, and he knew all its sounds. The cat door only swung in one direction, he'd rigged it that way, and the raccoons, even with their clever hands, could not escape. He'd counted on that, and also the fact that they wouldn't know windows could be broken.

Slowly, calmly, he got dressed. He took out his pistol, loaded it, and filled his pocket with extra bullets. He'd written his doctor's phone number in black magic marker along his forearm, in case he needed a rabies shot.

When he kicked the kitchen door open, the raccoons looked up, frozen, then tried to make it under the table. Eddie aimed carefully, for he did not want to hit their faces—he wanted to preserve their black masks. He shot them down, but he did not let them suffer; once he'd slowed them all, he put his foot across their bodies, one at a time, across their shoulders, and twisted their necks until he heard the snap. Then he set the raccoons on the chairs, out of the way. He put his gun in his pocket and set to cleaning up all they'd done.

It is true that he had drawn those raccoons in, that he'd stuck marshmallows along his windowpanes and cut the cat door though he had no pets. In the same way, he fed the deer in his fields, all autumn, and then, come hunting season, he'd curl up out there in his camouflage sleeping bag, his compound bow in his hands. That's how he hunted. Some might ask what kind of hunting that is.

Successful, Eddie would say. I hunt with my mind, you see. The stalking takes months—it's more work than it seems because you can't see it all. He'd tap the side of his head as he paused. I'm moving toward those deer since before they were born. They have no idea, right now, that I've been in their future all along.

Now, sometimes, people wonder what happened to Eddie, when it's certain whatever happened was all his own doing. I can promise you that.

He spent his afternoons at the A.C. Tap, a roadhouse set out alone on the highway between Sister Bay and Bailey's Harbor. His license had been suspended, but it didn't matter much because his car was hardly running, almost altogether finished, at the time. The police and Eddie had an agreement—he drove his tractor pretty much wherever he wanted, just so he stayed off to the side of the highway, the yellow reflective triangles on the fenders. Most afternoons his tractor sat there, parked outside the Tap.

Inside, he rested his huge hands, the thick fingers barely bending, on the bar. His face was bright red, like a mask, his eyes buried. Hours went by where he didn't say a thing, just sat there with a pickled egg and a turkey gizzard set on a napkin in front of him. No one else could eat those things slowly, and certainly not without a chaser.

Harley, the bartender, turned up the jukebox's volume with a switch under the bar when he liked the song. Otherwise—there weren't many left that he could stand and their number was fewer each day—he turned the volume down. He and Eddie understood each other. Some said they'd seen Eddie taking pills, but Harley knew this was not true.

Newcomers to the Tap would sometimes try to engage Eddie in conversation. When he answered them, and this was rare, they struggled to understand the connections of his response.

Looks like the Packers finally got that fool Mandarich, they'd say, full of goodwill.

Eddie wouldn't even turn to face them. You don't see Pabst coming out with a dry beer, he'd say. Or a red beer, or a beer made of ice.

One night he tipped his tractor into a ditch, driving home. The next morning they found him curled up in one of the tractor's back tires, eight feet off the ground. He was asleep, a light rain coming down, his hands folded flat like a prayer beneath his cheek. He said the whole thing had happened so slowly that he just climbed up as it went over, like a tipping sailboat, so he would not be trapped beneath it.

Like I've said, Eddie did not have time for most people. He sought my friendship—he turned to look down the bar and I understood he wanted me to move closer. Lots of folks up here don't like me because I came from New York, but I see their condescension as part of an inferiority complex. They distrust anyone who doesn't live the same place they were born.

You're a mechanic, Eddie said.

I am, I said. With my eyes closed I could tell you what's wrong with every vehicle that passes. Five minutes with a wrench and I can make anything run better.

Engines, he said. Ever do any work on clocks?

What?

You know, really fine things. Small things.

Motorcycles, I said, but it's all the same to me, the size. Sometimes parts are a little harder to get at, is all.

But you're inclined that way, he said. You have a mechanical bent.

We sat in silence as he thought all this over. He tricked a lot of people into thinking he was slow, a little touched. In fact, he wasn't even much of a drinker. He could nurse a beer until it was room temperature. He let me know that night that he thought I was special, worthy of his confidence.

Then he told me he had a bunch of raccoons he was working on. He said he might be interested in seeking my assistance. That's how he put it. He told me how he was a taxidermist, and then went into a description of a place there'd used to be, a park with otters in a pond and a bear that drank bottles of soda, where chickens played tiny pianos and ducks did arithmetic. All this had made money, Eddie believed. He saw an opportunity.

I don't get the connection, I said.

That's where you come in, he said. And you can have all the money.

What he wanted was for me to work on the raccoons and the other animals he'd taxidermied. He wanted me to put motors in them, to see if we could make them twitch and walk, wash food they'd pretend to eat, climb trees in slow motion.

I'm not in it for the money, he said.

Why, then? I said.

Human kindness.

What do you get out of it? I said.

I want to see it, he said. That's all.

I'll think about it, I said.

The way he spoke of his work was something to see. He pulled at my shirt, jabbed his finger on the top of the bar, his whisper rising smooth as he told me that he wanted to get back the feelings, like when you see an animal you've never seen before. Some piece of that, he'd say, and the whole time he talked he leaned toward me, really wanting me to understand, to share his excitement. The words came fast—diluted borax cleaned out body cavities, preserved them, and a frog's whole body could be taken out through its mouth, the frog turned inside out, and he wanted to try that with something bigger, so the skin and skull would kiss each other, joined at the lips, the eyes in one head and missing in the other.

At the time he first told me all this, I believed he knew something, that he possessed some skill. The truth was he'd just take the guts out of animals and fill them with sawdust, if you call that taxidermy. He'd lose track of a wing in the midst of doing a duck or pheasant and just leave the wires poking out in hopes he'd find it again; he used actual marbles, the kind kids play with, for eyes, and often they didn't match—one kitten's eye would be clear with a ribbon of colors inside, the other solid red; he'd stitch a snake from tip to tongue when you should be able to turn them inside out and back again with no need of thread. Turn any of those animals over and they'd vomit sawdust. You'd be hard-pressed to identify what you had left in your hands.

Still, his words were catching, full of excitement, and the better I got to know Eddie, the more we talked, the more questions I had about myself and where I was headed, what I was willing to do and what I wanted. I listened because he took the time to talk to me—it started that simply.

Skin without sensation, Eddie would say, laughing as if I understood. That was one of his favorite sayings, and I would nod, swigging at my beer. It was less about combustion, which I knew, than electronics, which I had to learn. All wires and batteries, hybrid appliances, but that's not what I want to talk about here.

Eddie slowly won over every pet within five miles of his house; don't ask me how many of them disappeared. He claimed natural causes, roadkill. He had no pets himself, except his chickens, and they were not merely for experimentation. The pickled eggs behind the bar at the Tap are all his—he gets a percentage of every one that's sold.

Sure, there are a few things I'd like to tell him now. Little things I'd like to say to someone, you know. I remember how I was sick one time, laid up for almost a week, and as I lay in bed I heard the tractor's engine, from a distance, coming closer, stopping just outside my window. I listened to Eddie walk in and out all the rooms of my house until he found me.

You're alive, he said, and when I nodded he just turned around and walked back out.

What were you planning if I wasn't? I said, but all I could hear was his footsteps, in and out of the rooms as if he had to retrace his path.

In a moment he was tapping at the windowpane. Know where to catch some bats? he said. I'd sure like to work on some bats.

I waited until the tractor started up, I listened to it fade away in the distance. I climbed out of bed to check on my dog, out in the yard. She was all right, my dalmatian-girl, watching me. If she's not chained, she'll run away from me, perhaps all the way back to New York. She cringed when I waved at her. It was not until I went into the kitchen that I saw Eddie had left me a dozen hard-boiled eggs.

True, his chickens had all seen him do it a million times, but they always trusted him when he went out among them. Then his arm would jerk out and he'd have one by the neck, caught between his thumb and forefinger, the rest of his fingers over its eyes. Windmilling his arm, he'd get the chicken's body going in a circle, its feathers a blur of white, and then he'd snap his wrist back against the momentum—the body would roll kicking along the ground, the chicken's severed head in his fist.

Sometimes he dislocated his shoulder killing a chicken, and he'd have to pop it back into its socket. It was one of these times, when he was already in a foul mood, that the woman showed up. She was driving one of those new convertibles; she pulled up and parked right next to his tractor. He was certain, as she got out of her car, that she was lost and needed directions.

That thing hanging on the wall of your barn, she said.

He saw that she was wearing rubber beach sandals and some sort of poncho. Probably, he conjectured, she wore nothing but a bathing suit beneath it. She was pointing to the wall above him, where a line of dark shadow ran diagonally across the rake. The rake was fifteen feet wide, to be pulled behind a tractor, covered in rust. It had not been used for twenty-five years.

Well, he said, coming through the gate. That there's a very important implement.

I'd just like to lay that thing down in my garden, the woman said. Plant some flowers around it.

Eddie saw the money in her hand. Let me show you some of the other things I have, he said, opening the door into the barn. Leading her in, he touched her arm just above the elbow, probably with the head of the chicken, which was still in his hand.

Old machines lie broken, rusted and tangled on that end of the barn. Eddie switched on the light and it was cut by spiderwebs, the bird's nests plastered around the bulbs. The teeth of swathers shone in the light, the long-necked blade of the plow, the weighted section of chain-link fence that, dragged behind the tractor, would break up the cowpies that covered the fields every spring.

How tall would you say you are? he said.

Five-seven, about.

Good, he said. Have any children?

Three, she said. Why?

Pretty good, he said. Pretty good.

For now, she said, speaking before the silence could grow, I'll just take that one outside on the wall.

It's a rake, he said.

I wouldn't know.

We rural folks use it for raking the fields, he said.

I told you I didn't know, she said.

There's a difference between joking and making fun, he told her. He told her that all the fields around his house were his, that he needed all his tools, which was a lie—he'd been selling his land off in circles that closed down tightly around him. There were only a few acres left, and he'd had to crowd his junk closer with every sale.

Maybe you could come back another time, he said, and we can discuss that rake.

I'll leave you my number, she said.

Give me your address, he said. You'd need it delivered, in any case. Not that I've made up my mind.

I can come by again, she said. I've driven past lots of times, you know, before I stopped today. I've seen you out in your yard. I've been planning this.

What's that supposed to mean? Eddie said.

Nothing, she said. Only that it wasn't just an impulse, coming here today.

Eddie leaned against the wall of the barn, uneasy, the chicken's head still hidden in his fist.

Call it whatever you want, he said.

I will, she said.

And so the woman left empty-handed, not even having seen the other side of the barn, where his animals were, hidden in the darkness, always ready to leap from the walls at the flick of the light switch. He showed it all to me—the squirrels with shrunken heads, their lips stitched tight, the pickling jars afloat with baby animals. He was making animals with mismatched heads and bodies, with multiple heads, with heads and hands that were parts of machines. There were dogs with green glass teeth, badgers with butcher knives for legs, deer with antlers of wrenches and screwdrivers, and he could get them all going on pulleys and lines, flying through the air and fighting with each other. Sometimes he would play his records as he did it, set it all to music.

Or perhaps he did take the woman further, he did show her his animals. I can just see her transfixed face as he went on about how an artist might see a person or place and imagine them in paint—all color and form and estimates of materials, necessary techniques—and how that's how it was, how he practiced by imagining the shapes beneath the skin, trying to tell what it would take to make an animal be itself, to have the correct impact, make a true emotional impression. Yes, I'm sure she'd be taken in by that, though I really doubt that he did show her, that he would; he was so careful about who he shared that with.

I'd go out there, driving him home if he got rained in at the Tap, then I'd pick him up the next day, so he could recover his tractor from the parking lot. Sometimes I'd have to search for him. Once I found him down in a ditch, picking over a dead horse that was half rotted away, plants and flowers growing through its bones. He looked up at me, just pulling his suspenders of orange baling twine up over his shoulders. It seemed impossible he could breathe down there.

That horse is too far gone, I said, standing upwind.

The skeleton, he said. I can do something with it, make it dance. The worms will help me. You'll make a little engine, a kerosene burner.

I could hear the bugs from where I stood. Looking out across the fields that Eddie once owned, I could see the wooden boats, abandoned and rotting in the trees. I'd heard people sold drugs out there.

Those days, I'd get Eddie away from his house, from whatever thing he was doing, and we'd go out driving. Now I drive by myself, cruising in my Datsun. Some mechanics drive the best cars possible and others get their kicks from those that are just making it, on the edge of total failure without giving in. I go to the beach up at Europe Bay, or just to Appleport, and try to skip stones through the chop. Or I throw them so high, end over end, that they hit the water silently with no splash and slice straight to the bottom without losing momentum. I think about all the money I'm saving and consider moving west or getting more settled here. Ships line the horizon, on their way to Michigan, or north through Huron and Erie, back to the dams and locks, the canals of New York. I realize I don't know as much as I once suspected, that I cannot go back there, where I came from. I've lost some bluster.

If I find children on the beach I challenge them to contests. Usually they don't dare. I tell girls to watch me and they pretend not to.

When Eddie was with me, we didn't stop at the beach. We just drove back and forth across the peninsula, laughing and talking, a six-pack on the seat between us. There's a hole rusted

in the floorboards on that side and the ground slides by. Eddie
would pretend his foot was stuck, then he'd get serious and
confide things to me. I was in his confidence then.

Did you ever, he'd say, see people that look so familiar that
you begin to suspect maybe they're someone you've known before and they're in a very slight disguise, trying to trick you for
some unknown reason?

That's too much, I'd say. Horse-poisoner.

Up here we know what's going on, he said. People come up
from the cities and think they understand.

I'm from the city, I said.

Case in point, he said, and we had a good laugh over that.
I've never had a problem with people acting superior, just so
they count me as one of their friends. That's how it was with us,
and it was because from the beginning I could see he was lonely
like I was, and that we were together out there with the winter
always coming.

At the A.C. Tap, the level of pickled eggs in the jar hardly
changed. Harley stopped telling people not to sit on Eddie's stool,
when it used to be every day he'd listen for that tractor coming. I
still wait for him in there, some days; I tell Harley how Eddie
called the woman foolish when he told me the story. As I drink,
I wonder if she makes him bathe, if he turns the water black in
the tub—there was dirt deep in the lines of his face, after all, not
just around his mouth, like someone who chews, but up on his
cheeks, around his eyes and, I suspect, all under his clothes. Like
the arms of old wooden chairs, how dirt gets down in the grain. I
drink Pabst, though there are other beers I prefer.

You look familiar, I say to people. I know you from somewhere, and they let me know I'm mistaken and swivel away.
They show me the backs of their heads.

I've been told there's a woman for me, somewhere, made just for me, and I'll let her seek me out, for a change. If she finds me I'll put my dirty hands all over her skin, I'll mark her up good. The fact is, there's something about me that people don't like. I know that, I'm no fool. Eddie saw past it, though, and I know he was honest, that he held no false sentiments.

Once, sitting at the bar, I said, Let's stop acting so stupid, and after a long time he set down his beer and looked at me.

Good idea, he said. You start.

That's how he is, exactly. He didn't even smile when he said it. The thing is, it's quiet around here in the winter. Business slows down and you have to make up ways to pass the time. I've taken my car apart piece by piece and reassembled it; I've walked all the way down the peninsula, out on the frozen lake, from island to island. I'd go and visit and he'd show me what he was working on, maybe like the bass he caught ice fishing, a wire running in its mouth and out its anus so it could slide great distances, out of trees, so it could carry messages or frighten visitors. When he showed me these things, he kept checking my reaction, and I saw the looks he gave me, beyond disappointment and into anger or pity. While I got a vicarious kind of thrill from seeing him so excited, I fear that I didn't understand his animals like he did. This was enough for me, this half sharing; perhaps it was not enough for him.

At the gate to Eddie's drive, the sign simply says BEWARE— the bottom half, whatever it said, has been torn away. The time I went over there, when I finally decided to check, was a couple weeks after his disappearance. I missed him. I miss him.

Something had gotten in and finished off the chickens. All that was left were white feathers in the fence. I was careful in his yard, fearing traps, springes left for animals. Any piece of ground might hide a pit, covered over, sharpened stakes pointing up from the bottom. No, I did not underestimate him—it's wrong not to respect a friend, and I know how he hunts.

I pushed the kitchen door open and stood on the threshold. The strange handprints of raccoons marked the walls, the ceiling, in jam and molasses. I saw the shattered plaster of the walls, the holes where the bullets had gone, and on the table were pieces of raccoon and other parts—wires and switches, batteries, an egg timer with its cover ripped off—strewn all together. A raccoon's face had been stretched on a circular knitting needle, flat and tight, its eye sockets empty.

Standing there, I decided it was unwise to search through all the rooms. I know the sound of an empty house. Instead, I went around the outside, fearing the whole time that this was what he'd expect from me, that he'd thought it all out, what I'd do, and he'd planned for it. Through the window, sunlight slanted across his empty bedroom. Two beat-up ducks hung above the door; one had wire for a beak, the rest torn or fallen off, lost behind a piece of furniture. The walls were solid yellow, *National Geographic*s stacked five feet high.

I warn Harley of my suspicions. Eddie might poison the woman slowly, dress her again so you wouldn't see the stitches, rig her up somehow, all full of sawdust, chipped marbles for her eyes. I say all this, but I don't voice the other possibility—that the two of them are keeping company, driving somewhere together, shoulders touching in the sharp corners. Talking to each other.

Harley says the only thing that's certain is that Eddie's disappeared. He hardly even listens. Sounds to me, he says, like this is all about you, something going on in your head. He just moves further down the bar.

All I know is I crossed from Eddie's house over to his barn and stood outside. A chicken with razorblade claws would slice out of the darkness on a piece of fishing line, slashing at my face if I swung that door open. The horse skeleton, an insane marionette held together by wire, hooves sharpened like knives or coursing electricity, would gallop after me. The barn was full of the faintest sounds. I stood outside that door and I could not stop shivering.

DEATH'S DOOR

Paintings of ships hung on the walls. Caught in the white lips of waves, bold amid the waters. Thomas could not bear to look at them. Outside, it was raining. He listened to the old man, Edvar Christiansen, hold forth about the relative ease of saltwater fishing, how those men had the tides for a friend, not to mention trade winds, how everyone knew that salt pulled the teeth of the waters' cold.

"I would not know," Thomas said.

Fifteen minutes before, Edvar had poured himself a glass of

milk and set it down on the table, where it remained, untouched. His bare arms were folded across his chest, and the skin looked gray, mummified. His beard was going from yellow to white; it did not seem quite clean. The old man's slicker hung from a nail by the door, and a smaller slicker, his grandson's, hung below it.

"You'd know better than anyone," Edvar said. "I'd think you would, having lost people to the water."

"I don't really think about it," Thomas said.

"That's a lie I'll let pass." Edvar picked up the glass of milk, then set it back down. "I'd be ashamed," he said. "The thing of it is, my friend, I'd be ashamed to fish saltwater, to be honest. I need a challenge." He slapped his own chest. "Out there, though, they kiss the first salmon of the year and who can blame them? It's a handsome, strong fish, while what we have here, these whitefish, are an unwholesome-looking thing—bottom-suckers, they are, mouths so weak and trashy no one would kiss them."

"Was it a good year?" Thomas said, watching the rain against the window.

"Oh, yes. Fine. Don't get me wrong, I'm a happy man." He smiled, and it was hard to believe his eyebrows were not a handicap to vision. "Good things happen to me," he said. "These days all the little things, all the conspiracies that used to set me off, they just make me laugh. You, for example, are bound to ask for money, more money, this year."

"True."

"Extortionist son of a bitch!"

Thomas looked down, laughing with the old man. He watched as Edvar tried to light a candle, but the match and matchbook would not be still in his hands. It did not seem possible he would unfold the nets into the waters again next year, yet last September such a future had also seemed impossible and now they were in it, through it, back again. Arthritis had turned Edvar's hands into claws that could steer his boat and not much more. He needed them both to turn a doorknob. His wife had always mended the nets, but she'd been gone three years; this was how the task had fallen to Thomas. They had met among the gravestones, Edvar asking, Where have all our dead friends gone? and Thomas answering: They're under the ground. Unless they're underwater.

It seemed natural that he would mend the nets, inevitable, though he'd never done it before and had to learn. Some found it easier to hang the big nets to work on them, but there was no way to do that here. They lay out across the fields and now he had to wait for the rain to let up before he could return to them.

The windowpane was thick, old and uneven, hard to see through. Out by the barn, the boy was jumping on piles of lumber, lifting boards and then chasing the mice or snakes, whatever he had uncovered.

"He'll get wet," Thomas said.

"Boys do." Edvar laughed again, the candle alight.

One narrow bed was visible through the doorway into the bedroom. It was the only place to sleep, as far as Thomas could tell, which meant the old man and the boy shared the bed, slept together. Green wool blankets lay heavily across the mattress. Above, flowers were pressed flat inside a frame.

"He starts school this month," Edvar was saying. "I'll be all right, though. I'll be all right."

"The rain is easing," Thomas said.

"The thing is," Edvar said, "that there's hardly anyone left and there's no place like it, here on the peninsula. You go south and it's a regular clusterfuck, Milwaukee or even Chicago, and north—hell, what they say about the upper peninsula of Michigan is a hundred percent true. A stupid people has risen up there."

He fished mostly the bay side, but right on the tip, north of the town of Gills Rock. Sometimes he strayed around to the east and through Death's Door, where the water rushed the gap and the wind funneled through, between the peninsula and Washington Island. That stretch claimed endless boats, it pulled them down to the bottom.

"Here I go," Thomas said. "Wish me luck."

"May the heavens hold," Edvar said.

Thomas opened the door and stepped outside. It was not the wetness that bothered him, but the feeling of being surrounded that the rain brought on. He could not imagine being on board a boat with a swell moving beneath him, the horizon tilting and unsteady, everything sliding away, rising and disappearing. Perhaps it would be like riding atop a whole dark night, though the old man argued that the ground itself wasn't much different, once you started thinking like that. Thomas walked across the wet field. At least anything coming after you from these depths would come more slowly, would not be so cold.

Thomas could not swim. He had never learned and doubted he ever would. He had no desire to fight with the water. Many locals could not swim—it was a point of pride, really, to leave swimming to the tourists and the summer people. He had friends who snorkeled whole days in waist-deep water.

A row of clove hitches ran the length of the headline. He walked them, then stepped onto the net. It was heavy with tar, the knots just orderly tangles, abraded and broken in places. He sat down where he had left off. The knots were oily and smelled faintly of fish. Looking back, he saw the old man chase a chicken across the yard, around the side of the house. Farther, the treetops slapped each other, making space, spun wild by gales on the lake, the cold waves a mile away. Thomas liked to work on the nets. He wondered to himself—how deep has this knot gone? What has this square of mesh held? What else might be brought to the surface? Rusted bicycles, dead bodies, lost creatures. There was always the chance that the nets could become snagged and tangled on a sunken ship or even that the people, the skeletons below, might take hold of these twists and pull down, hoping to find new company, to take the boat all the way to the bottom.

He felt the boy on the net before he saw him—shoes too big, the excess of belt slapping around his thighs, hopscotching across and then standing close, watching. He was soaked through, as if he'd been submerged fully clothed. His hair was slick on his head. He did not seem cold at all.

"Can you swim?" Thomas said.

"Of course I can swim. Everyone can swim."

"Yes they can," Thomas said. He let the boy sit close and he felt the softness of the small, smooth fingers that tried to follow his own, which were thick as the necks of bottles. The boy had a nice way of leaning, not at all self-conscious, as if it were a natural thing for people to touch each other.

"I could teach you," Thomas said.

"That's all right," he said.

Thomas was afraid the boy would leave. He leaned back against his small body, felt the smooth skin of his face and all the time to come, all the time remaining. I am eight times as old as this child, he thought. Do I know eight times as much? No. Not nearly.

"My father went to the desert," the boy said. "He went away. In the desert there's no water and there's no animals."

"And your mother?" Thomas said. "Where is she?"

"She's my friend," the boy said. "She took me to Washington Island. We rode bikes. They drive cars right on the boat out to there."

"So I've heard," Thomas said. "I know they do."

Then the old man began to call from the yard; he was holding the chicken in his hands. The boy stood and ran across the net. Thomas watched him go, then took a fid from his pocket and worked a long splice, forcing the openings and tucking the opposite strands against the lay, marrying them. Done, he pulled it tight. A splice like that could be the strongest part of the whole net. Each year, incrementally, the nets were a little more his.

When he looked back he saw the old man was hypnotizing the chicken. Edvar lifted it in a slow, smooth circle, a blur of white. Up over his head, down low as his waist. He set it on the ground and the boy squatted close. This was the first year the boy had been here. Perhaps he was also hypnotized, Thomas thought. How could Edvar know what he had, appreciate it, know what to do?

———†———

There was still a day's work left in the nets when the rain returned. It came tentatively, then in sheets. Thomas ran for the shelter of his truck. He honked once to let the old man know he was going.

The peninsula was only five miles across, yet he could go months without seeing the water; he knew all the roads that kept their distance. As he drove south, the hook swung down from its frame on the back of the truck. He used the hook, the hydraulic lift, to move the gravestones he carved, and also, now, to pick up the nets once they were folded. Then the nets would fill the whole barn, rising six feet from the floor. In the spring they would yield dead snakes, flat and brittle, birds with wings outstretched or folded in on themselves; the nets caught beer cans and candy wrappers all winter, condoms that had frozen and gone fragile, yellowed like old tape. When the nets were done each year, Thomas knew the winter was really coming.

He drove away without looking back. Here and there thin spirals of smoke rose up. People burning leaves. There was no one on the highways. The season was over, or so they said; it was disconcerting to think there were nine months of twelve when there was no season at all. He went toward the lake side, down into Bailey's Harbor, close along the shore, tempting himself. The waves rolled in, hiding behind buildings and then there again, always on his left. He had paced the shore, helpless, waiting for news, as the water filled their mouths. He had waded to his knees and called their names, his wife's and his daughter's. Annie, he called, Sara, until he was hoarse, as they spun downward, until he could no longer feel his legs.

It was three o'clock and already turning darker; the rain didn't help. Thomas kept driving, turning inland again, toward the middle of the peninsula. The A.C. Tap was out on the highway, miles from anywhere, a great producer of drunk drivers, a place people went to shirk their responsibilities. Thomas just wanted to get a look at the boy's mother, and he knew somehow he'd find her here. He parked next to the tractor of Eddie Polenka. Eddie had lost his license, it had been suspended long before, and John the Sheriff let him drive the tractor to the bar. Only in daylight, though, and only if he stayed way over on the shoulder of the highway.

Thomas shook the rain from his jacket. He breathed in the smoke. Eddie and Alan Johnson looked up at him without saying

a word. Hank Williams, Jr. and Sr., were singing "There's a Tear
in My Beer." In the poolroom a whole drunken softball team—
most likely the Catholics or Moravians—were celebrating the
end of the season. They all wore their jerseys. A glass broke
somewhere and Harley cursed from behind the bar. Thomas did
not say anything. He had learned in these places that the only
thing he hated more than talking about himself was listening to
others. Everyone always understood your troubles better than
you could. Not only had they all been through similar experi-
ences, they'd dealt with them more successfully.

"Now Thomas," Alan Johnson said, as if he'd just recalled the
name. "How's that truck of yours working?" He was a mechanic,
new in town. His hands, resting on the bar, were filthy; grease
marked his cheek, where he'd scratched an itch.

"Fine," Thomas said.

"Those damn hydraulics," Alan said. "Been a while since I
had a problem like that, that lift, where I really had to figure.
Where you been, anyway?"

"Busy. The nets and everything."

"Busy?" Alan said. "Maybe we could hang out sometime. You
can't be that busy."

"I am," Thomas said.

"Go ahead and make me feel desperate," Alan said. He
turned away, back toward Eddie Polenka.

Barbara Anderson was throwing the beanbags, playing the
game with a blond woman Thomas did not know. He turned on
his stool and watched them. The woman kept looking over at
him; he stared back at her. She had the boy's sharp face; he
recognized it. Some things were just not right, he wanted to tell
her. What would become of that boy?

When the game was finished, she sat down next to him.

"What's your name?" he said.

"Ingrid," she said. The edges of her teeth looked sharp. "What's yours?"

"Thomas."

"Thomas," she said. "Did you want to buy me a drink?"

"No," he said. "I thought you were someone else."

"So what?"

"Let's play again," Barbara Anderson said, calling Ingrid away.

Harley came down the bar and stood in front of Thomas for a moment without speaking.

"You don't want anything to drink," he said.

"No," said Thomas.

"I could get you a soda or one of those non-alcoholic beers."

"Right. I appreciate your concern."

"Seriously. You don't want anything at all?"

Thomas just looked away, up at the cribbage board made from a toilet seat, at the Packers' schedule hanging on the wall—everyone was prepared to be disappointed again. Every season the days of Bart Starr were another year further in the past. Thomas looked down the bar.

"Let's stop acting so stupid," Alan Johnson was saying.

Eddie Polenka just sat with a Pabst Blue Ribbon in front of him. Some night soon he would tip his tractor over on himself.

"Good idea," he said to Alan Johnson. "You start."

"Harley," Thomas said. "I'm looking for a woman named Ursula."

"One in particular?"

"She's got a boy that's the grandson of Edvar Christiansen up in Gills Rock."

"That Ursula," Harley said. "Yes. Lives on A, in her folks' old place. Just north of Jacksonport. Not many houses along there."

"That's all I need," Thomas said, standing. "Thank you."

"I didn't do a thing," Harley said.

The rain spread into puddles; it filled the metal seat of Eddie Polenka's tractor. Thomas sat in his truck for a moment, watching through the window, the softball team in the poolroom. Someone shoved someone else, some wild punches were thrown, and as he considered going in to help break it up he realized the men were only horsing around, smiling and hugging each other.

He shifted into reverse, backed out, then turned south. Clouds hung low over fields. Silos rose like towers. He passed the gnarled and empty branches of orchards and he remembered being warned of the cherrypickers, immigrants from somewhere, brought up the peninsula in the backs of trucks. That was long ago, when he was a boy. Now machines came and shook the hell out of the trees until all the cherries fell from the branches, until they were all caught in nets.

He passed the house once, then circled around. It was set back on the lot, at the end of a dirt driveway. He parked behind an El Camino with rotten boards stacked in the back. On a stick in the middle of the yard a wooden duck spun its windmill arms in opposite directions. Thomas walked under a birdfeeder made of a plastic jug. He stepped up on the porch.

When he pushed the bell he heard no sound. He turned and watched the duck, then knocked on the door. After a moment he heard something inside.

A woman opened the door and stood looking out at him. She was tall, with wide shoulders, her hair so blond it barely held color, and long, pulled back out of her face. He had not expected the wrinkles at her eyes, and then they were gone again. He tried to see past her, around her, into the house. Jars full of beach glass covered one windowsill.

"Did you want something?" she said.

"Yes," he said, trying to figure where to start.

"Well?"

"Something's burning," he said.

When she turned away, he hesitated, then followed her back through the house. For a moment he wondered if he had the wrong person, but still he followed. In the kitchen he watched her take the burnt piece of toast and throw it out the back door, into the rain.

"Who are you?" she said, turning to face him.

"It doesn't really matter who I am," he said.

"I see," she said. She went around him, back into the other room. He wondered if she might call the police, or go out the front door and drive away, leave him there. He stayed where he was, standing in the kitchen.

"If you were going to follow me in here," she said, returning, "you could have at least shut the door."

"True," he said.

"Sit down," she told him, and he sat at the table. He watched her take out the bread. Green tomatoes lined the counter; they would never ripen.

"I could offer you a piece of toast," she said.

"I'd take it."

There was one photograph of the boy, under a magnet on the front of the refrigerator. Thomas did not say anything. He wanted to take hold of her shoulders and shake her.

"Cherry or raspberry jam?" she said.

"Raspberry," he said. "My name is Thomas."

"I like the seeds," she said.

He nodded, looking up at the knots in the macramé plant hanger above her head. He wondered if she had tied them. He wished she would sit, but she remained standing. She crossed the kitchen, looked out the window, then turned back on him.

"That your boy?" he said, pointing.

"Yes."

"Live with you?"

"He's up in Gills Rock," she said. "With his grandfather."

Thomas knew if either of them mentioned the name of anyone on the peninsula the other would know it. He did not want a sense of false familiarity between them. He thought of the boy sleeping in the same bed with the old man.

"That can't be healthy," Thomas said.

"Compared to what?" Ursula laughed. "All that nuclear family business has nothing to do with anyone I've ever met. Everybody doesn't work the same way—that I know."

You, Thomas thought, you took him out on the ferry. A very safe thing to do, very wise. As she talked she paced, and he listened to her clogs on the linoleum; he watched the thick wool socks at her heels and ankles. He had come to let her know that she would regret how she was handling all this, that it was not too late.

"Everyone needs different things," she was saying. "We're not the same to start with, and then different things happen. You and me, for example, that's something we'll never know."

"What's that?"

"Nothing normal," she said. "But I believe we'll find our friends or they'll find us."

In a way he wanted to disagree with her, just to keep her talking. Certainly his own experience hadn't borne all this out.

Once she asked him why he was here, then he would tell her. He would let her know where she'd gone wrong.

"What's your truck for?" she said, standing at the window.

"Monuments," he said.

"What?"

"For picking up the stones."

"Monuments?"

"Gravestones," he said. "We call them monuments. I cut them and I carve them."

"I see. You decorate graveyards." She smiled at him, then looked out the window.

"It's not right," he started to say, but she wasn't listening, she was already talking again.

"Listen to this crazy story," she said. "One night, there wasn't much of a moon, and I was out in the woods, wandering, and finally I came to the edge of a thicket of trees and I saw the rows of white markers. It was after midnight and I was scared at first but I kept walking, like I knew I couldn't be hurt. I was alone and there was a kind of murmuring, the closer I got. Have you ever felt like that?"

"I'm not sure," he said.

"I don't know how much time passed. I stood still and the air around me started to change; it smelled sweet. I was ready for the spirits to take me when it happened."

"What?"

"I was stung by a bee."

"At the cemetery?"

"No," she said. "I'd thought those white frames were gravestones, but I was nowhere near the cemetery!"

"The hives," he said. He thought of honeycombs peeled from

frames, curling over a knife. He had seen it once, or at least a picture of it.

"It was something," she said.

"I bet."

"Have to go to work."

"Not right now," he said.

"I do," she said. "Night shift. I'm a supervisor at the cherry plant."

Thomas wanted to ask what she was doing out there in the first place, alone in the woods at night, but already she was leading him to the door. She lay her hand down low on his back.

"Goodbye," she said. "Thanks for stopping in."

Thomas splashed out to the truck, listening to her laughter, uncertain if he had said what he'd wanted to say to her. He turned onto the highway as the rain picked up, and he headed for home. The autumn was not a busy time for him; it was not much of a season for dying. February was suicide season. That was months off.

———†———

Driving away from Ursula's house, he was frustrated at how he had not said the words he planned to, how he'd lost the heat of his anger. She'd done it with the story, the beehives like gravestones, and he'd let himself be taken in.

The rain slashed at the windshield and Thomas circled the grid of country roads, past dairy cows and golf courses, closer and closer to the cemetery. Most nights he appreciated the rain, for it covered the sound of the lake as it carved caves in the cliffs, smoothed walls, raked pebbles across the shore. The waves called to him, loudest in the storms. He feared, if given the chance, he would throw himself deep in the water. When he heard the waves he prayed for the silence of ice—ice that climbed the shore to splinter trees and claim decks from houses that dared too much, ice that crept through the cemetery all winter, the water and cold finding seams and breaking stones apart.

He did not slow at the gate, but only downshifted as he drove out among the gravestones, down a row between them. He imagined bodies underground, expelling hoarded breaths beneath the truck's weight.

The truck idled as he swung out, rattling through the chains on the flatbed until he found the crowbar. Water filled his eyes, wind whipped around him. Turning, he stabbed the earth with the sharp tip of the bar, dragging cables from his other hand. Some headstones resembled statues, angels and crosses and marble books, hands reaching up and down from heaven. Shapes rose from unfinished stone as if they were trapped there, as if they had been inside since the beginning. To him, all this was unnecessary, showy and redundant. The names were enough. Like a promise. Dig here, they said, straight beneath where you are standing, and you'll find this person, whatever is left.

ANNE ELQUIST   SARA ELQUIST

He had cut the names of his own young wife, of his little girl, yet their bodies were not below the stones, not safely in the earth. They had gone down on the ferry.

Now he pried their stones from the earth, one edge at a time, and worked the cables beneath the slick, cold marble; he attached the hook and lifted one stone, then the other, onto the back of his truck. Black squares of dirt were left behind, red worms twisting themselves into tangles.

Wet, covered in dirt, smiling, Thomas drove out of the cemetery. The stones were so heavy the flatbed almost touched the
dual rear tires. The whole truck rode low; his headlights angled
up into the stars.

After the rain of the day before, the grass in the field had grown
to hold the nets. Thomas had to drag the whole thing a few feet
with his truck, to free it, before he could get to work. He wondered if, given time, the nets would sink slowly through the
ground, following their urge to find the depths and comb them
for what lay hidden and buried there, to bring it to the surface,
out into the air and light. He retied a whole line of Edvar's
wife's knots, where other repairs had changed the spacing and
wrecked the tension. It had been three years since Edvar asked
Thomas to carve a knot into his wife's gravestone—a simple
mesh knot like the ones in the nets—and finally Thomas had
relented. It was from that argument that he had come to mend
the nets each year.

Thomas sat in the sun and worked all morning, until he was
as good as done. His truck rested, parked to one side, still low
under the weight of the gravestones. A blue tarp covered their
shapes, their names, and now he had decided what to do with
them, what would make him feel better.

The nets spread all around him, full of holes that could be
trusted. Neither the old man nor the boy came outside. The light
cut through the trees, changing its angles. Thomas lay back,
thinking that a person rolled in the nets could never escape,
never get loose. Their arms would be pinned to their sides, their
ears bent back. He wondered how it would be to be rolled up

with someone you loved, your bones knitting together, your skin drying and learning the knots. He thought of Ursula and it surprised him, the notion of being tangled with her.

At the sound of their voices, he turned his head to one side, then the other, but he could not see Edvar or the boy. He closed his eyes and thought of them in bed, imagined their conversations. The first people to come here, Edvar might say to his grandson, these were my grandparents, even before that; they were covered with white hair and they came in boats with sails made from the skins of whales. They carried knives of walrus tusks. Fish leapt into their boats. They were happy to be here, for no one had liked them where they'd come from. Over time, we even lost our hair, you see. Those were the people who built this house for us. They could see us coming, the two of us, they expected us to live here now.

Thomas wondered who awoke first, and if they stayed in bed, waiting for the other to rise. He wondered about his own little girl, what she might tell him now. He wondered if, in his sleep, Edvar stretched his withered arms to hold the boy close.

He drove slowly, watching the water, listening. The waves kept coming, rows and rows. The lake never tired, and it pulled at him, but he turned away, inland; in the rearview mirror he saw the whitecaps still rolling after him.

The first time, he passed Ursula's house at fifty miles an hour; then he turned and passed at thirty, then even slower. Her car was not in the driveway, and the only movement was the wooden duck, spinning its arms. Looking up and down the empty highway, Thomas pulled the truck onto the driveway, halfway onto the lawn. He climbed out and turned, taking hold of the metal hook, loosening the cable through the pulleys. If he left the stones in her yard that would show her the words he could not say; it might force her to care about what she had, if she saw what it meant to lose something.

"Had the feeling you weren't through with me," Ursula said. She came around from the other side of the truck, not from the house. Thomas tried not to seem surprised.

"What can I do for you?" she said. "Another piece of toast?" She shook her blond hair, hugged the cage of her ribs.

"Listen," he said.

"Let's go for a ride," she said, heading around the other side of the truck. She opened the passenger door and climbed in, then slammed it and waited for him. He opened his door.

"Quite a load you're hauling," she said, not turning around to look.

"Right." Thomas accelerated down the highway. "Where to?" he said.

"I know who you are," she said, bending her knees to rest her feet on the dashboard. "I knew yesterday, too; I was just playing along. My boy tells me all about you."

"I see," he said.

"This time of year I like to go to the harbor, down on the bay side." Ursula rolled down the window, stuck her head out, then turned back toward him. "The water looks harder, the surface of it, and the salmon and trout come in shallow and they're all beat up and tattered. They slide along under the few boats that are left and they circle the pilings. Some kids try to shoot them with arrows and stab them with spears, so I stop that—at least when I'm there I do."

"All right," Thomas said.

At the harbor, most of the slips were empty, the boats taken out and stored for winter. The sun faded toward dusk. Sailboats rested on trailers. The water kicked into foam along the pilings.

"Drive out onto the dock," Ursula said. "See if you can make it out to the end."

In the middle of the dock, a boathouse stood, its wooden sides weathered, covered with the names of boats, letters in all colors of paint. LAURA, SPINDRIFT, WHISPER. Thomas eased the truck forward, his rearview mirror close to the wall; Ursula looked out her window, down into the water.

"Right to the end," she said.

A lone fisherman sat in a folding chair, holding a pole; a dog, a dalmatian, rested next to him, its snout hanging over the edge as if it was sniffing for fish. As they passed closer, Thomas saw that the fisherman was Alan Johnson. Alan waved coolly at the truck, then looked back out over the water. His line stretched to a red and white plastic bobber, which rose and fell in the low waves. Farther out, miles away, were the dark shapes of islands.

Thomas turned off the ignition and opened his door, swung his feet onto the dock. Ursula came around the front of the truck and stood next to him, close to the edge. As he looked out toward the islands, the low waves sliding in, she took hold of the tarp and pulled it loose; it blew along the dock, edges scratching the concrete, settling against the wall of the boathouse. The sailboats' rigging rang in the wind. The two marble gravestones sat on the truck, exposed, the names dark with shadow. Ursula did not say a thing.

Reaching for the hook, Thomas flicked the hydraulic switch and gave himself some slack. The cables were still wrapped around the stones; first he attached Anne's, lifted it, and pushed the metal arm around, so it hung over the water. He let the cable out a little at a time, until the water darkened the base of the stone, and then the whole thing eased below the surface. Once it hit bottom, the cable went slack and the hook came loose. He raised it again.

"Now hold on," Alan Johnson said, standing, moving closer. "Children swim here, you know. People dive off."

"Is this your business?" Ursula said.

"I know you," Alan said, as if only just recognizing her. "We met before, remember?"

"No," she said. "And so what if we did?"

Alan began to answer, but when he looked at her face he turned away. The dalmatian skittered along the edge as he pulled at its leash. He reeled in his line and folded his chair; not looking back, he disappeared around the other side of the boathouse.

Thomas had not slowed at Alan's words. Now he had Sara's stone aloft, and he lowered it down next to her mother's, through the cold water.

The hook came up empty, and he wound the cable back onto its spool. He stood next to Ursula, looking down, and he could make out the white marble, the stones glowing ten feet underwater. He had set out to show her something, and she had twisted it this other way around.

He glanced at her, then back to the water. On a bright day, perhaps, the names would be legible; over time, though, plants would grow to fill the letters. Currents would wear down their edges and leave the stones smooth.

THE TREASURE STATE

MIGRATION

The tiger's face filled the windowpane, looking in, its breath fogging the glass. Turning, tail hooking out behind, the big cat moved lazy and slack-hipped across the ice, toward the others. The clouds rested only twenty feet above the ground, as if the whole world had a ceiling. Only wind or snow could clear the clouds, and neither was likely soon.

Claudia looked out the back window, watching her livestock. She could not see down into the valley or up the slanted bench to the mountains' peaks. The air's pressure had increased, tightened down between the clouds and earth—it made her feel claustrophobic. She turned, crossed the room, and sat down at the table, closer to the woodstove. Three kittens slept in a box, taking in the heat. Their striped sides rose and fell.

The ranch was thirty miles from Gardiner, fifty south of Livingston, set up in the mountains. Doug would be back in two days. He'd never returned early. He could make it all worthwhile, talking like they were pioneers, out where no one had thought to be before. When she was with him, around other people, Claudia felt she was in on something, that she lived outside the world of others and inhabited one they could not imagine. Now, sometimes, she felt that way even when Doug was gone.

Technically, he always said, who knows if it's legal? But you can bet they'll draw up a whole new law if we get any attention up here. A couple years is all we need—we'll make the money, then we'll be out of danger. Only way anyone finds out is if we slip up and do something stupid.

Claudia wasn't about to. She turned a page in her book, touched the photograph of Dian Fossey with a table full of gorilla skulls, then scratched at the long scabs on her forearms. Out the front window, eighty yards away, she saw that Patrick—the older brother of the ranch manager from down the basin—was stuck. He was delivering a load of fenceposts; stacked atop one another, they looked like quills.

Patrick tried to use one of the posts as a lever, to free the truck. Claudia could have easily driven down and pulled him out, but she figured he was finding it more entertaining than frustrating, and she enjoyed watching his struggle. He slipped and fell, then stood again. He was over fifty, but dusted his knees like a child before once again taking hold of his lever. Claudia watched his four dogs come halfway to the house and sniff the air; they barked at each other to show their bravery, then ran back toward him. Rounded, bundled like an arctic explorer, he circled his truck.

In the next photograph, Dian Fossey stood with an arm around an ape's shoulder, its hairy arm around hers. Gorillas were so much stronger than people, and perhaps, Claudia thought, they also had the ability to be that much more gentle, their range increasing on every side. She read on, about Dian Fossey's technique of imitating the wild gorillas to draw them in, how Dian understood animals better than humans.

Claudia did not claim an understanding of either, but she did claim some agreements, some working compromises. And unlike Dian, who sought places where the animals hadn't been driven into the corners, Claudia did not need a safari—here she was, back in Montana, on the ranch where she grew up. She had returned a year ago, with Doug, after her father had finally passed away. The first thing they did was sell all the cattle and half the land. She tried not to think of all the fences that remained, used for nothing. In all the miles of barbed wire, there was probably not one strand she hadn't mended, and now so many were left snapped and snaking loose—whole posts pulled out by the elk that tore through the fences, followed each other single file, now through the clouds, stupidly trusting whichever one was in front, blind, an easy target for anything big enough to take them down. The elk used to come and feed off the haystacks when she was a girl, but now they did not come so close.

"Quiet," she said to the kittens. The clouds had tightened her nerves. She checked her watch, knowing it was feeding time, that they were right. Standing, she set aside the books—Dian

Fossey and Jane Goodall, *Canine and Feline Urology, Manual of Feline Behavior, The Mammals*—and went back toward the kitchen. She filled the sink with hot water, then set the bottles there to warm. There was a knock on the rooftop, and she listened for another that did not come. The stovepipe, she decided, or a loose shingle—the ice got under and cracked them sometimes. She put the teapot on the burner.

It always took a while for the bottles to warm; she had time to check out back. Her wool pants were covered in alfalfa, blood and spit, their suspenders backward; one strap came up between her breasts, splitting into a Y at her clavicle, forking over her shoulders. Feathers leaked from her down jacket, where duct tape patches slipped.

She expected the cold, the air rushing at her eyes. The tigers and lions just watched her—they knew it was not feeding time—but she could tell they were also unnerved by the clouds. Long golden tails rolled and unrolled of their own will. Yawns revealed teeth. A few cats disappeared down the alleys between the fences; the structure was all a little haphazard, but the cats didn't stray as long as they were fed.

There were twenty lions and tigers, maybe twenty-five— Doug had taken some of the bigger ones with him, separated in the trailer as he drove the long way to Texas, all the back roads, hoping to avoid any trouble.

Claudia petted Hondo's head, scratched the tiger all the way down his spine. He half sneezed in pleasure, steam rising. It had taken some time to get used to their breath, but Claudia loved the cats. Hondo licked her pantleg; she'd read their tongues could take flesh from bone, but she knew how gentle they could be. The books also said they could leap thirty feet—she'd never seen that, though of course all these cats were drugged, fed

tranquilizers in their meat. All except Victor, the male lion, who
needed his energy to do his thing. He was kept in a separate
cage, and now he was pacing, watching her. She felt Hondo's
ribs under her hand, the slow rise of his heart. Something, a
dead bird, lay on the ground in the middle of the pen. None of
the cats showed any interest.

Doug believed they were twice as ferocious when they were
taken off the tranquilizers, that it was from withdrawal and also
the release of all that restrained wildness. They didn't forget the
jungle, he said, even the ones born right here. He argued that it
was all genetic, that memories were passed down. He tried to
breed Victor, the lion, with the female tigers, believing people in
Texas would pay big money to shoot and kill something they
would never find in the wild.

Ligers, he said.

Now Claudia watched the big cats go in and out of the garage, where heatlamps burned, multiplying the power bills. She
listened for a rasp as they breathed, any sign of pneumonia. In
her mind, the hunters always missed, and the cats ran free,
escaping, crossing the border south and seeking their climate, the
memories of their ancestors. She didn't like to think of Texas.

As she turned to go inside, something solid slapped her between the shoulderblades and knocked her down so fast she
could not get her hands up to catch herself. Her shoulder, then
her head hit the ground. She lay there, eyes closed; when she
opened them, her vision doubled, then righted itself. Five or six
cats had circled close, watching. They backed up when she
moved her arm.

The bird was struggling next to her head, its wing broken.
Claudia caught it by the foot and it turned and pecked at her,
the sharp beak right through her down jacket. Sitting up, she

pinned its wings with her fingers; the bird whistled, trying to turn its head, its heart speeding. Its eyes were dark red. Claudia covered them with her hand. She wrung the bird's neck in one motion, felt the whole thing go loose.

When she looked up, she saw there were more birds, all black and white, those red eyes. Some ran for cover, staying close together, their bills long and sharp, heads bobbing on well-oiled necks, wings out for balance, legs straight as if they had no knees—others were still falling, as if they'd been thrown from just above the clouds and their wings weren't strong enough to slow the force, to catch themselves before the earth broke their bones. They rolled off the roof, some already dead, some able to run. The cats crowded together, confused and afraid, running for the garage.

Claudia stood and went back toward the house. She swung the door open into a terrible screaming, and it took a moment for her to realize it was not coming from inside her. It was the teapot—sputtering, choking itself, almost boiled dry. She set the dead bird on the counter, then took the kettle off the burner. The sound did not stop, but only changed. The kittens were howling, hungry. She pulled their bottles from the sink, then went to sit by them, next to the woodstove.

They were already as big as house cats, and they scratched at her hands, impatient. Once they had all had a little milk, she picked up the phone; first she called the operator to get the number, then she called the Department of Fish and Game. She told the man who answered what had happened, and she tried not to let him know where she was. She did not give him her name.

The man asked her to hold on, and as she switched bottles she picked up the dead bird and twisted its head around on its loose neck, then untwisted it. She opened the beak and looked inside, touched the film closing over the dead red eye.

When the voice returned, she set the bird down. She let the kittens play with it. The man told her he thought he knew what was going on. He asked if she had low cloud cover, and when she said yes, he guessed she was up in the basin. There was nowhere else the clouds would settle like that. The birds were water birds, migrating, and they'd mistaken the clouds for a lake or pond when they were high above it. They'd followed each other down. It was a whole flock, he suspected, and they could not take off from land. They needed a body of water.

Claudia tried to prevent him from sending someone up to help her, but he just said there wasn't much going on in Gardiner, that they had time and men to spare. She half listened as he went on about snowmobilers getting lost, about frostbite, about some antler-collecting fool from Lodge Grass who'd frozen to death, unwilling to leave his hoard behind.

"I hardly think," she said, but by then all he'd say was that they were all government employees down there, that they had to earn their salaries. He hung up as she protested.

Pulling the Audubon book from the shelf, Claudia found the page, then lay the dead bird on top of its picture. White feathers on its stomach, black on its back and a cap on its head. An eared grebe, certainly, its blood running down the book's binding. If someone did try to find her, it would not take long. There were only four ranches in the basin, only one farther up. Claudia tried to think.

There was a knock at the door. She closed the bird into the book, then opened it again. She slid the kittens' box under the table and, looking around the room, closed the curtains over the back windows. She checked the kittens again.

When she opened the door, Patrick stood there, smiling, his dogs close behind him. He was a big man, his stocking cap pulled down so far it hid his eyebrows. His boots were obviously from two different pairs.

"Is it dead?" he said.

"What?" Claudia said, then realized she was still holding the bird.

"Got stuck down there," he said. "Got the posts out here now."

Claudia just looked at him, at his dogs all sniffing the air, whining, staying close to his legs. He looked behind him, then back at her.

"Lock them up," she said. "Your dogs. In your truck. We have a situation here."

She watched him lead them out, hold the door for them. They were closer to the cats there, emboldened by being inside the truck. She'd woven black plastic through the fences in front; the dogs could not see, but smelled the tigers and lions. The dogs barked behind the windshield, climbing over each other, their teeth showing.

"What?" Patrick said.

"Follow me." She led him back through the house, out into the maze of pens. A few of the cats had caught birds, or had been eating dead ones; blood covered their chests and paws, feathers stuck to them as they cleaned themselves. The birds had settled into four or five groups, spread around along the fences.

"Have to catch them first," Claudia said. "Round them up."

"Are they tamed?" he said.

"I mean the birds."

"That'll be easier," Patrick said.

Claudia expected him to say something about the cats, but he did not; perhaps he already knew. She told him what to do.

"They're not dangerous," she said, but he was already walking through the middle of them. He kicked at a stack of metal posts that were frozen together. As he began setting up a narrowing alley of chicken wire, Claudia walked the pen with a long-handled shovel in her hands, finishing off the injured birds, the only ones she could catch. At one end of the pen there were bones from deer and other carcasses long since picked clean. The birds' heads rang on the flattened blade of her shovel. She turned and headed back. Still the clouds were not lifting.

Patrick pounded the posts with a length of pipe. When he stopped, there was no sound at all. He did not speak, and Claudia appreciated his silence. The two of them circled the pen from opposite sides and drove the birds before them; it was easier than she had hoped—once a few started in one direction it pulled the others. She slipped on the ice, almost fell, regained her balance. Birds came out singly and in pairs, from hidden crevices, running with their tails up and wings out.

"Hey there," Patrick said to them. "Whup, whup."

He pulled the loose chicken wire across behind the birds, and then Claudia went looking for boxes. There were ninety-three birds, five boxes worth. The cats just watched the whole operation, close under the clouds, a little anxious about what might fall next.

Claudia dragged the boxes inside. She went back out and Patrick was still standing in the middle of the pen, staring at Victor. The lion paced and stared back, shaking his sorry mane.

"Come in and get warm," she said.

"All right," Patrick said.

Inside, she watched him pick up one of the kittens; it bit through the thumb of his glove and he did not seem to notice.

"What are we doing?" he said.

"Waiting."

"What for?"

"To see if someone comes."

They both sat there without taking off their heavy coats. Claudia wondered how things got so complicated, what Doug would do, what he would say when he returned. The birds shuffled against each other, their feathers sliding along the inside of the cardboard boxes. She was sure they would fly out of the boxes—though she knew they could not do this, it kept surprising her. Here they were, pausing in their migration, caught short of where they wanted to be. She looked out the window, down toward the abandoned trucks. The Case tractor slowly rusted, a tin can over its vertical exhaust pipe to keep out the wet.

"Are you thinking?" Patrick said.

Claudia watched the red eyes of the birds jerk in their sockets; they could look at her from all angles without moving their heads. She remembered when she was a girl, twenty years before, when Patrick had first moved out here to live with his brother. He would show up to visit around dinner, walking with the dogs he had then. He was a young man—he stopped just to say hello; he never said much, always turned down anything her mother or father offered. Eventually, he stopped coming, and later his brother apologized, saying he had not realized about Patrick's visits or he would have stopped them before. Now Patrick petted the sleeping kittens, looking across the room at her.

"I like your hair," he said. "Used to be curly."

"That was a long time ago," she said.

"You're still Claudia."

She stood to put a log in the woodstove, and then heard the dogs, still in Patrick's truck, as they began barking.

"Someone's coming," he said.

She looked out the window and saw the green Fish and Game truck rolling slowly up the drive. She took the kitten from Patrick's hands, then hid their box back under the table.

"Bring all the birds outside," she said.

Claudia ran out the door, down the stairs of the front porch and wildly across the ice, to intercept the truck before it got too close. It stopped, the driver's door opening.

"You're the one with the birds?" the woman said, slapping her hands together, looking up at the clouds.

"Yes," Claudia said.

"Talked to your neighbors down below—even they weren't sure who was up here." The woman wore tight snowpants, a parka with a fur collar, sunglasses with leather at the temples. It was not that bright. A thick blond braid snaked out the back of her Fish and Game cap.

"I'm Dana," she said.

"Don't know why they sent you," Claudia said. "Everything's under control." She looked back at Patrick, bringing out two boxes at a time. Fortunately, he had parked his truck and the trailer of posts across the fence, where the cats' pen stretched around the house.

"Those are some tall fences," Dana said, looking in the same direction.

"They are."

"Where are they?" Dana said.

"Where are what?" Claudia said.

"The birds."

"Oh," Claudia said. "He's bringing them out."

Twenty feet away, Patrick set down the last box, then walked over to his truck and tapped through the windows at his dogs. She did not like him so close.

"I guess I'll just take them, then," Dana said.

Claudia looked down at the frozen ruts in the ground, the jagged marks of chains, then up into Dana's face.

"No," she said.

"I came all this way."

"It happened on my land. It's my responsibility."

"To be honest," Dana said, "this is my first week. I'm just trying to do my job."

"I appreciate it," Claudia said. "But I don't need your help."

The two stood looking at each other, Patrick coming closer, then standing silently, the third point of a triangle. He looked at Claudia, then Dana, then Claudia again.

"All right," Dana said. "I'll just drive up here and turn around."

"It'd be easier to back out," Claudia said. "I don't need you leaving ruts further up there."

She helped Patrick load the last boxes into the blue pickup. He climbed in back with the birds and she eased off the choke, rolled down toward the road. The cab of the truck was full of grit and junk, wrappers and tools. The gunrack behind her head held a shovel, two kinds of hammers, a long-handled ax. Probably there was a gun somewhere in the truck, loose under the seat, caught in the springs, tangled in baling twine, lost in a feedbag.

"Hang on!" she shouted, and Patrick shouted something back, words she could not understand. He crouched there, hardly out of the wind, as if he could feel no cold. In the rearview

mirror, Claudia watched the woman's truck, and then she saw
something else. She pulled over, rolled down the window.

"You let the dogs out," she said.

"Well," Patrick said.

"Well," she said, "we can't leave them behind. Loose like
that."

They waited until the dogs caught up, trailing steam, tongues
slapping up over their eyes. They scrambled at the side of the
truck, climbing from the tire, claws scratching at the side of
the bed as Patrick reached to grab each one by the collar.

"Got enough room?" she said.

"Yes."

The road was steep, cutting back and forth. A couple weeks
before, a hunter had gone off the edge, pulling a trailer with
four horses in it—it was a miracle none of them was killed.
The lucky man led them out the escape door in the front
of the trailer, and some others from town managed to pull the
truck out backward. The man hitched everything together
again, at the bottom of the hill. Claudia had watched the horses
rear and resist, showing white all around the edges of their
eyes before they finally got back into the trailer.

The clouds had hardly lifted down in the valley; as she descended, she could just make out the Yellowstone, jerking back
and forth, its banks expanded by ice. Looking back to the road,
she brought the truck around a corner and almost hit a man
walking a dog. The man gave her the finger; the dog, a dalmatian, was almost invisible against the dirty roadside snow—Patrick's dogs were wild in back, barking at it, no doubt trampling
the birds.

Claudia drove on. They crossed the bridge, the water low, the river narrow, and it shook just a little under the weight of both trucks. It always seemed more rigid in the winter. By the high-way, tall green metal boxes stood, where everyone who lived up the basin brought their garbage, where sometimes there was something—kitchen scraps, lambs or even calves that didn't make it—worth scavenging. Claudia turned left at the green boxes, out onto the highway. Behind her, Dana, who should have taken a right and headed back toward Gardiner where she be-longed, also went left and continued to follow.

"Bitch," Claudia said, knowing she could not force a confron-tation, that she'd have to play along to help this pass.

She drove on, up Paradise Valley, the highway parallel to the river. There, the current would be too strong for the birds. The clouds were higher here, but still only a couple hundred feet up. In the back of the truck, Patrick was yelling something to his dogs. Claudia scanned the side of the highway, for roadkill. She did this out of habit; she could always come back later. Now that they were away from the ranch, all they had to deal with was the birds. One thing at a time, she told herself.

She parked on the side of the highway, up above the pond where, in the warm months, the swans and Canada geese gath-ered. Now cattails and weeds stuck up, strangled by ice.

"Cold," Patrick said, climbing down.

"You're cold?" Claudia said.

"Yes."

She turned and looked back into the cab of the truck. She found two more right-handed gloves and put them in her pocket. In a moment, she felt Dana standing behind her.

"All this crap in here," Claudia said. "Friend of mine got in an accident and all his injuries were from things flying around the cab."

"I bet."

"You carry a gun?" Claudia said. "Didn't think so."

"Just thought I could help." Dana stood there, answering a different question. "That's why I followed you."

Claudia took the ax from the gunrack. She looked down toward the frozen pond, then at the birds, then at Patrick.

"You two carry the boxes down there," she said.

As soon as Patrick moved away from the truck, all the dogs leapt from the bed and began chasing each other out across the field. Dana dragged a box behind her. She stopped at the fence, next to a sign that said KEEP OUT.

"I don't know," she said.

"Where in hell are you from?" Claudia said.

"Arizona."

"Well, I'm from here."

"I know that."

"We're saving these birds." Claudia was almost shouting. "You don't even have to be here."

Dana lifted the box over the fence, then climbed through.

Soon they had all five boxes on the bank of the pond. Patrick shuffled off after his dogs. The ax in her hand, its heavy head dragging along the ice, Claudia walked to the center of the pond and turned a slow circle—cattails, the highway, cattle again, ice in their tips, the cold air, the sky above. A car slowed, up on the highway, then sped away again.

She raised the ax above her head. Her feet wide apart for balance, she brought the ax down into the ice. Splinters caught her in the face and neck, and she swung again. She liked the pull in her back, the solidity of the ice and kick it returned. Five swings and she broke through. The ice was four inches thick; she lifted out the slabs with the flat of the blade, trying to keep her

gloves dry. It all came easier once the surface was broken. The
water was dark beneath the ice, almost black.

When Claudia stopped to rest, she looked up and was almost
surprised to see Dana still standing there, next to the boxes of
birds.

"Let me," Dana said. "You've done enough."

"No," Claudia said. She did not want to turn the ax loose.

"Maybe you could give your husband a chance, then."

"Who?"

Dana pointed to Patrick, returning across the field with his
dogs. They fanned around him, dark against the snow.

"He's too heavy to get out here," Claudia said. She raised
the ax again, moving toward the bank, chopping out a narrow
canal.

"Cold," Dana said, running in place.

"Arizona," Claudia said, over her shoulder. "What do you
have down there? Snakes?" She swung the ax, kicked a triangle
of ice along the pond's surface. "We've got snakes here, but that's
just the beginning. This isn't even a cold day."

"Listen," Dana said, "I came out here to help you."

"Arizona!" Claudia said, the ax over her head, ice all around
her.

"There's no reason to be such a bitch about it," Dana said.

Claudia stopped swinging. She turned all the way around.

"This here has nothing to do with us," she said. "It's the
damn birds, all right?"

She kept chopping, turning her back again. Patrick shouted
something from across the pond, waved, and disappeared into
the cattails.

"You raise cattle up there?" Dana said, her voice quieter now.

"It's a cattle ranch," Claudia said. "It was."

"I'd like to see it," Dana said. "On a day where there's some visibility."

Claudia dropped the conversation, concentrating on her work. When she finished, she walked to the nearest box and picked out a bird. The rest looked up at her, frost in the plumes on their heads, their evil red eyes revolving, their necks never still. She stared back at them for a moment, then knelt down and dropped the bird into the water. It slipped, tried to climb out, and finally decided to swim. Instantly more graceful, it went down the canal, to the middle of the pond, and returned.

"I don't know," Dana said.

"I'm back," Patrick said, his thick body looming closer.

Just then the bird turned again. It sped up, kicked its black legs out, and splashed until it was running on the surface; its neck out straight and parallel to the water, it pulled itself into the sky.

Kneeling, Patrick picked another bird from the box. He looked up at Claudia and she knew he would do anything she asked him, anything at all. The bird slipped into the water, testing the canal, splashing into flight. A dog barked, then another. Claudia realized, watching the bird rise into the air, that Dana's arm was around her, holding her close. Claudia's left arm was pinned against Dana's body; in her right, she still held the ax.

Another bird followed, then another. They gathered, circled, and waited above; they would fly south—magnets in their heads, compasses spinning circles through their breasts—and keep going, passing over Doug as he drove north, as he returned to her. They would fly over Wyoming, Colorado, even Texas. There, on the land spread out far below, they would have to watch everything that happened to the lions and the tigers.

BEYOND LUCKY

The man was wearing a jacket from a band uniform—gold brocade around the buttons, epaulets of gold twine on the shoulders, the whole thing a cold, leathery blue. The woman next to him wore a turtleneck tucked into leggings, orange moonboots, a down vest too small to close around her stomach. They stood by the pay phone, at a service station set out on I-90, eating ice cream cones. It was not yet noon.

Sue was pumping gas, watching them. Tire tracks of ice shone and circled and crossed each other in the parking lot. The hood of her car was frozen shut, so she did not check the oil. On the way inside to pay, she passed close to the couple. They pretended not to watch her pass.

The radio inside seemed to be switching from station to station. Next to the cash register were magnets in the shapes of all fifty states, packets of powder that promised to cure hangovers. The man behind the counter had a cigarette burning between his fingers, another in an ashtray. He paused as if he wasn't going to give Sue her change; she stood there until he finally counted it out.

Now they were standing by her car, waiting for her. Two clouds of steam rose from their faces, as if they were on fire, burning from within. Sue put her money away before stepping closer. A cardboard suitcase rested on the ground between them. They did not say anything, and they were looking neither at her nor each other—their eyes only confirmed the fact of their presence there in the parking lot, standing close to her car. Sue did not speak, either. The sides of her car were stained with lines of salt; dirty black ice choked the wheel wells. She wondered for a moment if the man inside was watching them, and then she wondered why that would change anything. There were no other cars, no animals on the ground or birds in the sky.

The two of them still did not say anything. They just stood there, waiting. Sue judged by appearances—she was no fool. The man's moustache looked unplanned, and his jeans were so tight she could watch his skinny legs shiver. The woman was so pregnant it seemed she might lose her balance, that standing required an effort. She looked as if she could give birth at any moment, as if she would. It was this fact that did it.

"All right," Sue said. "Get in, then."

Sue gave them her real name, and there's no reason to

change it here. The story reflects well on her, after all. That winter she'd been teaching some art classes at a community college far from where she lived. She was on her way home after a two-week stint, tired from acting the expert, making proclamations about art, projecting a certainty she knew was simplistic. When she told this story later, to friends, she was a little ashamed at having been so trusting, yet there are certainly far worse things to be.

Sue pulled onto the interstate and accelerated. The engine bucked in complaint, straining with the weight of the new passengers. The man had not let her put the suitcase in the trunk, and now it crowded his feet. In the silence, she heard the rasp of his coat rubbing against itself. She decided it was not up to her to speak first; she was already giving them a ride, after all. She hit the washer fluid, then the wipers. They scratched the liquid into frozen lines. Pretending to adjust the rearview mirror, she looked at the woman in the backseat.

The woman's stocking cap was made from the cut-off sleeve of a sweatshirt—the wrist cuff hung down toward her ear, and Sue almost expected to see a hand there, reaching out. She checked the road, then looked back again, and the woman had taken off the cap. Her hair was bright pink, in tight curls. It was gathered into two short pigtails, like horns, above her temples. She looked back into the mirror, at Sue, with no expression at all.

"Ambidextrous," the man said, stretching out both arms.

Sue let that go.

"If you need me to hold the wheel," he said, "let me know."

"What?"

"You know, to hold it steady. If you want to do something with your hands or something."

"I'll let you know," Sue said. She'd noticed that all the whiskers were thicker on one side of his face, as if that side was continually in shadow. It was like those psychology photographs that divide faces in two—one half friendly and trustworthy, the other sinister and anxious to do you wrong. The left side, the friendly one, was turned toward Sue.

"Karma," he said. "Some say that's how hitchhiking is. The day'll come when you need a ride, and now you've earned it."

"I'll keep that in mind."

"Scott," he said. "My name is Scott."

"What's your name?" Sue said.

"I just told you," he said. "Scott."

"I meant your friend," Sue said.

"Chrissie." The woman did not turn her face from the window to say it.

The sun glowed faintly from behind the clouds, too weak to ever get very far up in the sky.

"Mind if I smoke?" Scott said.

"Yes I do."

"No problem," he said. "Probably don't have any smokes, anyway."

They kept driving, west. He offered to split the gas money, and was clearly relieved when Sue said that was not necessary. A half hour passed before they saw a truck coming in the opposite direction, a kind of proof that there was life where they were headed. Scott talked in bursts, then sat silently, stretching his arms. He told her they hoped to make it to Bozeman. The day before, he claimed, he'd been riding with a trucker and seen antelope with some kind of orange plastic all tangled in their horns.

"Right," Sue said.

"From road construction," he said. "Why would I lie about that?" He smiled at her, waited a long time before speaking again. "This car—you found it dependable?"

"Pretty much so."

"Yes," he said. "I bet you have." He rolled down his window for a second, let a cold slice of air inside. "Listen," he said. "I'm going to let you in on a secret."

Unclasping the suitcase, he did not open it all the way, but only a few inches, as if it held things he could not let Sue see. He pulled out a solid wheel of tickets, a foot across, and held out the loose end, smiling.

"Lottery," he said.

The outermost layer of tickets unrolled enough to reveal that the ones underneath had no numbers stamped on them. Scott did not seem to notice the blank tickets, and Sue did not say anything.

"State lottery or what?" she said.

"The lottery," Scott said. "The big one." He shook the disc of tickets in the air, then put them away again. "Beyond lucky," he said, "and I know what it is to lose hope. This was in a 7-Eleven, you know—I saw that the little door was open, back behind the counter, and she distracted them, down by the frozen food. She acted like the baby was coming—it was perfect. Probably took hours before they realized what we got away with."

Looking in the mirror, Sue could not tell if Chrissie had fallen asleep or had only closed her eyes. She wondered if the story was true, if Chrissie would say anything if it wasn't.

"Montana," Scott said. "I'd like to settle out there. Lots of celebrities do, you know."

It was four in the afternoon and it was already getting dark. Sue remembered how, setting out this morning, she had dreaded the boredom of this drive. She would welcome boredom if she found it again. The farther she went, the more anxious she was. At last they came to a town, back among other people.

"I'm stopping here," she said, pulling into a truck stop.

"Pancakes," Scott said. "I know I could use a little something." He jumped out and slammed the door before the car stopped moving, then opened the door and grabbed the suitcase.

When Sue stood, she realized for the first time that Scott was shorter than she was. A long white Cadillac was parked next to her car, and he was walking around it, leaning close, shading his eyes to see in through the window.

"Riding in this here," he said, "you wouldn't care if you ever got where you were going."

"Maybe there's someone here who might be going closer to where you're headed," Sue said. "Maybe even that car."

"Then you'd have to drive alone," Scott said. "Couldn't do that to you."

Chrissie followed the two of them into the truck stop's restaurant. It made Sue uneasy, how quickly the three of them had become attached, a unit. At the table next to theirs, a red-faced man was speaking in a loud voice.

"Can't say I've ever been this far from Wisconsin," he was saying. "Out here it's a little claustrophobic. Fear of the marketplace or whatever. Would take days to find a decent body of water."

The specials were on the blackboard, every other word misspelled. The menu wasn't much better. Up near the ceiling, a model train circled its tracks, following the walls around and around, disappearing and emerging from behind a clock made of a shellacked slice of tree stump.

"Used to be such a drunk," the red-faced man said, "I had to drive my tractor to the bar."

The woman with him said something, but she was not facing Sue, so Sue couldn't hear. The woman had a long fur coat and it was draped over her chair. Chrissie had turned around and was stroking the coat, petting it. Sue was afraid the woman would notice.

"Come in, Sue," Scott said. "Hello in there."

"What?" she said.

"I was asking if you drank."

"Not really."

"Me neither," he said. "I like to stay sharp."

She watched Scott tie the fringe of his jacket, the epaulets, into knots and untie them again. He cut his pancakes into small pieces—all one direction, then across at right angles—before eating them. Sue thought of what he'd said about the antelope, of driving with the trucker, and she wondered if he'd even been with Chrissie the day before. She thought of their theft of the tickets, the trick they pulled, and, looking at Chrissie, she began to suspect that Chrissie was not actually pregnant. Sue could not see Chrissie's stomach very well because of the table between them.

"Tea," Scott said. "I never figured what kind of people drink tea."

"Now you've met one," Sue said.

The red-faced man and the woman in the fur coat stood to leave. It looked like the coat was made of foxes, forty or fifty; Chrissie turned to watch it go.

Sue saw her car waiting outside, resting in the parking lot. She could not finish her chicken sandwich. Chrissie reached across the table to take a potato chip, then another. When the bill came, Scott paid his part, not quite all of it, in quarters. Sue made up the difference. On the way out she tried to get a good look at Chrissie, but Chrissie held her vest in front of her stomach.

"Well," Scott said, swinging the suitcase. "Let's get after it. Want me to drive? Might get there sooner."

Sue just shook her head, then stood for a moment, giving them another chance to change their minds, to disperse. Scott opened the back door for Chrissie. He climbed in himself and honked the horn until Sue opened her door.

She drove back to the interstate. At the edge of the town they crossed a pair of railroad tracks and Scott suddenly threw up his arms, pressed his palms flat against the roof, and lifted his feet from the floorboards.

"Do that," he said. "And you're going to get laid tonight."

"I don't believe in that kind of thing," Sue said, hoping he was not thinking of her.

"Getting laid?" he said.

"Whatever," she said. Sometimes, she thought, you had to help people in spite of themselves. Even in spite of yourself. In any case, she was driving in this direction—they weren't really putting one over or taking advantage of her. She only wished she could help Chrissie and leave Scott.

"I might sleep a little," he said. "That all right with you?"

"Fine."

"If it isn't, you know, you can say so. It's kind of a trade-off, after all—the ride for the conversation, for the company."

"Sleep," Sue said.

Low walls of ice funneled the headlights. Sue listened to Scott's breathing slow and find regularity. She began to think of Chrissie, in the backseat; whether or not she was actually pregnant, she was certainly being used. Sue wouldn't have picked up Scott if he was by himself. Now she slid her left hand back between the side of the seat and the door. She felt the nylon of the moonboot and reached up higher, her wrist bent and her hand upside down. The backs of her fingers touched Chrissie's leg and she scratched up and down, trying to send a signal.

"Do you know you're touching me?" Chrissie said. "I'm trying to sleep."

Sue whispered over her left shoulder. "Do you need help?"

"To rest?"

"Are you in trouble?"

"Watch the road, please."

"I am," Sue said. "I have to."

"I don't mean to sound rude," Chrissie said. "It's just that I'm hoping to bring a child into this world."

"Yes," Sue said. "I'm watching the road."

"Reckon," Scott said, sitting up straight. "Reckon we're getting close."

"What?" Sue said.

He leaned his forehead against the windshield, squinting through it, and raised his hand to point at the square green sign that rose up only to fall away behind them.

"Yes," he said. "Only seven miles."

"To where?" Sue said.

"Where you live," he said. "Your home."

Now Sue saw he held the car's registration in his other hand, her address printed along the top. He had to have taken it out of the glove compartment, though she had not seen him do it. She tried to think of a lie; none came.

"It'll be a pretty cold night," Chrissie said, whispering as if talking to herself in the backseat.

"All right," Sue said, thinking aloud. She took the exit, her exit, and coasted to the stop sign. She eased the car through the town, its quiet streets. What had been slush, now brittle ice, cracked away beneath her tires. They passed one other car under the trees' bare branches; its headlights seemed too pale to do any good.

Her house was completely dark, the walk and driveway unshoveled, papers all over the porch, mail jammed in the slot. She led Scott and Chrissie around back and opened the door into the kitchen. She hit the light and an old grocery list ruffled on the refrigerator's door, close to her hand. Dishes from before she'd left were still stacked in the sink.

"Make yourself comfortable," she said. "Have to check the furnace." Down the stairs, she knew that if she was alone she'd be worried that perhaps someone was in the house, had broken in while she was gone; now that fear had turned into a kind of hope. The furnace was fine, the basement empty.

They were settling into the living room as she went all the way up to the second floor. She heard light switches, the front door opening, a sound like firewood being stacked.

Unfortunately, there was no one upstairs, either. The drawers of her dresser were still open from her hurried packing, her bed unmade as if she'd just climbed out of it. She would like to climb back in, and she had no reason to believe they'd do anything more than fall asleep on the couch downstairs—yet she also had no reason to believe they'd stop at that. She was so tired her mind leapt ahead of her.

Chrissie had found a washcloth, wet it, and spread it over her stomach. She was sitting on the couch with her shirt pulled up.

The sight of Chrissie's stomach, the pink skin stretched out, was a great relief to Sue. She was ashamed to have suspected anything else.

"These things were frozen together," Scott said. He'd brought in the newspapers, all in plastic bags; he brushed the powdery snow from them and it disappeared, melting into the carpet.

"Are you tired?" Sue said.

"Slept in the car," he said.

"I'm nocturnal," Chrissie said. "Pretty much."

"Have to find the most recent one," Scott said. "Find out when the lottery numbers are announced. You only have a few days to claim it, you know."

"My roommate, Jim, should be back tonight," Sue said. Her roommate's name was Tina and she was out of town until March.

Scott opened newspaper after newspaper, spreading them out on the floor.

"Would you like some tea?" Sue said.

"I figured you'd get around to that," he said.

In the kitchen, Sue listened for their voices in the living room. It was silent, and she realized she hadn't heard them say a word to each other. They were traveling together, but beyond that she couldn't tell. She could certainly afford to help them a little, she told herself, that this was the kind of thing that makes us human.

Chrissie had taken off her moonboots. Her pink feet were bare. She lifted the washcloth and her navel stuck out like the tip of a finger. Sue sipped her tea; she looked away, then quickly back, trying to catch Scott and Chrissie making eye contact in that instant. They did not.

"Haven't had a shower in a week," Chrissie said.

"I'm sorry," Sue said. "Go right ahead. It's at the top of the stairs."

"I'm fine," Scott said once Chrissie was gone. "I'm not the kind of person who gets very dirty."

"I see," Sue said, then she heard Chrissie calling down the stairs. It shocked her a little, for she had not heard Chrissie raise her voice—it was almost as if someone entirely different had broken into the house or been inside all along.

"Towels," Chrissie called. "Clean towels."

Sue moved slowly, then hurried, thinking that perhaps the time had come, thinking she should call an ambulance, someone. She took towels from the cupboard on the wall, ran up the stairs, knocked on the door.

"Everything all right?"

"You can come in," Chrissie said.

The two rubber bands were twisted like red spiders on the tile next to the sink, but Chrissie's hair still stood up in its horns. Her breasts rested on her smooth, round stomach; a dark line ran from her navel to her pubic hair.

"This will be my first child," she said.

"I have a niece," Sue said. "That's all."

Sue tried to look away when Chrissie turned around, but her eyes only found the mirror, and it was there, too. Extending straight from the tip of Chrissie's spine, a tail hung down two or three inches—almost an inch wide, tapering to a point, red hairs along the edges. Sue took a long look, to be sure, then stepped back into the hall and slowly shut the door. She stood there until she heard the water running.

She found Scott in the downstairs bedroom, which she used as a studio. His back was turned to her; he stood in front of a piece she'd been working on when she'd left, a two-by-three-foot charcoal drawing on paper, a female nude with arms outstretched, face upside down and looking out, either floating, rising from, or sinking into dark water. Scott kept lifting his arms as if he would touch the surface. Sue listened to the fabric of his coat scratch against itself. He spoke to her without turning around, as if he'd known she was there all along.

"You work with nude models?" he said.

"Sometimes," she said. "When I can afford to." She wondered if he knew about Chrissie's tail and decided that he must.

"What about when you can't afford to?"

"What?" she said, then, "I use photographs, or memories, or mirrors."

"Mirrors?"

"Forget it," Sue said.

"I can hold myself perfectly still," he said. "Like I'm in a trance. Usually when I get my clothes off things head toward the action side, but I could do that, I think, pick up some cash."

"I could find you a real job," Sue said, suddenly taken by the desire to contact someone outside this situation. "I could call a friend of mine who's in charge at the lumberyard."

"Whoa," Scott said. "Whoa, whoa. All that talk about the job was hyperthetical, anyway. Remember the tickets? You start giving us charity and that changes our whole relationship, you know, that puts you somewhere where you'll start acting all up yourself and better than us."

"That's not how I meant it," Sue said.

"Whatever," he said. "All is forgiven."

She decided she had to make the call, regardless of not having a cover. This was her house, after all, and she could call whomever she wanted. She went into the kitchen and picked up the phone. She'd almost expected that the line would be dead, and it was.

When Sue returned to the living room, Chrissie was sitting on the couch, fully dressed, a towel around her head. Scott sat in the easy chair across the room.

"Where's your roommate?" Chrissie said.

"He'll get here." Sue sat down. She checked her watch; it was only ten o'clock.

"Kindness," Scott said. "You can't count on the kindness of strangers, you know, but it's sure nice when it happens." He pulled another chair over and put his feet on it.

Sue knew they were in a kind of standoff, and to acknowledge it would more likely heighten than defuse it. She had no idea what was at stake, only that she was a hostage in her own house. She would outwait them. They held sway over the darkness; she was counting on the sunrise. Scott sneaked glances at Chrissie through half-closed eyes—Sue saw that, or thought she did. She began to wonder if she'd had it backward, if actually Chrissie was exerting some control over Scott. Sue pretended not to notice that Chrissie was staring at her, tried not to shiver under the weight of her eyes.

"There's plenty of time," Chrissie said, twisting her hair back into position. "I'm not really due for a week or so. Thinking of getting a tattoo of a zipper, whether or not it's a C-section."

"Time for what?" Sue said, surprised at the sharpness in her voice.

"Hormones," Scott said. "Easy now. She's just got all these hormones coursing through her right now."

Sue closed her eyes only to rest them. She checked her watch again and again, surreptitiously, so she'd know she hadn't fallen asleep, so later she could account for every ten minutes of the night. She recast all that Chrissie had said, tried to think back through all that had happened. Somehow the radio had come on, the disc jockey sending songs out to truckers and back home to their wives. Scott was asleep. Sue could no longer tell if Chrissie was staring at her or into some middle distance. Hours passed, and Sue willed them to quicken.

She thought how Scott had said he could hold himself perfectly still, and she imagined drawing him—nude was how he wanted it, and she'd take off his pants, catch the tremor in his thin legs. She would leave him the band jacket, that was all, bare from the hips down, his skeleton showing through his skin; she'd coil tickets around his bare legs, unrolled possibilities, half his face in darkness. She'd do him in charcoal or she'd hold him in colors, paint him, and as she wondered through her palette she came to the pink of Chrissie's hair—Chrissie, whose eyes lay heavy on her now, in the dim room, trying to read her thoughts—and she would not give Chrissie that hair, would not show her skin or anything beneath her clothes. The moonboots, yes, and a thick fur coat, a long one, and fur leggings, an Eskimo hood that closed around to hide her face, bury those eyes. Sue was not asleep. She chose her palette, swaddling Chrissie so she could hardly move, so she looked like a Sasquatch, a powerless missing link, lost out on the highway, an ice cream cone in one gloved hand.

Then there was light along the windowsill. Sue stood and went upstairs. Searching her closet, she found some of her largest clothes—halfway down the stairs she realized Chrissie hadn't asked for them; she didn't know what had moved her, except it was happening already. She set the clothes on the couch next to Chrissie, who didn't thank her, but just started to pull her turtleneck over her head.

"You can change into them in the other room," Sue said.

"Fine," Scott said, waking up. "I'm fine. This jacket's warmer than it looks."

"Good," Sue said.

"Where's that roommate of yours? What's his name again?"

"You didn't hear him come in?"

"No," Scott said. "I sure didn't."

Sue took a scarf and her coat from the closet. She put them on and stood by the front door, waiting.

"Going somewhere?" he said.

"You can't stay here," she said. "I have meetings. People are coming here to see my work."

"You're no different," Scott said. "No different than the rest. I could feel you turning that way."

"I've done enough," Sue said as Chrissie returned. "Let's go."

"Let's go?" he said, still sitting on the couch. "Let's go?"

Chrissie stood silently, her eyes on the floor. She seemed harmless now, as if the morning had either weakened or restored her.

"I'm going out and starting the car," Sue said. "It has to warm up. If you're in it by that time, I'm driving to the train station. If not, the police station."

"Jesus Christ," Scott said. "As if we're not all friends here—about which I now see I was mistaken."

"I'm going," Sue said.

"Hold on," he said. "Wait. It's clear you don't trust us enough to leave us alone in here. You don't trust us at all."

Sue was not drawn in. She stood in the doorway until Scott

stood and walked past her, outside. Chrissie followed, and the two of them waited by the car, steam rising from their faces. They seemed less helpless, somehow, than they had the day before.

Sue did not wait for the car to warm up, and the engine rattled, cold, the fan spinning wind around them. In the rear-view mirror, she saw Chrissie was staring out the window. Scott concentrated on the road ahead, as if trying to memorize the circuitous route Sue was taking. She didn't want them to know how close she lived to the train station.

"Just drive with us," Scott said. "The three of us could travel together, and then we'd just see what happened."

"I don't think that would work out," Sue said.

"All the way last night at the restaurant I saw you turning this way," he said.

At the station, Sue gave him twenty dollars. She bought them tickets going west.

"Know anything about the lottery?" Scott asked the station master.

"Got some lucky numbers today?"

"Plenty," Scott said.

Chrissie checked her hair in the window's reflection, then pulled on her cap and followed Scott to the train.

"Goodbye," Sue said as they climbed inside, Chrissie holding Scott's arm for balance. Sue walked all the way along the train, her hand on its cold metal side, and she tried to see them through the window, see them sit down. When the train began moving, she waited, expected them to be looking out the window at her waving goodbye. They were not.

Now she could drive straight home. She wanted to believe they could make it, yet she was glad they were gone. The town was beautiful in the morning, the snow clean and white, perfectly friendly people on the sidewalks, dogs on leashes, bulbs already planted and just waiting in the frozen ground.

She slept until evening, when she found they had stolen her roommate's quarter collection, over fifty dollars' worth—later, she wondered about Scott paying all in quarters at the restaurant, as if he'd already stolen them. There were ways time moved while she was with them that Sue would never untangle. Also, they had taken her charcoal drawing, somehow carried it out right in front of her. Even if they'd rolled it up she couldn't imagine how they had done it or where they were taking it.

Despite all this, she still admits she would do it again, if presented with the two of them out on the interstate. And as it is reassuring to know that there are people like Sue, those who stop to help, it is also important to realize that that baby, that child, walks among us now.

HELP WANTED

Two women with long, thick braids down their backs were doing
loads of laundry where every piece of clothing was purple. The
portholes in the dryers were solid, spinning purple; at first, seeing that—and the two women, both all in purple—I believed
something had gone wrong with my eyes. My frame pack rested
at my feet, my dog sleeping next to it. A man reading a newspaper sat on the other side of the laundromat.

One of the women dropped a sock and I picked it up.

Favorite color? I said.

We like it, she said. There was a purple ribbon in her hair.

I'd gone in there to get out of the cold wind, then decided to wash what clothes I carried. My car had failed to make it across the Dakotas, which was no surprise. I took off the license plates, pried the VIN number from the dashboard, and rolled that strip of tin into a ball. It rattled inside the dryer, now separated from the car by five hundred miles.

I poured some dog food into my cupped hands, but she wouldn't eat it until I put it on the floor. In cold weather, hitchhiking is easier if you have a dog along; people are more likely to sympathize with an animal than another person. There are no short rides in those states.

She sheds, doesn't she? The man with the newspaper was standing closer now. With a dalmatian, he said, what you got is a short-haired dog without the benefits.

I don't know about that, I said.

This town, he said. Livingston. Would be the windiest town in America if the population was higher.

I didn't understand, but I didn't comment. Turning away from the man, I fed a five-dollar bill to the change machine; among the quarters were two slugs of smooth metal. The dryer wouldn't take them.

A piece of paper tacked to the wall said HELP WANTED! MECHANIC NEEDED. ROOM + BOARD +. No other details, no phone number, just a map. The two women folded all their purple clothing, not even looking at me. I want to talk about women, but there in the laundromat nothing more passed between us. I pulled the map off the wall, folded it, and put it in my pocket. Then I sat down and waited for my clothes to dry.

———┼———

I stood on a bridge, looking down into the river my last ride had identified as the Yellowstone. Shards of ice three or four feet across spun past, pieces of trees whose branches must have raked the riverbed.

This was the furthest west I'd ever been. The gravel road turned off from the highway forty miles from town. My dog ran ahead as the road climbed; it was impossible to tell what time of day it was, the gray clouds hanging low. The road narrowed, turned to switchbacks, and straightened out again. Two pickups came out of nowhere, bouncing half sideways through the frozen washboards, just missing us. Dogs barked from the bed of one, and then we were alone again.

The higher we climbed, the more snow there was; we walked for an hour, surrounded by ranch land, snowfields where cattle stood in clusters, shivering together. My dog was tired. I tried to pick her up, to carry her, but she wouldn't let me.

First I saw the line of cars, trucks and tractors, then, as we came closer, the dogs began barking. At the gate, a sign said NO TRESPASSING!!!!! The sign was prefabricated, but the exclamation marks had been added. Next to the gate, a dead deer was caught halfway over the barbed-wire fence, its hind legs hooked back, its chest collapsed, its head down on the ground.

The dogs were all on chains, so twisted and tangled around each other that they couldn't move much. They went from side to side, all together, like a confused crab. I knelt close to the deer—it was both frozen and desiccated—and saw how the plants had been dug up by its dying hooves. Its flat tongue stuck out, cold and pale; its eyes had been pecked

out and dried blood spidered around them like another set of
lashes.

Looking for something? a man shouted.

None of the people who lived on that ranch wore purple, though
I rarely had the opportunity to see many of them at one time.
Perhaps thirty people lived there, including the children; they
were always up to something, always busy. It was never clear
what they were doing, and I was told that was not my concern.

Duane, Cousin Duane, made it understood that I was not to
speak or interact with the women. He told me they left the dead
deer by the gate to discourage visitors. And don't wander, he
said. Don't stray.

You all don't trust me much, I said.

Either your dog's got to be tied up with the rest or you have
to keep her close, he said. Can't afford to tangle with the neighbors—anything that happens might bring in the government.
We don't need any extra attention.

I'll keep her close, I said.

Hell, he said, we lost a dog not too long ago, found the
remains. At the very least, we got wolves out there, no matter
what the Department of Fish and Game says. Me and Cousin
Hollis did some recon at night—we had some infrared scopes,
you know—and we saw some pretty strange things.

Like what? I said.

Nothing you need to know about.

They called each other Cousin, but I understood early on that
they were not related. Cousin Duane's words were all half whispered, conspiratorial. His face was red, chapped all around his

dark beard. He always wore the same stocking cap and it had unraveled along one side so locks of his dark hair poked through. He told me he was forty years old.

I'm not the head guy, he said. Don't be mistaken. It's just that I'm responsible for you.

So you must be pretty high up, I said.

No, he said. It's not that important, what you'll be doing.

I asked what was important, whose concern that was.

Cousin Duane just laughed. We're not doing anything illegal here, he said, not even anything very interesting. There's just no reason you have to know about it. You'll be getting your information on a need-to-know basis. Fair enough?

Fair enough, I said.

You're not a curious person?

Not necessarily, I said.

Meals were delivered to me, out at the shop. I heard a knock at the door and then, when I opened it, no one was there. Just a tray holding a sandwich, a bowl of soup going cold. The sun shone a couple hours a day, slicing down. Standing, holding the tray, I looked past the line of stranded vehicles, snow drifted against them, that I was expected to resurrect. Usually the clouds were low, so I couldn't see the tops of the mountains. Aspens grew thick along the stream. Sometimes elk moved in single file, leaping fences as if they were an inchworm, all connected.

I studied the footprints left in the snow outside my door. From their size, I determined that a woman delivered my meals.

It took a week to figure what all I had in the shop. Tools and torches, snowshoes, canned food, plenty that didn't belong there, survival equipment like tinfoil blankets and those boy scout saws that are just razorwire stretched between two stainless-steel rings. I organized it into bins and boxes, broke it down into things I could use and things I couldn't. I pounded long nails into the walls and hung baskets, old bicycles, broken chairs out of my way. Tire chains, chainsaw chains, patches of chain-link fence all went together, following a logic known only to me.

Cousin Hollis and Cousin Duane would come in sometimes, watch me without saying a word. They'd bring in shovels with broken blades for me to weld, ask about the feasibility of attaching some sort of giant screw onto the front of a tractor. I suspected they used my shop late at night, for reasons unknown. Usually the men were gone all day, returned in the middle of the night, and left again before sunrise. I won't even speculate on all I didn't understand, all the questions left unasked; it was not my job to ask questions, nor to interact with the women.

There was a woodstove in the shop, and I would have preferred sleeping there, next to it, but that was not allowed. My bed was in an old travel trailer that had no tires; its axle rested on cinderblocks, its tongue on a caved-in aluminum trough. The propane heater threatened to snuff its pilot—each time I fell asleep I ran the risk of never waking. I lay awake listening to the radio I'd salvaged, all the company I had. The reception came and went, and this made it almost worse than no friend at all.

She moved so quietly that even when I set out to catch her I failed a few times. The shop had no windows on that side; I could not see her coming. Finally I drilled a hole in the wall.

She carried the tray in one hand, a baby on her other arm. The woman's hair was bright red, on the verge of pink, tight curls pulled into two points above her temples, almost like horns. In a situation like that, the one woman you meet can seem preordained, inevitable and perfect. I waited, then opened the door before she could knock. I wore my heavy welding gloves—burnt and dirty, speckled with metal—so she could not just hand me the tray.

Come in, I said.

I can just set it down here, she said.

No, I said, holding the door, careful to stand exactly where she usually set the food. Come in.

She stepped inside, set the tray on a table, then began circling the shop, surveying the piles I'd made. We both stood so still I could hear her breathing and my own, the baby's and the dog's.

What's your name? I said.

When she came to my dog, she put the baby down, inside a tire that lay empty, on its side. She petted my dog, scratched hard at the base of her spine, above her tail, so she stretched her back legs. I moved closer. I shook the gloves off my hands, letting them fall to the floor. The baby made no sound when I picked it up.

She's a dalmatian, isn't she? the woman said, and I agreed, though that was obvious.

The baby did not cry, it just looked at me with its dark blue eyes, its lashes half an inch long. With my fingers, I searched its mouth for teeth, following the smooth gums, and still it remained quiet. It reached out its perfect hand and gently tugged on my hair. It looked deep into my eyes like it could hypnotize me, turn me whichever way.   .

He likes you, she said. That's a new one.

He's beautiful, I said, and he was.

His name is Alan, she said.

That's my name, I said.

Is it now?

I guess it's both of our names, I said.

The baby reached out his arms to clasp his mother's neck, and for a moment, with his little body against mine, the three of us were connected.

My dog went missing. I was half worried about her, mostly concerned they would discover I'd lost track of her. On my hands and knees, I kidded myself that I could follow her footprints. I walked slowly down the line of abandoned vehicles, then further, hiding behind an old privy. I waited there to see what would happen, if anyone would follow. No one did. I sprinted, stumbling where the snow's crust gave way, making it to the first line of trees. The snow was shallow beneath the branches; icicles pointed down.

It was difficult, trying to call her without giving myself away. I followed the stream, past irrigation turnouts and head-gates, around places where the water had backed up and sloughed over, where long sheets of ice now stretched down the slope. I could see where animals came to drink, all different footprints overlapping each other, dark water sliding below the holes they'd made. That's when I heard her.

It was like nothing I'd heard before. She wasn't barking. I thought she was in pain, caught in a trap or something worse. I tripped and kept on. I was right underneath her before I saw her, noises coming up from her throat, her mouth motionless. She was standing on the branch of a tree, ten feet above. The tree's trunk was slanted, at an angle to the ground, yet it was still not easy to see how she'd gotten up there. She looked down at

me, her legs trembling, hair up along her spine. I held out my
arms and she jumped down, into them.

Well, the woman said, her voice behind me.

I turned. Her dirty wool pants were rolled thick at the cuffs,
her down jacket patched with duct tape. I had never seen her
before.

I've been watching you for a while, she said, holding out her
binoculars. And I can't figure out what you're doing. I do know I
don't like it. You're on my property, for one thing.

Lost, I said.

You part of that outfit up the road?

I was looking for my dog, I said. She got lost.

The woman looked to be a little older than I was, though her
clothes hid the shape of her body. Her dark hair blew across
her face as I tried to see it better. I could tell that she was talking
tough, that her words were mostly bluster, and I wanted to see
why. She stood there, looking at me, and my dog leaned against
my legs, trembling; before then, she had never liked to touch
me.

I'm Claudia, the woman said. I'll show you the way back.

We walked down out of the trees. Below, I saw a house, a
tangle of wires and tall fenceposts off to one side and behind it. I
noticed how Claudia tried to stay on that side of me.

That your house? I said.

She did not answer.

I stopped walking and squinted against the glare. The sun
came out just then, calling shadows, and through the fence I saw
a dark shape move out from behind the house, into the light,
then turn again, pacing.

Go down that way, she said, pointing across untouched snow-
drifts, toward the dark line of the road.

Think I'll go closer to your house, I said, then take your driveway.

Well, she said.

Look at my boots, I said, not slowing down to argue. Now we were closer. I almost tripped over my dog; she was trying to stay between my legs. Claudia just watched my face, not saying anything.

The tigers stood thirty feet away, inside the fence, clearly visible. There was nothing to say, no words to cover them. Standing still, they watched us approach. We walked around the side of the house, and all the stone of its foundation looked burned, as if one house had been lost to fire and another built in its place. Claudia opened a door in the tall fence.

Ten feet away, steam rose from the two tigers' mouths. Their tails slid back and forth, twitching along the dirty ice. Black lines like crescent moons circled their milky blue eyes; like small horses, so close, they stretched and their claws unsheathed to rake at the ice. They watched me as if they were bored already, not hungry, yet they seemed thin, ragged, their colors paler than I'd have expected. One yawned, showing its teeth; I smelled rotten meat and something else. I would say mange, but I could be wrong.

Come in here, Claudia said. They're drugged, in the meat I give them.

No thank you, I said, closing the gate, staying outside. My dog stood halfway between me and the gate, frightened of both directions, almost invisible in the dirty snow.

Kneeling, Claudia scratched the head of one of the bigger tigers. It rolled over, showing where the stripes ended and its fur turned soft and white. Its long whiskers hung limp around its mouth, and its tongue slipped out, licking at her.

Can't they take flesh from bone with those things? I said.

It's a question of pressure, Claudia said.

All different kinds of wire encircled the yard, mixed with aluminum siding, forklift pallets balanced on their ends. I pointed to a hole in the fence, a dark path leading through it, worn through the snow. Claudia didn't even look up.

That's so they can get to the stream and drink, she said. I can't carry all that water up here, and my pipes are frozen solid.

They're loose, then, I said.

Claudia laughed. Her shadow and my own were cast perfectly onto the white wall of the house; I watched our silhouettes as we talked. The tiger's shadow was twenty feet long, dark along the ground. He paced again, crossing our shadows, blending the three of us together.

I feed them, Claudia said, so they don't go far. And they're not exactly wild animals.

I stood transfixed as the tiger arched its back—loose skin hanging along its belly, the tail slowly rising, hanging motionless, then cutting the air—and circled Claudia, rubbing against her legs.

You do work up there, she said. I saw you coming, walking straight down from that outfit.

Well, I said. The truth is I'm doing some mechanical work for those folks.

But you're not one of them, she said.

I just don't give out information unless I have to, I said.

Discretion, she said. I'm very glad to hear that.

Just then my dog ran into me, right into my legs. Claudia laughed as another tiger came up from the stream, through the fence. It paused to look at us before passing by.

———†———

My radio had disappeared around that time and no one seemed
to know anything about it. It made me a little uneasy not to
know what was happening in the world, and also that no one
beyond half a mile—except Claudia, yet at that point I wasn't
sure she counted—knew where I was.

One day I did not wait for Chrissie—that was her name—to
deliver my lunch. I went over to the main house, making a wide
arc around the dogs. All their necks were rubbed raw because
they could not keep themselves from straining against the ropes.
The broken antlers over the door looked fragile and old. I
knocked and there was no answer. The knob turned in my hand,
and I almost expected bells to ring, announcing my entry, as I
opened the door. The silence surprised me.

The kitchen was empty, immaculate. I felt the ammonia in
my eyes and nose, burning cold in my lungs. Alan's crib stood in
one corner; I could hear Chrissie whistling out back, along with
the birds. Through one door I saw a long table, surrounded by
fourteen chairs. Down the hallway, all the doors had numbers
painted above them. The doors were locked—I tried them, shirt-
tail in my hand to prevent fingerprints. I had no idea what I was
looking for or expected to find.

Back in the kitchen, I opened every cupboard and drawer.
Flour, candles, canned vegetables. Newspaper lined one cupboard; I read about a train that had been derailed and spilled
poisonous chemicals into a field. The date had been torn off. Out
the window, my dog, loose, was taunting the others; she'd get
pulled into the fray and all of them would try to hump her until
she struggled beyond their reach again.

She's a flirt, Chrissie said, coming in behind me.

Last thing I need is puppies, I said.

Chrissie set Alan down in his crib. She was wearing the felt liners from her boots, an apron that looked like it was made out of bandannas. Her skin was so pale that I could see the blue veins in her face, the shadows of the bones in her arms; her skin made me believe the color of her hair was true.

Isn't your dog spayed? she said.

I don't know, I said. I don't think so. She wasn't always mine.

Sitting down, I took Alan out of his crib. I set him on my lap and he made no sound. Even then I was thinking of a time when he would understand the words I'd tell him, and I wondered what those words would be. About the best kind of person to become, perhaps, or how to make friends. He watched me without changing his expression. His feet were bare, his toes perfect and smooth.

You shouldn't be over here, Chrissie said.

Saved you a trip, I said. Sitting there, I saw how my dirty footprints circled the room, went through both doorways, gave me away. There I was.

Which one? I said. Which one is your husband?

Who? Chrissie said.

Alan's father, I said.

Oh, she said. His father's somewhere else—long way from here.

I see, I said. She opened the refrigerator and I reached out and untied the bow at the back of her apron.

You got grease on it, she said, retying the bow.

You ever get lonely here? I said.

What? she said.

Could it get you into trouble, my being here?

You're only the mechanic, Chrissie said. After all. It's not like anyone's watching me.

The baby stared into my face as if his vision could go deeper and deeper inside me. I believed Chrissie was interested in me, and found it frustrating that she would not admit it. I wanted to tell her more about myself, that I wasn't only the mechanic—yet to those people I was only the mechanic; to be something else to her would take more than words.

I hoped to get six vehicles running by cannibalizing the seventeen they had. I also handled the other problems that arose, pounded out dents with Cousin Hollis, tried not to ask any questions. The vehicles that came in—and the men, too, some days—were covered in thick red dirt, like clay. As if they had been burrowing.

At night I heard hands flat on my trailer, someone checking on me. I flicked the light on, then off again, to let them know I was inside. Then I waited another hour before I sneaked out. And I did. Piece by piece, I took the pump I'd found and fixed, and I carried it up into the trees, hiding it where I could find it in the daylight. The snow had melted a little, exposing long strips of land, islands and spits that made it easier for me to move undetected. Part of it was I had to show myself I could get out when I wanted, that I wasn't entirely trapped, and I also needed to talk to someone who lived beyond that world. Not all the reasons I brought Claudia the pump were based in self-interest—I did believe it was best if her tigers were fenced in, if she didn't get tangled with the Cousins and vice versa.

Been thinking about this, I said. Thinking about you down here.

Likewise, she said.

The day we put it together I tried to stay close to Claudia, tried not to turn my back to the tigers. My dog watched from inside Claudia's house, her head at the window.

We sank the pump into one of the stream's pools. The extension cords and hoses had to be kept outside the fence, so they wouldn't be chewed. As we worked, I asked Claudia questions, and she answered the ones she cared to.

We're raising them for game farms, she said, for hunting down in Texas.

She did not want to talk about it, nor about her husband, who had gone down to Texas to make a delivery. That's all she told me about him.

In one corner of the pen was a pile of bones. Forklift pallets propped up on their sides formed long alleys, catacombs. The lion was in a cage of his own because he was not drugged, I learned, so he could be used for breeding purposes.

Ligers are always a goal, Claudia said. Money in them.

Further down the alleys, beyond the lion, I thought I saw two tigers feeding on the carcass of another.

That's an elk, Claudia said.

We fixed the gap in the fence, stretching new wire, and then the tigers were trapped inside and could no longer roam. Claudia said she was pretty sure we hadn't fenced any out.

If so, they'll come back, she said. Coffee?

Sure, I said, but once we were inside she handed me a beer. That was fine with me. I settled on the couch, looking around at the room, at all the books, the record player, and I couldn't see any signs of a man. The tall walnut gun case was full, though, one glass door hanging open.

On the television, some woman was talking. Three tiger cubs slept in a box by the woodstove, my dog sitting anxiously on the other side. Perhaps she was allergic to the cubs; something about them made her sneeze.

Band-aids circled all of Claudia's fingers. She was maybe ten years older than I was, wrinkles at her eyes, a couple gray hairs. She stretched her overalls over her shoulders, then dropped her wool pants. Her long underwear—men's, with the Y-front crotch—bagged at the knees.

That's Mother Claire Prophet, she said, pointing to the television. Leader of the CUT.

The cut? I said.

Church Universal and Triumphant, she said. Mother Claire channels, through some old dead guy, some spirit. She talks to Abraham Lincoln, Albert Einstein, Marie Curie, Alexander the Great, you name it.

What do they say? I said.

They warn her of the nuclear threat, Claudia said, and they tell her not to trust those Russians, never to believe all the hype about the cold war being over.

People believe this?

You see them around, she said. They dress all in purple.

Standing, Claudia went into the kitchen, then returned with warm baby bottles of milk. She sat next to me on the couch, a tiger cub in her lap. Kittens, she called them. The news came on, and we made a joke of the weatherman's name. Our shoulders were touching.

That Claire woman, I said, she sure has plenty of people to talk to. Smart people. You just have me.

Fishing for compliments? she said. I have the cats, you know. They listen.

I began to ask about her husband again, but she cut me off. Then the cub bit the nipple in two and milk spilled all over. Claudia went down the hall to change her shirt. I watched the sports, learned something about high school girls' basketball in Montana towns.

Come in here, Claudia called.

What? I said.

There's something in here I want to show you.

I went. Claudia had taken off her wet shirt. She turned to face me, and I saw the scar below her bra—four stripes, like claws. She shook her head once, her dark hair sliding over her freckled shoulders. I wasn't sure what she wanted me to see. Below the scar, her skin was pale, smooth above the waistband of her long underwear. She pulled her hair away from her face and watched me, her mouth a thin line; her expression was calm, as if she were still fully clothed and we were still watching television.

The bed was king-sized; it filled the whole room, and the twisted bedclothes looked as if dirt had been tracked through them. In the mirror, I saw Claudia's back reflected and, further in, myself, standing in the doorway. My feet would not cross the threshold.

She still wore her heavy wool socks, the same long underwear. She crossed the room in quick steps, grabbed my belt buckle in her hand, and walked me in, turning my back to the bed. Unbuckling my belt, she pulled my pants to my knees, then pushed me backward. Neither of us said a thing. I tried to lift my hands, to touch her, but she slapped them away. The skin of her fingers was rough and dry. Her one hand was over my face, fingers in my eyes, and the other worked me into the front of her long underwear; the fabric twisted and gathered around as she led me further in.

Cousin Duane crossed the shop and crossed it again, always returning to the dartboard. He lifted tools and then set them down. He fed a log into the stove. I was welding a tailpipe and it took a little attention, the torch so close to the gas tank. I took my time, to be sure I was calm, because the way he was jerking around, throwing the darts hard and then yanking them from the board, made me anxious about what he was going to say. I felt him turn toward me, saw the flash of his face.

You like it here all right? he said.

I stood. I felt slow, heavy, in the leather apron; the welding visor was tipped back on my head. I could tell he knew I'd been visiting Claudia and there was nothing I could do.

You going to fire me? I said, full-knowing this was the best I could expect.

I just want to get a few things straight, he said.

My head tilted back to balance the visor, I saw the hooks all along the beams, and it occurred to me that a man could be hung there, easily enough. I did not find this reassuring.

Know anything about those CUT people? I said, suddenly believing I could hold him off with questions.

That's a cult, he said, snorting. Bunch of people without their own minds.

Are you a patriot? I said.

I just want to get some things out in the open, he said.

Do you all pay taxes? I said.

Enough, he said. What I want to say is we like the work you're doing for us. What I wanted to say is we've noticed something else.

I see, I said.

Cousin Duane took off his stocking cap, balled it up in his fist, then put it on again.

What it is, he said. I've noticed it and Cousin Hollis has, and some others. It's things with you—well, between—things between you and Cousin Chrissie.

Well, I said.

It's potentially all right with me, he said, with us, but you should know we've noticed.

Good, I said. I figured you had.

I mean, we want to grow, but not only for growth's sake. We look after our own. And I want you to realize I don't laugh at cults or satanism or whatever to weaken them, because I think they're strong or something—I laugh because I think it's funny. Know what I mean?

I think so, I said.

Hell, Cousin Duane said. When it comes to all that, we're even on this side of something like the Mormons.

I had screwed heavy hasps, locks on the inside of my trailer door. Of course I knew daylight was no promise of safety.

One night I heard the same sounds I'd grown used to, the flats of hands on the side of my trailer. I flicked the light on, off again, but the sound did not let up. It whispered along one side, around the corner, under the window, and up the other side, someone's hands only inches from where I lay in bed, only a half inch of aluminum between us. There was a knock at the door.

Chrissie stood there, the baby Alan in her arms. I stepped aside, trying to stay calm, to appear comfortable.

Have a seat, I said.

There's nowhere to sit but the bed.

I know that, I said, sitting beside her. I heard the shake in my voice.

I need to talk to you, she said.

Why didn't you knock before now? I said.

What?

Go ahead, I told her. I want things open between us. Seems like lots is happening that we don't talk about.

Well, she said. I want to tell you that I followed you, these days, down to that woman's house. I watched you through the windows, everything you did.

Where? I said. I could not think of what to say, and it seemed as if silence might be best, if I just played innocent and let her tell me what she'd seen. Waiting out the silence, I tried to count how many curls were pulled into the pigtail closest me. I looked into Alan's beautiful eyes. I tried not to imagine Chrissie following me—she might have seen me blindfolded, tied down, a hood over my head. Or, even worse, Claudia unzipping my fly and jerking me off, neither one of us looking away from the game show on the television. When I came it was as if we were aiming for the spinning wheel, the pile of money.

Well, I said to Chrissie, uncomfortable under the baby's gaze. I was only visiting.

I saw you do some unnatural things, she said.

Chrissie, I said.

I followed you, she said. I saw it. She moved Alan beyond my reach just as I held out my arms.

You're telling me because you feel bad about following me, I said, hoping. All I wanted was to hold her close, to put my arm around her, around the three of us.

I'm just telling you to tell you, she said. That's all.

The blue veins forked through the backs of her hands, to her fingers. Her lips began to shape words, yet no sound came. She had words for me, I knew, only she was afraid to say them. The skin of her face was translucent, turned toward me, then Alan, then returning to me.

Why then, I said, did you follow me in the first place, if you're just telling me to tell me.

I'm keeping an eye on you, she said. Don't you know that by now?

Why? I said, and she was already standing.

Goodnight, she said.

It might seem obvious that Claudia and I would do it like animals, on all fours, like tigers, but we did not. In fact, I never saw her with her clothes off. She never let me touch her.

She would tie me spread-eagled to the bedposts so I was caught in the animal hair and strange smells of her sheets. She would leave round circles of bite marks on my back. I won't pretend I didn't like it; I happily took whatever she'd give. No one else ever touched me.

You're at my mercy, she'd say. You wouldn't let me tie you up if you'd betrayed me.

Blindfolded, hobbled by a rope between my ankles, hands

behind my back, I sought her. Only to have her come and go, separate her touches with long minutes, suddenly leap behind me with rattles, icicles. This was my pleasure, and always I felt the tigers around me, though I did not see them and I cannot be certain. When the blindfold came off I did see them sometimes, at the window, looking in. Somewhere beyond them, Chrissie also watched, though I did not know that then.

And it was only then, once I knew she had seen me, that I could see myself and what I was becoming. Still, it was not easy to stop things with Claudia, not cold. She had not done me wrong, perhaps she needed me, and it's possible we helped each other. More than anything, I believed I was not a person who could be inside another—abandoned to gasps and moans, shivering naked and struggling for pleasure—and not feel some attachment. That I still believe.

Cousin Hollis shot it. From what I could understand, it had been loose, up in the trees. There were five or six men across the yard, more than I'd ever seen before, gathered in the daylight. I could not hear what they were saying, but I could see Hollis describing the shot, recounting his every action. Words, pieces of the conversation, came to me. Snowbank. Gut-shot. Son of a bitch.

I hoped the tiger was not Hondo or one of the others Claudia especially loved. The men gutted it on the far side of the yard, then led the dogs, all snarled together, to the pile of entrails. They were done in ten minutes, then set to licking the red snow and each other.

Hey, Alan, Cousin Hollis called. Your dog want any? We set some aside.

No, I said.

This kind of bullshit, Duane shouted at me, walking closer to lower his voice. Exactly this is what draws the government. You know anything about all this? Seen anything?

Sure don't, I said. Haven't.

We've been watching all this for a while, he said. Hell, I could care less what they're doing down there, but we've got women and children here, unprotected, know what I mean?

Yes, I said.

Not that it's for you to worry about, Duane said. This we can handle.

Over to one side, Chrissie stood on the porch, watching everything. First the tiger, then turning her head in my direction. It was then I knew that she had not told—that she was keeping an eye on me for her own sake, not for the Cousins'.

Later, they hung the tiger in my shop, from its hind legs. Its tail snaked limp between its legs, skin gathering at its shoulders, its front paws hanging like worthless paddles, the whole thing spinning a little, meat still on its bones and its brain thick as suet in its head. I sat as far away as I could, squeezing sparkplugs with a pliers, one after another, until the porcelain shattered.

The next day, all that remained of the tiger was the dark stains of blood and bile on the cement floor of my shop. I did not ask questions. I stripped one of the last remaining transmissions from a Chevrolet; I cleared red clay from the air intakes of the Case tractor. I did not lie in wait for Chrissie to deliver my meals, nor try to waylay her. I did not speak unless spoken to.

On the third day after they killed the tiger, I stepped into the cold sun and crossed the yard, an easy hour before my lunch was due. I did not knock, but just opened the door into the kitchen. Alan sat alone in his crib, fixing his blue eyes on me, silent. I knelt there, staring back, close to him, breathing his breath, and for a moment I considered taking him with me, just the two of us. Perhaps that's what he wanted; perhaps he planted that thought in my mind.

Alan, Chrissie called, her soft voice coming down the hall. Alan, she said. I reached out and put my hand flat atop his head. Still he did not make a sound.

Answer me, she said, her voice louder. I'm not talking to the baby.

She must have been waiting for me, somehow watched my approach. I stood and turned toward her voice. I stepped into the hallway.

Come closer, she said, talking through a closed door.

I leaned against it, anxious, thankful that the time had come. I would take her away. Soon we would be moving. The daylight was the safest time.

Open the door, she said.

The overhead light shone down; three other lamps lit the walls. Chrissie stepped toward me, then stopped. I said something, but it made no sense, and my arms slapped around me, beyond my control, electrical.

All I could see of her skin was her bare feet, the palms of her hands, her neck and face. Everything else was tiger—tiger legs attached to her wrists and ankles, claws overhanging, the tail loose and switching as if the floor was water. A ribbon tied under her chin held the tiger's head atop her own, the teeth above her brow. Stripes bound her.

No, I said.

A few red curls spun loose below the tiger's jaws. Chrissie's palms were held out to me, fingers trembling, paws shaking loose.

Isn't this how you want me? she said.

Listen, I said, but I had nothing to say after that. I saw the tears on her face, and for a moment I thought the Cousins had put her up to this, and then I knew they had not. I had led her here myself. The tiger skin was still fresh, not dry or fully tanned. I could smell the blood, the wet fur. In that silence I thought of Alan, waiting in the kitchen, and Claudia, counting her livestock.

Alan, Chrissie said, on the verge of sobbing. She moved toward me, then back again, confused, finally sitting down on the floor. The inside of the tiger skin shone red and white, all blood and congealed fat.

Chrissie had followed it all through to the end, answering everything she watched me do, and now all that was left for me was to betray her, to turn her away from where I had led.

I have to think, I said, my hand on the doorknob. I thought I could leave this place, I said, but now I see that's wrong. It's best if I get back to work.

Whoever picked up those tools was in an improved situation, because I left the vehicles in better shape than I found them. At the gate, next to the bones of the deer, I turned and looked back. If Chrissie was watching, she was hidden somewhere out of my sight.

I left around noon, the sun all around me, my dog at the end of a long rope, pulling me faster through the ice and mud. Cows and their new calves slowly turned their heads as we passed, descending the switchbacks. Below, the river appeared, hid itself, then showed again.

Claudia's house looked like any other from the road, as if nothing out of the ordinary happened there. My dog tried to go that way, out of habit, and I held her back. A new truck, one I had not seen before, was parked out front, a long, mud-splattered trailer behind it. I ran away, in the other direction, alongside my dog, picking up slack and then pulling her along.

The river drowned out my footsteps, my voice when I spoke out loud, saying I'm sorry, Alan, I had to leave you behind.

Swollen, crashing under the bridge, the water ran ten feet higher now. We crossed to the other side, then waited out on the highway, watching the cars pass. Within an hour we caught a ride with a cattle truck going south through the park, cutting across Wyoming and on into Idaho.

THE BEEHIVE STATE

THE SUBMARINERS

We were in Utah. We'd crossed the Wyoming border an hour before, descending the canyons toward Salt Lake City. The café where we'd stopped for lunch was in a narrow canyon, set up there by itself with the highway pressing close to the front door.

I returned from the restroom, and the woman who'd driven me into Utah was no longer sitting at our table. Out in the parking lot, her car was also gone, which was neither much of a surprise nor a disappointment. It would slow me down, though, and I did want to get through Utah as quickly as possible. Now my dog dragged my pack slowly around the parking lot, tied to it by her leash; the pack's metal frame slid like the runners of a sled across the ice and cold blacktop. I watched this through the window, past my reflection—my hair flattened in a swirl around my skull, from wearing a stocking cap on the highway, the whole night before, waiting. My lips were chapped, my nostrils tender from blowing my nose.

One triangle of toast, its edge yellow with egg yolk, remained on the woman's plate. Cream spidered in my coffee. Circling, the waitress held up a fresh pot—its spout orange, decaf—and I shook my head. The waitress had a hooked nose, a blond braid down her back. I thought she'd liked me when she took our order, that she'd even flirted a little. The bill rested, unpaid, on the table; I lay my wallet next to it, to allay any fears she might have. I was the only person left in the restaurant. The legs of the empty chairs and tables, made from tree branches, forked and twisted.

Outside, my dog sat atop the pack, to stay off the cold ground. Steam rose from her snout. It seemed to be getting dark out there, though it was only a couple hours past noon; the narrow canyon didn't give the sun much of a chance.

Anything else? the waitress said, suddenly close. I'm balancing the till.

No, I said. I took out some money.

Everything all right? she said.

Great, I said, all dignity and confidence. Standing, I counted out the money, leaving her a tip; I turned and went out the door.

I tried to hitch a ride, but in twenty minutes not one car passed. My dog sat watching me. This was the very canyon the Mormons came down, the back of the menu had said, led by Brigham Young. Its popularity had certainly waned, if the traffic was any indication. Standing in a tight shaft of sunlight, I moved inches at a time to avoid the cold shadows. Through a sliver, below the curtains—they had been closed now—I watched as the waitress came and went. Her feet, then her legs, her waist when she was up close.

When the sun deserted me, I took another sweater from my pack, saving my cap in case things got desperate. I rubbed my dog's ribs, trying to warm her, to encourage her. I unzipped another pocket and spilled some dog food onto the ground. She sniffed at it, suspiciously, then ate it.

Jogging back and forth on the road, I jumped up, bounced on my toes, shadowboxed; I reminded myself what real cold was like. Wisconsin, North Dakota, Montana.

Remember, I said to the dog. Those days I had to put a sweater on you?

I heard the door open behind me. The waitress stood there, keys in her hand.

I need a ride, I said.

She looked around, but there was nowhere else to go, no one to appeal to. I could tell she was thinking of the cook, or whoever else was still in the restaurant. Hers was the only car in the lot. She went around to the other side and I tried to follow, but she kept the car between us. I stood still before we made a full circle.

Just toward the interstate, I said. Something like that. West.

The dog, too, I imagine.

Yes.

All right, she said. Might be a long time before someone else comes by.

We put my pack in the trunk of the car, next to a shovel and a bucket of salt. She told me her name was Liza, that she lived

down in the city. I had to climb across, since the passenger door
was broken. My dog, in the backseat, started getting involved
with a bunch of bags and wrappers from fast-food restaurants; I
gathered them and put them under my feet. We were driving,
descending the canyon.

Strange, Liza said, how she just left you like that. You do
something that made her take off?

Well, I said, this is better, anyway. You are.

Now you're making me nervous.

My name is Alan Johnson, I said. I offered her my driver's
license, but she didn't look.

You wouldn't be hard to identify, she said. Unless you got rid
of the dalmatian.

I only met that woman last night, I said. Hitching. On the
interstate, in Wyoming. I think maybe this was as far as she was
going. We just talked a little, then she slept while I did some
driving.

Easy, Liza said. I believe you.

Part of a word, written in some past condensation, resur-
rected itself along the window. I waited, but it remained illegi-
ble, so I crossed it out with my finger. Then I rolled down the
window and stared up at the cliffs of the tight canyon, trying to
keep rocks from shearing loose and falling down to crush us.
Liza's fingers—thin, white, without rings—held the steering
wheel. I sat next to her, trying to come up with a compliment
that wouldn't seem obvious. I wanted to say she seemed like a
kind, sane person, but I feared that would sound suspicious.

Saved my dog from an accident, I said. That's how I got her.

Hit by a car? she said.

I told her all about how my dog fell off a cliff, how I'd never
especially liked her, and how the feeling was mutual. Early on

I'd even considered selling her, tried to give her away, but eventually all that seemed less possible, as if we were supposed to be together.

Sounds like you like her now, Liza said.

We're used to each other, I said.

Fate, she said. You can't always choose who you spend time with.

True, I said.

And it was true that we had crossed almost the whole country together; in fact, I believed the dog had grown attached to me, and I took her attitude as a kind of sign, a gauge that said I was right to be feeling better about myself. Or perhaps this was a projection, for I knew I had grown more fond of the dog.

Liza drove, both hands on the wheel. The softest hairs, like down, grew on the back of her neck.

Cracked serpentine belt, I said, pressing my ear against the dashboard. Could go anytime.

It's not my car, she said.

We came out of the canyon, down into the clouds. She told me it was because of a temperature inversion, the pollution—the clouds like a ceiling that held the smoke, exhaust, and cold air down.

We're part of the problem, then, I said, meaning the car's exhaust. On the left, we passed what seemed to be some kind of zoo, and that distracted me. Peacocks sat atop the chain-link fence; a herd of little deer ran along a fence; an elephant stood in the snow, tossing cold hay over its back, and then it was gone. Liza did not slow. Now there were cars around us, passing and falling behind.

I like to think I'm part of the solution, Liza said.

What? I said.

And you, Alan, I really don't take you for part of the problem, either.

Thank you, I said.

Sometimes a person will say one word and you immediately realize that you'll know them for a very long time. That's how it was when Liza said my name. I just sat still, holding that realization. We took a couple turns, into a quiet neighborhood, perfectly spaced trees in front of small houses and apartment buildings. Broken branches lay strewn here and there, piled in gutters. Without warning, Liza parked on the side of the street.

I can't wear this uniform for another minute, Liza said. This'll just take that long.

I followed her, leaving my dog in the car. At this lower elevation, most of the snow had melted away; it was only left around the borders of the yard, in the tree's shadow.

Inside the door of the building, piles of mail sat untouched. A flight of stairs ran along a wall of windows, with an identical stairway on the other side, through the glass. At first, I took the windows for a mirror and I climbed haltingly, searching for my reflection, doubting myself for a moment. Liza was also lost; I reached out and touched her leg.

Yes? she said.

Lost my balance, I said.

The door of the apartment swung into a narrow hallway that doubled as a kitchen. I doubted the oven's door could open all the way; pans hung low, from hooks in the ceiling. The room widened. Liza threw her apron over the back of a chair.

Hold on, she said.

Who's the guy? a man's voice called from the next room. All I could see over the back of the couch was the red bandanna on his head; then he turned a little and showed his dark eyes.

He's Alan, Liza said, shouting from behind a door.

I just stood there by the table. I heard Liza pull her dress over her head. I heard zippers and snaps.

Welcome, welcome! the man said, his voice surprising me again. My name's Rick.

I stepped into the room. Some kind of motocross played on the television; the sound was turned off. Motorcycles jumped up again and again, the course just a series of jumps set in a circle. Man and machine hung in the air, weightless for a moment until the earth pulled them down. Insert pictures showed the faces of the racers, and they all looked the same; all sporting little beards that made them look like teenage criminals.

Losers, Rick said. He had a beard just like theirs. He wore sweatpants, a t-shirt, mismatched socks. Out the window, behind the television, I could see down onto the street—my dog in the car, her tail sticking up behind the windshield.

Ride a motorcycle? I said.

You crazy? Rick didn't turn from the screen, as if the racers' pictures were actually a reflection of his face.

Liza returned, her hair loose now, wearing jeans and a sweater with reindeer knit across the front.

I'll see you later, she said.

How's that? Rick said.

Alan needs a ride downtown, to I-80. Hitchhiking.

Hell, Liza, Rick said. I have to go out anyway. Relax, for hell's sake. Now he looked up at me. I'm ready, he said, swinging his feet to the floor, reaching for his shoes, tying the laces. One second, he said, then went through the doorway Liza was standing in. He returned with a backpack in one hand and a sweatshirt in the other.

Good luck, Liza said.

You saved me, I said.

Now that's a little melodramatic, Rick said.

Liza, I said.

Rick stood half in the hallway, the apartment's door open. He jerked his head down the stairs, as if we understood each other.

Go ahead, I said. I'll be there in a second.

Go ahead? he said, but when he saw I wasn't moving he went on down the stairs. I listened to his footsteps.

I'd still be in that canyon, I said, if it wasn't for you. I tried to look her right in the eyes when I said it.

Pass it on, Liza said. You take good care of yourself.

In that moment I could have hugged her, and perhaps then I would not have left; she turned a little toward the television, though, and I saw that in her mind I was already gone. Nothing would be gained by dragging it out, and certainly not with Rick waiting.

Outside, he leaned against the idling car. I descended the strange stairway, into the cold, and found him there.

That's your dog, I take it, he said.

Yes.

Good, he said, as if this was a relief.

We began to drive, Rick cursing the fast-food wrappers—my dog had gotten into them, licked them clean—and simultaneously explaining how the late snow had caught the new leaves on the trees, the weight breaking the branches, bringing them down. My dog panted, her head stretched into the front seat between us, her breath full of yellow teeth.

Not too smart, your dog, Rick said.

No, she isn't, I said, defusing the insult in agreement.

All the cars around us had dark lines of dirt and salt along their metal sides, black ice encrusted in their wheelwells. The sky was solid gray, settled just above the tallest buildings; the traffic tightened in their shadows. Rick checked his teeth in the rearview mirror.

Ugly city in a beautiful setting, he said. Not that you can see it much today.

You from here? I said.

Certainly, he said, laughing. Now look at that rinky-dink affair—he waved at the temple, a small castle surrounded by office buildings, a golden angel blowing a horn atop the tallest spire.

You're not a Mormon? I said. I had been led to believe everyone in Utah was.

Oh, hell yeah, I'm a Mormon. Since I was born. You know, anymore, it's all turning to splinter groups. What would you say if I told you I got a brother down south with three wives?

I don't know, I said.

And if I said one of them's even the daughter of the other? What would you say to that?

You can let me off anyplace down here, I said.

We kept going, Rick holding tightly to the little backpack on his lap, my dog panting away.

So what do you think of Liza? Rick said.

She's nice, I said.

Nice? he said. What about her ass?

That was nice, too, I said.

You're talking about my sister, he said.

Sorry, I said. Really, this is fine. I can get a ride from here.

Hold on, Rick said. Trust me, here. Now, let's talk about Liza. I'm interested to hear your impression.

Where's the lake? I said.

What? Where'd you come up with that?

I've never seen it, I said, except on maps.

West, he said. I-80 goes straight past it, out across the salt flats. No one from here goes out there, really. It stinks, for one thing. Down the south end you got Saltair, a flooded set of buildings, then some kind of nude beach for fags—I heard about that, not that I'd know. That's all.

I knew I-80 would go west, across the deserts. It seemed we had taken a right turn, though, that we were heading north. I-15, the signs said. The sky cleared a little as we left the valley that held the city. A low ridge ran parallel to the interstate on the right; on the left, the land stretched out, flat.

Where you headed? he said.

California, maybe.

That'd be good for you, he said.

You don't know me.

Your hands, he said, and I let that ride. I asked him again if he would let me out and he told me we should go a little further. I searched out the window, past Rick, trying to see the Great Salt Lake. Squinting, I saw a glimmer of light, a thin strip that might have been water.

Somewhere out there was the spiral jetty, made by an artist. Once, in a museum where I'd worked as a security guard, I'd seen a photograph of it, read the description a million times. The water rose up and covered the spiral jetty, hiding it for years; when it subsided, the jetty surfaced, all covered in salt crystals. That was one thing I'd like to see. I imagined myself walking out from the beach, around and around until I was at the center.

Rick kept looking at the rearview mirror, then over his

shoulder, checking his blind spot. I couldn't tell if he was using it as a pretext to look over at me.

Weak, he said, pointing off to the right, at an old wooden rollercoaster, the kind that gets better, scarier each year—everything a little looser, bolts unthreaded, the rust at work.

Think someone's following us? Rick said.

I looked back. No, I said. Looks like everyone's pretty much going their own way.

Liza's not my sister, he said.

That's what I thought, I said.

The interstate seemed to have run out of exits. I imagined Liza sitting on the couch, in front of the television, brushing her hair, saying my name aloud, again and again, repeating it to herself. We drove in silence, passing a trailer that held a purple dune buggy. The buggy had tall black tires and its engine was visible through a cage.

Tits, Rick said.

What?

You never heard that expression?

No, I said, and then I saw the lake expand, suddenly visible off to the left. It shone, mountains rising up from its waters. We turned toward it, passing through a neighborhood of large gardens, yards with trampolines.

You ever been married? Rick said.

No, I said.

I knew you hadn't, he said. Me neither. What it takes to trust another person like that, I just don't know.

It might be all right, I said.

Rick laughed at that. I grew up with my brother, he said, and I sure as hell wouldn't trust him.

All at once, we were surrounded by water. Waves slapped the causeway, which was only two narrow lanes; water splashed up, leaving trails of salt on the windshield. Rick said the causeway had washed out ten years before. He said the lake never even got fifteen feet deep, that it was so salty you couldn't sink, that it attracted birds from all over. Avocets, great blue herons, eared grebes.

You some kind of naturalist? I said.

I've been to school.

Listen, I said.

You're not expected anywhere, he said. Relax.

To resist him, I decided, would only make matters worse, and perhaps my suspicions were only suspicions. My dog whined at the water. There was only one other car on the causeway, about half a mile back. Rick kept one hand atop his pack. He talked about brine shrimp, all linked together. I looked up. The sky was relenting, opening itself.

One time, Rick said. Listen to this—one time we were driving out here, going forty, fifty miles an hour, like this, and up ahead it looked like a van was driving in reverse, so fast it was hard to catch up. But when we did, we saw how there was a windshield there, and a steering wheel facing back, but it was like the front ends of two vans had been welded together. So we pulled around front, and you know what?

What? I said.

A clown was driving it. A fucking clown! The red nose and everything. We never found out why.

I believe it, I said, just to say something.

He told me the island was named Antelope Island. We couldn't see any, though he said they were there. A herd of five hundred bison, too. On the island, I looked back down the causeway and it made me uneasy; it would be better, I thought, to be surrounded by water, to have no escape and to know no one could follow. Or to be surrounded by land. One or the other. The causeway left us somewhere between.

Well, Rick said. I thought this was something I'd have to do by myself. Guess I was wrong about that.

Dirt roads forked away, south, across the island. There were no buildings. We climbed a rise and kept driving, gravel kicking under the car.

So you've been here before, I said.

Plenty of times, he said. I've had lots of times here.

The parking lot was empty. Rick stopped and turned off the ignition; then he got out of the car and walked away, leaving the door open. My dog jumped over the seat and went after him. I followed.

Rick stalked ahead, the back of his bandanna loose, flapping, a red triangle. He seemed a little more tense, testier, saying something softly, words I couldn't make out. I tried to stay behind a little, so I could keep an eye on him, not turn my back. The tiny rounded paths of mice forked here and there in the dried grass, from stone to stone. My dog stuck her snout into every hole, her tail slicing the air.

Stone's pretty soft, Rick called back. You can carve on it, if you want to sacrifice a knife.

We climbed higher, up a steep path, where huge slabs of rock lay atop one another, forming natural altars. Rick disappeared into the ground, down into a tiny cave. He looked out at me, his face at the level of my feet.

When I was a boy I found a book down in one of these, he

said. Something about the sexual habits of animals. Plenty of pages ripped out, but still pretty good.

I heard the sound when he dropped the keys, then listened to him curse as he tried to reach into the crevice where they had fallen. It seemed possible that we would spend the night on the island, huddled together in the car.

As Rick grunted and swore, trying to reach deeper, I climbed atop one of the larger rocks and looked down, over the curve of the island, its white beaches and sharp peninsulas. The water blended into the sky, denying any horizon, and far off I could see the mountains, the peaks hanging like solid clouds. Snow stretched like octopi over the pointed tops.

Finally, Rick said, reemerging, holding out the keys. You keep these, he said. I got no pockets.

He could have put them in his pack, but I did not point this out. I took the keys.

Buffalo point, he said, climbing up next to me, turning a slow circle.

Where are they? I said.

Over there somewhere, in a corral, he said. They've been out here a hundred years, though—whole herd brought out on a sailboat, almost capsized every time the wind gusted.

That was before the causeway, I said. It stretched out below, a dark, thin line connecting us to the world.

About that clown, I said.

That was a true story, Rick said, so calmly I believed him.

Jumping down, he paced back and forth, bending and then standing again.

Need a place that's sheltered from the wind, he said.

Beyond him, my dog ran along the slope toward the beach, flushing seagulls from the rocks. Rick unzipped his backpack and took out four packets. They were letters, all bound together with string, and the top envelope of every packet was marked with the same handwriting.

Setting them down, he leaned the packets against each other; they did not burn easily, being too closely packed together. With his fingers, Rick separated them a little, and the flames rose. Pages flapped loose, revealing the same handwriting—slanting left to right, leaning backward, covered in exclamation marks— just before they went to ashes. Rick leaned close, his face illuminated, as if he wanted to read them one last time.

My dog, I said, but he didn't hear me. He didn't notice as I backed away.

The wind came cold across the lake, thicker and saltier than the ocean. I smelled sage, also, as I kicked and stumbled through the bushes, whistling for my dog, realizing this also let Rick know where I was. The light was starting to give out. I could not see or hear my dog, yet I knew she would find me—I'd only used her as an excuse to move away from Rick and whatever he was doing. I kept on, shivering, trying to stay on the path, and when I came around the edge of a slope I was surprised to find myself just below the parking lot.

I opened the car door and sat there for a moment, listening as the wind spent itself and started again; I fit the key into the ignition, but I did not start the engine. I'd like to think that even if I'd had my dog with me I wouldn't have left Rick there, but that's probably not true. I would have gone back to Salt Lake City, perhaps even tried to find Liza, or I would have found I-80 and driven west across the salt flats, out into the desert. Instead, I sat in the car and thought about the letters Rick had burned. When he set the match to them I had believed for some reason that they were from Liza, yet now I realized they could be from someone else. I thought about those letters because it seemed wonderful to me that one person, alone, would feel moved to write down words and send them to another. And now they were lost, lit on fire.

I closed the door of the car as silently as I could and I went back up the narrow path, choosing my steps carefully in the darkness.

I only found Rick by his silhouette; I climbed up behind him. He slapped the stone and I sat down.

Why did you bring me out here? I said.

Company, Rick said. The moon, he said, and there it was, pale, a sharp crescent over the mountains. Our feet hung in midair, and below them the ground was dark where the letters had burned.

I wonder where she is, he said.

I don't know, I said. Who is she?

Talking about your dog, he said.

My dog, I said. Yes.

This was all underwater, he said. Once. You find fish fossils, trilobites way up in the mountains. The whole city, the damn temple and its secret rooms, the Capitol and the car parks—the water filled the canyons and those highest ridges you see were islands, at best, like this one, but right here where we are was under, too, a mile below the surface.

Without warning, he took my thumb in his hand.

That's your will and your reason, he said, then flattened out my hand. He leaned so close, for a moment I thought he was going to kiss my palm. Heart line's better than your head line, he said. Forget about fame and fortune.

Next, I said, you'll tell me how long I'm going to live.

Until you die, he said, so close I could feel his warm breath on my fingers.

Now the causeway was hardly visible; I could just see a car, its headlights pointing away from us as it headed in from the island. At that moment I knew my dog was gone.

You're going to lose something, Rick said, letting go of my hand. Of course, he said, that's a pretty all-purpose fortune.

I guess so, I said.

He put his hand on my shoulder to push himself up, then stood. He moved his hand so it rested atop my head, and we stayed like that, both looking out over the lake and the causeway, for quite some time before we started down to the car.

NIGHT

No, Marinda is not asleep. She watches the dark cracks along the wall as the furnace kicks on in the cellar. She lies in the darkness, listening for Opal and Matthew in the next room. The adobe walls are too thick to hear much of anything. Reaching from under her blankets, Marinda feels the cold floorboards with the flat of her hand. The wind comes down across the snow on the ridges, it funnels through the canyons; shingles slap up and down on the rooftop and winter seeps through the windowpanes. Matthew likes to say they live in the shadow of the mountains. Opal always complains of the cold; she has come up from Arizona, with her daughter, Grace.

"Are you awake?" Grace says.

The girl is seventeen, half Marinda's age. Marinda does not answer. Instead, she thinks of what Matthew once told her, that some things are a pleasure and others a duty—now she imagines the calluses on his fingers as they run over Opal's skin.

There are three single beds in the room, and one, Opal's, is empty. Grace turns over and over again as Marinda pretends to sleep, as she tries not to listen. In the beginning, when she married Matthew in the Salt Lake temple, she had not been sure her faith was strong enough. She did not know if she truly believed they were sealed together for eternity or if they would have children in the celestial kingdom—children she'd bear without pain—or that Matthew would preside like a god, like God Himself, over another world, and she would be there by his side, looking down at wives just like her. She believed his faith would be enough to carry them both if all this were true. She had been content to concentrate on this life, the mortal one; she had not been worried about the latter days, let alone eternity.

"Aren't you cold?" Grace says.

Marinda shivers. She watches the dim white square of the light in the ceiling, the dark shadows of insects. Her feet are frozen and she pulls them up, hugging her knees. The wind howls, smoothing the corners of the house. She is stronger than the girl; she imagines leaping up to straddle her, suffocating her with a pillow.

"Are you asleep?" Grace says.

"Quiet," Marinda says. "Keep it down, or I never will be."
She imagines Matthew and Opal resting in the next room, per-

spiration turning cold on their skin as they try to catch their
breath. She listens as Grace climbs out of her bed and pushes it,
the wheels squeaking along the floor, until it bumps Marinda's.

"What are you doing?" Marinda says.

"You like me," Grace says. "I know you do."

Now the beds are touching, close together. The girl's face
flashes in the darkness, then her fingers pulling back her hair,
then her teeth.

Now they live two hours south of Salt Lake, closer to the
Manti temple, which looks more like a fortress than a church.
They came here after Matthew met Brother Jacobsen, at some
church function. Brother Jacobsen wears cowboy boots and
claims four angels came to him. When he broke with the main
church, a few others, Matthew included, went along. There are
seven families now; the number is always growing.

Brother Jacobsen says even the true church could be cor-
rupted by money, diluted by government. He claims that Presi-
dent Woodruff sold out the church for statehood, back at the
turn of the century when they'd abandoned the practice of plural
wives. Brother Jacobsen never calls it polygamy. All he wants, he
says, is to return closer to the truth. Sometimes he bursts out
with a loud, sudden roar, to show he is the lion of Israel, the one
mighty and strong who will set the church aright. Facts cannot
explain his charisma.

Marinda had not liked the move, and she had said so. At first
she'd missed their neighbors, their friends, going to church like
they had in Salt Lake. Those were simple concerns, though,
before the women began calling for Matthew.

Can't you ask them not to? she'd said.

No, he said, surprising her. Can I doubt their revelations?

Their revelations? she said.

Can you say God did not speak to them?

And He told them to call you on the phone? she said.

Matthew had not been able to meet her eyes, but still he had nodded. She told him it did not feel right to her, and he smiled sadly. This was when he began raising his voice to her.

Your temporal, worldly concerns are only slowing you down, he said. They're slowing me down.

From what? she'd asked. Whose words are those?

I think God is trying to tell you something, he said. I think he's trying to tell you to make room.

Matthew could say these words as they sat together in the sunshine; on the steps of the porch with his arm around her, these words came as even and slow as if he were making sense. He promised that all this was necessary to reach the highest levels of existence in the next life. He pointed to the wives of Abraham and Solomon, Jacob and David, Joseph Smith and Brigham Young. Still, she had fought his revelations, she had not consented to another wife crossing her threshold.

"I feel sorry for you," Marinda says to Grace, the two of them alone in the darkness of the bedroom. "That's not the same thing as liking you."

"I don't think my mother's coming back tonight," the girl says.

"No," Marinda says. "She's not."

"We all do our part, I guess."

"Everything that's asked of us. Now sleep."

The girl keeps on, whispering about her life before, in Arizona, of finishing high school, of everything still to come. In the next room, the bed shifts, its wooden legs scraping the floor. Opal believes her popularity has to do with performance or attractiveness, but Marinda knows this is not it. It is Opal's fertility that Matthew likes, and Grace is proof of that.

Other people—in the main church and outside, also—believe all this has to do with sex; that is not true, not strictly. It has to do with reproduction, yes, but it does not touch on tenderness. Marinda has failed to have children, though the doctor said it is not a physical problem. She remembers Matthew out in the yard, under a gray sky, pointing upward and shouting that he could see spirits without bodies, that they needed tabernacles to inhabit.

We're not a factory, Marinda had told him.

In a factory, they make machines, he said. No machine harbors a soul.

He had been offended when asked to undergo an examination himself; then, once he'd passed, acted as if he'd been exonerated, as if he'd triumphed, through force of will, over a terrible and false accusation. In those days he had taken Marinda's temperature every morning, he had come home from work at noon. He rose above her in desperation, then would not let her turn over once he'd climbed off. Stay on your back, he'd say, keep your knees up; he'd even take her ankles and hold her upside down until she lost all feeling in her feet.

She tries to remember when Matthew had just talked to her with his head on a pillow, his face turned toward her. There is no tenderness between them, no playfulness as there was once. Now he has taken to wearing suspenders, growing his beard and shaving his upper lip in an attempt to look like Brigham Young. He speaks of a man down by Kanab who had an old motel, every wife with her own room, and it is impossible to know if he is joking. In the old days, he says, all the wives had their own

---

homes, even in different towns, and when she says that was over a hundred years ago he just laughs.

Truth doesn't change, he says. Truth is not bound by time.

Those aren't your words, she says, and he does not answer her.

Tonight, Marinda lies looking out under the blind, across to the neighbor's corral, where a horse stands balancing on three legs against the cold. Just that afternoon, she crossed the field; she walked to the fence and looked over at the old man who lives there alone. The eaves of his house were covered with antlers, stretching all the way around the perimeter. A cannon rested in the middle of the yard; it looked like it belonged on a ship.

Good neighbors make good fences, the man said to her, looking up. What we got here between us, I just don't know.

Does the cannon work? she said.

I got no use for things that don't work, he said.

Neither do I, she'd told him, but he had not recognized this as an offer of friendship.

Some things aren't meant to work, he said. Aren't meant to be.

What? she said.

Whatever you people are doing, he said, it's not my business, but that doesn't mean I like it. I've got to live next to it, after all.

He turned his back to her, descending a staircase that went into the ground, disappearing under his house, and Marinda had watched his head go down last; then she had looked up into the mountains, at the formation they call the Horseshoe, which is shaped like half a volcano's mouth. That is where the coldest winds erupt, like now, racing around the house, sliding frigidly through Spring City and settling into the cemetery, where rows of wives' stones stand behind the taller one of their husband. They are from the mid-nineteenth century, long ago. The women were so young, most outliving their husband, and what had they done then? Kept each other company? Hoped for an early death so they could join him and get on with it all in the next world?

Grace sits up. She takes the blanket from her bed and swings it over Marinda.

"What are you doing? Keep them for yourself."

"We'll share."

Grace slides across, under the covers, before Marinda can stop her. The soles of the girl's feet are as cold as her own. Marinda can smell soap on Grace's skin, dried tears, milk on her breath. She turns away so their backs are pressed flat together and warmth passes between them. They are sister-wives, Marinda thinks to herself—that's what they are supposed to call each other.

"Sleep," she says. "Sleep now."

"You like me," Grace says.

"I don't dislike you," Marinda says. The girl is too young to blame.

"You just have to accept it."

Marinda resisted all this even after Brother Jacobsen had come to her. One afternoon he came, without warning. Smiling, he stood confidently on the porch, rocking from his heels to his toes. He looked like a singer from a choir, his hair thin and blond, asking if he might have an audience with her.

She told him there was no roaring allowed in her house, and he laughed as if there were a joke, an understanding between them. That day he said all families needed harmony, that her consent to taking sister-wives would make everything run more smoothly. He circled their living room, walking like a man with twelve children and three on the way. He ran his fingers along the furniture as if he were testing its quality. Matthew sat listening, nodding his head to the words.

Do you think my wives are not satisfied? Brother Jacobsen had said, and Marinda knew she could not ask after their happiness without betraying herself. Still, she sensed something in Brother Jacobsen, squaring his shoulders to look at her. She had read how, in the beginning, church leaders had married each other's wives. He smiled at her, thumbs hooked in his pockets; she felt the time was coming, felt the pull of him.

If you consent, he told her, I can promise you'll no longer be barren.

Say something, she'd said to Matthew, who stared at the ceiling, then the floor. He raised his face to her.

Listen, he said. It's easier with your mouth closed.

What are we talking about here? she said, and the two of them just stared back at her. For a moment the house felt afloat, a little loose in the ground.

Yes, Brother Jacobsen had paced across the front room of this house, just like that, wearing shiny pointed cowboy boots, a blackness that reflected light. Marinda wondered which wife had shined them for him; at the same time, the thought of shining them gave her a strange thrill. She listened to his words and then she asked him to leave.

Out, she told him. That's enough.

Marinda, Matthew said. Brother—

Those who are the pure blood will accept my teachings, Brother Jacobsen said, turning on the porch. Those who are not will not. He walked halfway to his car, then came back and whispered a few more warnings. Low, so only Marinda could hear. He said he knew what she was thinking, that he would always be told where to find her.

"I didn't even like it," Grace says, still awake. "I wasn't any good at it, anyway—he told me I didn't know what I was doing. I prayed I'd get pregnant, then he'd stop."

"And your prayers were answered."

"Yes."

"Yes," Marinda says. "That's the power of prayer, all right."

She tried to think of Matthew alone with the girl, and found it easier to imagine than being alone with him herself. Now Marinda's touch had become a reminder of failure, a condescension he could not accept. They had understood each other, once. They had hiked in the summers, gone on afternoon picnics with no food, only a blanket for wrestling. Matthew had run naked on the red rocks, holding his fingers out from his forehead like horns, tossing his head from side to side; barefoot along ledges, he cast shadows down over where she sat clapping and calling. She misses that. There is plenty she misses.

As the wind keeps up and the furnace ignites again, Marinda realizes that she is holding on to the girl. The lengths of their legs press against each other beneath the sheets, behind their long nightgowns; only their arms and necks are bare, the skin of their feet touching. And then Grace loosens her grip and pulls both of their gowns up, bunched beneath their breasts. They clasp each other again so the smooth skin of their bellies touches. Heat gathers there. She feels the baby kick, Marinda thinks, then realizes it is the girl's heart or perhaps her own. She wonders if this will be the only world she'll know, and whether or not she can stand it.

Grace's breathing is warm and sweet and even. It slows. The house is silent. Marinda gently loosens the girl's arms, careful not to fall asleep herself. She waits a little longer, until she is certain she is the only person awake in the house.

Slowly, quietly, she pulls the blankets away from herself and swings her legs out, sets her feet on the cold floor. Grace does not stir. Marinda stands, opens the top drawer of the dresser and, balancing on one foot, then the other, pulls on the wool socks. She eases the door open and closes it behind her.

It is even colder in the hallway; Matthew closes the vents at night. It is too dark to see the pictures in their frames, but she knows most of them by heart. There are those of her wedding day, smiling by the seagull fountain on the temple grounds, and new ones of Opal in a bathing suit, of Grace when she was a child, not so long ago.

She opens the door and steps into the other bedroom, the room that was once hers. Matthew is snoring softly. The air is heavy, full of sweat and whatever else. Marinda steps closer. The curtains are open and the snow on the ground is glowing, casting light inside. She sees herself like a dark ghost in the mirror, arms out to break a fall or to hug someone.

They take up only half the bed, tangled like that. Opal's nightgown hangs from the bedpost and her leg hooks out, naked from under the covers, thrown across Matthew, holding him down. His head is thrown back, his beard hiding his throat, new whiskers sharp on his upper lip. He twitches in his sleep, like there is something loose in his body. Marinda pulls the blanket to cover his bare shoulder. Looking over the two of them, she is not angry with him anymore. She does not pity him because she does not know him. She leans close to stare into their sleeping faces, then turns and leaves the room.

The house seems smaller in the darkness. Matthew's black metal lunchbox rests on the kitchen counter, his thermos in the sink. The pans hang shining from their hooks above as she bends to take the money she'd hidden, taped under a drawer. From the closet she takes a blanket, Matthew's coat, a stocking cap, her snowmobile boots. Twice, she stands still and listens; there is nothing. She puts on the coat and hat and carries the boots out through the front door, straight onto the porch. Setting the boots down without letting the door close, she turns, back inside, and creeps down the hallway, into the bedroom where Grace lies sleeping.

Marinda sits down, one hand on the girl's forehead to wake her; she is ready to slide it down, to cover her mouth. Grace's eyes open in the dim light.

"I need your help," Marinda says, trying to keep her whisper low and calm. "Quiet."

She holds Grace's arm, leading her into the hall. From the closet, they take another blanket, more boots. Marinda closes the door silently; they stand on the porch, pulling on their boots.

"What?" Grace says.

"Shh."

Matthew does not trust Marinda with the key to the truck. She had it copied. Now she moves toward the truck, her head bent against the wind, her face turned down. She opens the passenger door and throws the blankets into the cab. She helps Grace step up.

"We're going to surprise them at breakfast," Marinda says. "We'll be gone a very short time. Quiet now."

Only when she walks around the back of the truck does she realize the trailer is still attached. There is a dead deer on the trailer; Matthew said it would be fine to leave it there, what with the cold. Its dark blood is frozen in puddles. Two crows feed on the carcass and there is white frost, maybe moonlight, in their feathers. She waves her arms and the crows straighten their wings a little, adjust their claws, then settle down again.

"I don't care what you do," she says, keeping her voice low. She has no gloves, so she can use only one hand at a time, the other inside the coat. The trailer's winch is frozen solid and she kicks at it, almost falling over, until it turns. The tongue will still not lift free of the ball, and as Marinda pauses, winded, she hears a door close. It is not a truck door. She thinks she hears footsteps on the ice. Bending down, she half crawls to the far side of the truck. Her fingers ache and the air is too cold to breathe, her breath too frozen to hold. She cannot run. There is nothing she can do but wait. No one comes.

Opening the door, she climbs over Grace, into the driver's seat. She eases in the clutch and, slowly, the truck rolls down the slope. The frozen gravel breaks and whispers beneath the tires. In the rearview mirror, the crows lift a few feet into the air, then alight again, holding on as the trailer pulls sideways, threatening to jackknife. The engine starts and she turns onto the road with the headlights off. They pass the neighbor's house, the horse still balancing in the corral and the cannon pointed into the mountains, poised to release an avalanche and solve everyone's problems. They roll through town, past dark stores, smoke snaking from chimneys where stoves burn all night. The wind shakes the lighted signs of gas stations. Both of the truck's tanks are full; Matthew is nothing if not dependable.

Marinda switches on the headlights and they cross the ice-slicked roads, the girl moving closer, shivering beside her.

"Are you trying to save me?" Grace says.

"Not exactly. Maybe partly." Mostly, the truth is, she wants to get away from Matthew, yet she also wants to take from him what he wanted and what he has done. If she does the girl a favor in the process, so much the better; Marinda even admits to herself that there is something about not being alone, something else about the promise of a child.

As they climb the on ramp to the highway, the deer slides from the trailer, tumbling stiff-legged and frozen across the shoulder, crashing through a snowbank, gone. Marinda watches in the rearview mirror as the trailer straightens itself, then she looks over at Grace.

"Stop crying. Stop."

"I'm trying."

There will be no clean getaway—every new move will spawn its own complications. Marinda watches a truck behind them and she thinks of Brother Jacobsen saying he could feel her thoughts, that he knew she was the type to run and he'd always know when and where. Now she is testing him, wanting to prove him wrong, wanting him to prove himself right. She accelerates and the trailer lashes back and forth.

"Hold my hand," Grace says. "Will you hold my hand?"

Marinda takes the girl's hand. The truck behind them begins to flash its brights on and off, so they reflect in the mirror; then it begins honking.

"We can't outrun them," Marinda says. "Especially with the trailer." She pulls over to the side of the highway and waits, looking out through the windshield. In a moment, she hears footsteps, then something metal—the barrel of a rifle—knocks at the window, right next to her head. The door jerks open, and she turns to face the man.

"Well," he says. "I thought he was running off on you ladies. Abandoning you. I was wrong."

It is the neighbor, the old man from next door. He wears a camouflage jumpsuit, a bright orange hunting hat. His gloves

are also orange; he touches her hand and she flinches at the
roughness.

"We're not going back," Marinda says. Grace is breathing
hard, shivering as cold air rushes in through the open door.

"I should hope not," the man says.

"Couldn't get the trailer off," she says.

"Hold on," he says. "I'll get it for you."

Marinda flinches again as he points the rifle at her, past her;
he reaches it up and sets it into the empty gunrack behind
her head. He closes the door, and then she feels the truck shake a
little as he unhitches the trailer.

"I can't stand this," Grace says.

"You can." Marinda rolls down the window at the old man's
knock.

"That's it," he says. "Don't come back."

"Your gun," she says as he turns and walks away, but she
knows that he means for her to keep it.

Sunrise is a few hours off, though behind her now the sky is
darker, up toward Provo; farther north, in Salt Lake, it is worse
on some cold days, when the dirt can be seen hanging in the air.
They sit still for a moment, silence setting. Marinda looks
straight through the windshield south, following the Rockies,
the Wasatch Range. The highway is a cool blue under the moon
and there is nothing on it but one eighteen-wheeler, creeping up
a distant incline. Yes, the sky is much clearer to the south, and
now they will begin to drive under it.

RESCUES

Martin had never found himself in a place like this, in a like situation. He was driving, away from his house, cutting Utah right up the middle, and the sun had not yet risen. His truck rattled north; it was a 1972 Ford with a yellow blade attached to the front, for snow, and the blade was now lifted over the highway, angled sharp to cut and spill the wind. Outside, the low hills swooped a cool blue in the moonlight, cut by sharp black trees, climbing into the shadows and bare faces of mountains.

Cows stood shoulder to shoulder, small and distant in fields, awaiting the sun.

Seventy-six years old, Martin was no vigilante. He considered himself a quiet old man, and expected others felt the same. He kept to himself, whatever that meant—perhaps that most of the time he was just too tired to deal with anyone else.

Next to him, in the passenger seat, sat the girl. She had not said a thing. As tall as he was, she wore a long flannel nightgown with lace up the front, cheap plastic buttons supposed to look like pearls; on her feet, a pair of snowmobile boots—black, red and white stripes along the sides, too large to be her own. Her dark hair hung down across her face; strands blew out, then settled. It was impossible for Martin to tell if she was asleep or sobbing.

"All your instruments are dead," she said. "On the dashboard."

"True," he said, surprised at her voice. "Everything works, though. Have to trust it." He paused, then risked a question. "What's your name?"

"Grace," she said, and turned away from him.

While he had seen her before, many times, they had never exchanged words, he'd never known her name. They lived next door to each other, actually, and had for a few months; Martin had lived there much longer, over forty years, in the small town of Mount Pleasant. He'd heard that his new neighbors were polygamists, and he had no reason to doubt it. It started off with one couple, and then another woman had moved in. Grace was the daughter of this second woman, this second wife. In the last few months, Martin had watched the house next door, though it was none of his business; it all bothered him more than he liked to admit to himself. So close, he felt like an accomplice.

"I'm pregnant," Grace said. "You probably already knew that, already heard it, anyway."

"How old are you?" he said.

"Seventeen."

Provo glowed faintly, off to the right, and then they were past it. He had no idea where they were going. They would just drive awhile, he thought. Driving was good for thinking. As they lapsed into silence, he reached under the seat and handed her the stocking cap he kept there. She pulled it on, down over her ears. Her knuckles were red, as if she'd been gnawing at them. Her cap matched the one he was wearing. Orange.

Martin drove. In the middle of this night—perhaps two, three hours before now—he had been lying awake in his bed when he heard footsteps, outside, in the frozen snow. Next, there was a car door, opening gradually, straining for silence. Martin must have been sleepwalking, moving without reason; he didn't know why he followed, why he took the shotgun and pulled on his clothes, why he shuffled into the darkness. All he knew was something was not right—either the man was abandoning the women, or something else—and for some reason he believed he could make a difference.

At first he had followed the other truck at a distance, but once it pulled onto the highway he tried to stay closer. In his headlights, he saw the outlines of two heads. He flicked on his brights, then honked, and the other truck accelerated, trying to outrun him. They were pulling an empty flatbed trailer, and that hindered them; still, it had surprised him when their truck slowed and finally stopped on the shoulder of the highway.

It surprised him more to see who was in the truck—this girl and the first wife, the last combination he had expected. The first wife was the one driving; when he saw her face, he knew she was behind whatever was happening, and he didn't want to cross her. They had had a few words, and he could tell she was as surprised as he was; he stood there, the shotgun in his hands. They were awkward, embarrassed, none of them where they were supposed to be. All Martin could think to do was to give them the gun, unhitch the trailer, and wish them well.

Yet when he returned to his own truck, the girl came running after him. The woman yelled something; the girl did not look back. She climbed into Martin's truck and did not say a thing until she commented on the state of his dashboard, over an hour later.

The other truck had kept going, south, and he had not tried to follow. He had headed back toward Mount Pleasant. When they got to the exit, however, the girl would not let him turn off the highway. She took hold of his forearm and held it steady so they kept moving north, as they were now.

"Why did you run back to me?" he said. "Why did you get out of that truck?"

"I don't know."

"Didn't you want to go with her?"

"I don't know," she said. "I didn't know where she was going. Maybe I thought it was safer this way."

"But you don't know me. I could be much more dangerous than wherever she was going."

"No," she said. "In the end, you'll go home."

Martin was heartened that she trusted him, for whatever reason; somehow, though, it was disappointing that she didn't consider him a threat. He was old, that was true, and he'd given away the gun. Hand to hand, she would likely overpower him. Still, he was sorry to find his weakness so evident.

The traffic thickened as they neared Salt Lake City. The

morning light turned the buildings gray against the mountains. Looking back to the road, he realized he was stuck in the right lane and, so guided, took the exit into the city; he drove through one light, then quickly under the shadow of the temple.

It would be better, he believed, to get out of the truck now—driving had done all the good it could do. To leave the truck, they would have to find Grace something else to wear; in silence, they circled until he saw a shop that seemed open. The girl did not resist his idea. She followed him inside.

Martin waited while Grace was in the dressing room. He wandered between round racks of clothing, plastic tags marking off sizes.

"Granddaughter?" the salesclerk said.

"No," Martin said, and immediately wished he'd said yes. Here he was, with a seventeen-year-old girl in a nightgown and snowmobile boots, early in the morning. The idea shocked him—he surprised himself, being here—and he shivered with new anticipation.

Grace returned, and stood in front of the mirrors. She'd chosen a heavy flannel shirt and a pair of jeans. Many of her faced Martin, while one turned away. He thought of the child inside her, all the children, and then he saw himself, behind her. Many of him stood there, small and distant, all taking off their orange stocking caps to rub at their bald, spotted heads. His insulated coveralls, faded camouflage, made him look like he'd been hunting.

After he paid for Grace's clothing, he hurried her back to the truck. They were driving again, across the city, into the foothills of the mountains. The sun was a cold white circle behind the haze; snow rested high on the ridges and peaks, but there was not much in the yards of the houses they passed.

"Where do you want to go?" he said, and wished he hadn't asked it. He didn't expect an answer, and he didn't get one; Grace's silence was both a frustration and a relief. She rubbed her pale wrists together, her hands clenched tight. Her nightgown now lay bunched up, on the seat between them as they drove farther, toward the mouth of a canyon.

"Look," he said, distracting her gaze from a statue of Brigham Young. He pointed to the right, the cages and fences of some sort of zoo.

"If you want to," Grace said.

The parking lot was vast, almost completely empty. Two metal leopards stared down from the pillars of the zoo's gate. Martin climbed out, then waited, watching Grace. Her face was sharp, her nose straight and almost too thin, fragile; the shape of her body was lost in the lumberjack clothing she'd chosen; she slid her snowmobile boots along the blacktop, sounding a reluctant rhythm.

"No need to talk about anything," Martin said. "We'll just pass a little time here."

"I guess so," Grace said.

He bought their tickets, then they walked in, past the drinking fountain lodged in a painted lion's mouth, past flamingos shivering as steam rose from their heated pool. Small deer followed along a chain-link fence, looking for a handout.

"You're not cold?" Martin said.

"Not yet," she said.

When he opened the door of the Feline House, warm air rushed out. It smelled faintly of shit and urine, rotten meat. The feral cats, the smaller ones, rested behind glass; their motions were so slight, so repetitive, the cats might have been dead, fitted with tiny motors or plugged in to unseen outlets. Martin followed Grace. Two young girls passed, a morning's worth of quarters sounding from the pockets of their dresses. One wore red tights, the other yellow; both had blond hair in messy braids, coming undone, and one chewed at the wax head of an ape she'd just bought from the Mold-A-Rama machine. Grace turned to watch them go.

The cage of the mountain lions was full of tractor tires, slashed to pieces, teeth-pocked plastic balls.

"Try to appear larger than you are," Grace said. "That's what the warning signs always said, down where I'm from. For mountain lions."

"Good advice," Martin said. "That'll cover most situations."

The big cats' ears jerked and their eyes went wide, then narrowed at the flash of the photo booth, which he had not noticed. Four pictures for a dollar, it said along one side. The drawn curtain hid the head and shoulders of the person inside; all that was visible were two hands resting on knees, a pair of worn combat boots on the floor. Martin suddenly felt an urge to have his picture taken with Grace, to be close together in the booth and then hold the four black and white exposures of their faces, faces caught in time. He would like her to sit on his lap, like to feel the weight of her thighs atop his own, her feet dangling around his ankles as she leaned back, closer, trying to fit both of their faces into the frame.

Now she was looking at him; she turned away as he noticed it, and he was repulsed by himself, surprised by the nature of his thoughts.

"Look," she said.

She stood in front of the tigers' cage. They paced, always turning exactly the same way, as if hypnotized or asleep; their tails pulled the air behind them into a current that spun around and around again, back and forth across the cage. Grace had her back turned to the tigers; she faced a glass case that held another big cat. Beneath the case, it said SHASTA, THE LIGER.

Martin leaned closer. Shasta looked pretty much like a lioness, he guessed, or a tiger without stripes. Her mouth was set between a snarl and a smile; a spiderweb spanned her teeth, motionless for lack of breath, and a hidden wire held her tail aloft. She stood transfixed, in mid-stride, as if surprised to find herself encased, as if she didn't know she was no longer alive.

"Read the plaque," Grace said, and Martin stepped back to do so:

"SHASTA" THE LIGER
May 6, 1948–July 12, 1972

Born at Hogle Zoo to "Huey," a male Lion and "Daisy," a female Bengal Tiger. This unique animal, the only Liger to be born and reach maturity in the United States, could not have occurred in nature since the ranges of the Lion (Africa) and Tiger (Asia) do not coincide. While a zoo is not normally the place to view mounted specimens, she is placed here on permanent display so that you and all future visitors will know that there indeed was such an animal.

Martin looked back to Shasta, and it was only then, in the reflection, that he noticed the man standing behind him and Grace. Martin turned, and the man smiled at him.

"That's something now, isn't it?" the man said.

"Yes," Martin said.

The man stepped closer. His face was red, puffy and lined, his eyes buried. Gray whiskers hid his weak chin, the dewlaps

along his neck. His mackinaw was frayed at the cuffs; his pants
were dirty, worn-out brown duck.

"Well," he said, leaning on the case. "Hell, there's only one
of them, so it makes sense they'd get the best guy to do it.
Taxidermy. I do a little myself—just an amateur, of course, you
know, got lots to learn."

Martin turned, as if to go, but he saw then that Grace was
listening, almost smiling, as the man went on, waving his arms,
his voice low and dramatic. Martin was tired; he welcomed the
distraction, the shift in Grace's attention.

"You see," the man was saying. "Hardest thing is to paint
this faded skin around the lips and eyes, and all that's perfect.
Heard about this liger from a man who cut my hair this morning—barbers can always be counted on for a conversation. I like
to talk sometimes; company, you know."

There was something soothing, mesmeric, in the way the
tigers paced. Then they began to roar, disinterestedly almost, as
if it were required. Loose skin swayed beneath their striped
necks. Their teeth were yellow, the points worn down.

"They're roaring at us," Grace said.

"No," said the man, pointing to Shasta. "They're roaring at
her. Look at her! She torments them every day, you know—she
won't respond, she never moves, she looks like a lion and like a
tiger and she looks like neither. Beautiful!" The man walked
around the glass case, shaking his head. "A lazy taxidermist will
overconcentrate on the show side, hide the stitches, all the mis-
takes on the off side. Not this guy."

Martin nodded to Grace, who smiled at him. They began to
walk away, back in the direction they'd come.

"Take care," the man said behind them. "Real nice talking to
you."

"Well," Martin said to Grace.

"Wow," she said, her voice low.

They passed the black leopard's cage, its spots visible only in the moments it turned, then under another display, objects behind glass. MUSEUM OF HUMAN STUPIDITY, the sign said above an array of coins and aluminum cans, five different knives, dolls' heads, arms and legs, shoes and laces, tampons, broken glass, razorblades. These had all been found in the animals' cages and pens. Farther along, the two girls were pacing back and forth with the mountain lion; they roared, trying to provoke it.

Martin opened the door, and Grace passed through, outside. In the sunlight, it was not so cold. Giraffes lurched their way around, eyes searching all the way down the valley, into the city. Martin walked beside Grace; they stopped along a railing. Below, an ice-choked stream ran through a gully.

"I have some relatives near here," he said. "Up near Bountiful."

He watched Grace's red knuckles gripping the railing. She let go, took off the stocking cap, then put it back on. She undid one button of her shirt and reached inside, over her shoulder. She pulled out a plastic tag, and it hung over her collar, still attached.

"Been scratching me," she said.

"Or I could take you somewhere else, a hospital or something."

"Why?" she said.

"I don't know," he said. "It's a place people go when they need help, I guess."

"You're not responsible for me," she said.

Martin looked out, across to the fake gray caves of the polar bear, and then the bear itself, more yellow than white, lumbering pigeon-toed toward a pool of water.

"I just said I was," Grace said. "That I was pregnant—it was the only way I could get him to stop, to tell him I was."

"So," Martin said, and then he couldn't think of anything to follow it with. He was thinking how quick she was—how hard, in a way. He had been fooled, not that this bothered him. He admired her for it. And while she said he was not responsible for her, he was, for he'd brought her here. She hadn't asked or told him to leave her, which he took as a sign that she wanted him to stay.

They sat down on a bench, along a chain-link fence. Above the fence, a sign showed how the carriage of a wolf—the tail, ears, straightness of spine—showed its rank, its dominance or submission. One picture showed a wolf rolling over to show another its stomach. Martin read the sign, then looked at Grace, who looked away. Her eyes were red, as if she held in tears or was hiding them from him. He sat on one edge of the bench, she on the other; he wondered if he should hold, comfort her, but now they had that space between them.

There was the sound of footsteps. The man they'd spoken with appeared, coming around a corner. He smiled, recognizing them, and kept moving in their direction.

"Matching caps!" he said. "I noticed that about you two, right off, but I didn't want to say anything right away."

"Why not?" Grace said.

"Just didn't," the man said, then sat down between them. He bunched his hands in the pockets of his jacket, crossed his legs, and turned his head to look at both of them. "Name's Eddie," he said. "Polenka."

"What?" Grace said.

"Eddie Polenka," he said. "My name." He uncrossed his legs and crossed them the other way—his heavy boots made this look like an effort. He looked into her face, then Martin's. "Everything all right here?"

"Fine," she said.

"Good," Eddie said. "Looked a little peaked." He lifted up his arms and groaned as he stretched. "Myself, I been traveling. Lived the same place my whole life and now I'm moving, traveling, loose."

"Where you from?" Grace said; Martin was only half surprised that she encouraged the man.

"Wisconsin," Eddie said. "Who knows if I'll go back there? Hoping to meet up with a friend of mine, somewhere out here, but now it's just me and a dog I picked up. Been all over and I like it all, only the other day I was up in Yellowstone Park, and some of that gave me the pip. They got it pretty much tamed down in there—you see what they want you to see. Rangers go out every morning and prepare the bison, herd the elk and moose, you know, it's a big show—and of course there's the main attraction, Old Faithful, jacking itself off every hour or whatever it is." He snorted, catching his breath.

Martin shivered, watching and listening. He saw how Eddie held, in his hand, the strip of photos, the four exposures of his own face—four tiny heads, each contorted into terrible expressions and grimaces, hands up like claws. Perhaps these were what Eddie's thoughts looked like as he talked, smiling the whole time. Martin was not frightened; he felt alerted, heightened. He kept his back straight, to show respect but no submission. He wondered if Eddie was dangerous, merely lonely, or at some intersection between the two. He knew that some people, after being alone a long time, would talk ceaselessly, as if trying to make up for past silences; others, like himself, forgot what there was to say.

"Ever been to the Grand Canyon?" Grace said.

"No," Eddie said. "Not yet."

"That's where I'm from," she said. "You really can't say you're traveling if you haven't seen that." She leaned out to look around Eddie, at Martin. "You ever seen it?"

"Yes," he said, relieved that this was so.

"Look down there," Eddie said, his voice a little louder to recapture their attention. "You know, if an Eskimo gets attacked by a polar bear, the only chance is to grab them between the legs, try to rip their balls off. Pardon me, young lady."

"That's all right," Grace said.

"Course," Eddie said, "of course you're screwed if it's female, but what else is new?" He laughed, turning to face Martin. "You married?"

"I lost my wife three years ago," Martin said.

"Lost your wife?" Eddie said, but his voice trailed off before he could continue, as he understood.

"She died three years ago," Martin said.

He had not meant to come out with that; he had no reason to be honest here, and speaking of Priscilla always seemed a plea for sympathy. Yet it was true that she was lost. He lived with her empty dresses, ate off her dishes, and never heard her voice.

"That Shasta," Grace said, filling the silence.

"She must have been sterile," Eddie said, adding distance from Martin's words. "Shasta. Like a mule, couldn't breed. Probably would have put all her energy into hunting, if she was out in the wild. Hybrid vigor's what they call that."

"Still," she said, "when an animal's stuffed like that, it never looks right. Because there's no motion, maybe, or the eyes."

"Maybe so," Eddie said, "but if you made them look just the same, and then you made them move just the same, what would be the point?"

"What?"

"Exactly. Now with my work, I'll tell you what I've done— made new animals, you see."

"New animals," Grace said. "I believe that."

"Dogs with wind-up jaws and flashlight eyes," Eddie said. "Squirrels that fight with glass tails, cats and skunks and badgers with interchangeable heads."

"So they're part real and part fake," she said.

"I wouldn't be too quick to call anything fake," he said. "That kind of goes against what I'm trying to do."

"Which is mix animals all up with each other," she said. "So what?"

"You're not shocked by that?" he said.

"I just don't see what's the point."

"The point!" Eddie said. He stood, as if he could not talk of such things while sitting. "The point is that it's something you never expected, brought together. Like Shasta, you see."

"Like mixed feelings," Grace said.

"How's that?"

"You surprise yourself," she said.

Martin looked back and forth between the two of them. What had started with Grace changing the subject had turned to something else. Now she was animated, her eyes bright and her face flushed. Cords rose in her neck. She and Eddie paused as their conversations crossed, then diverged again, talking past each other. Martin could not follow, but watched; the talking seemed to be doing both of them some good.

"I'm not judging you," Grace was saying. "It's no one else's job to make us happy."

"Certainly not," Eddie said.

"So, mixed feelings," she said.

"Nothing wrong with that—hell, it's impossible," Eddie said, catching his breath, sitting down again. "I don't know what other kind there is."

Listening, Martin turned and looked through the fence, up a slope to where some trees were growing. He searched for the wolves, but they were hiding, invisible. Eddie and Grace were slowing down, their voices lower. We are a part of all we have met, he thought. He'd read that on a sign somewhere, long ago, and back then it had struck him as trite and self-evident. Now he was not so sure. He thought he saw a wolf starting down the slope toward them, but it was only the wind in the trees.

"Let's go," Grace said. She was standing now, closer to him.

"All right," he said, getting to his feet.

Eddie remained on the bench. He did not seem surprised, nor disturbed by the suddenness of their departure.

"If you have time," he called out, "go to the ape house! That's something to see!"

It was almost noon. The day had turned colder; thick, gray clouds gathered above the mountains. Grace took Martin's arm and they walked past the seals' drained pool, the line of empty baby carriages waiting to be rented. The circular gate swung like two rib cages passing through each other, so a person could only exit.

"I'm ready now," Grace said.

They climbed into the truck and drove out of the parking lot, through the city, and turned south, back toward both of their homes. Grace smiled faintly, her eyes closed, planning ahead. The price tag hung out the back of her collar, square and white along her shoulder. Perhaps she was wondering where she would be now if she had not run away from the other truck; the other woman, the first wife, could be all the way through St. George by now, into Nevada or even Arizona. Grace rode next to him, her eyes closed. Martin did not disturb her until they were almost to Provo, more than halfway back.

"What are you going to do?" he said.

"I'm smarter than they are," she said.

"I know you are," he said. "I hope that's enough."

"There's a right way to escape, not sneaking. And my mother's there. I'm only seventeen."

"True," he said.

"When I go, I'll be a different kind of afraid," she said. "I'll know where I'm going, not just go where someone else wants to."

They turned off the highway, into the wide canyons. Martin squinted through the windshield as they began descending toward Mount Pleasant. When he pulled over, just a few blocks away from their houses, she opened her door and stepped out onto the road, her nightgown under her arm. She handed him the stocking cap, brushed the hair from her eyes, and looked into his. She did not linger; there were no second thoughts. She slammed the door.

As he shifted into gear, he waved to her, but she did not notice; her eyes looked ahead, unwavering, her mind elsewhere.

He drove home, then went inside and stood in his dark living room, not bothering to take off his hat or coveralls. He waited, watching from behind curtains, until Grace returned. She came slowly, without hesitation, through the gate and closing it behind her, disappearing into the house. He heard no raised voices, nor did he expect any. He knew she would not give him away, yet he also knew that, while he may have meddled, he had done everyone a favor. Or so they might believe.

Martin saw Grace from time to time, at a distance, but they never spoke again. He watched her through the slats in the fence, whispered her name as she did chores in the yard next door—her dark hair in a bun, clothespins in her mouth, she ignored him. He considered writing her a note, but he really did not know what he would say, and it was not wise to arouse suspicion, to put her in danger. Still, he knew he had done something, however small, that some light had been let in. She had seen a piece of the outside, where one day she would live.

Then she disappeared. This time Martin did not awaken— his neighbors moved without warning, in the middle of the night. He looked out his window the next morning and saw a couch resting in their front yard, on one end, taller than a man; it was surrounded by a few smaller pieces of furniture. This was all they'd left behind, the things that would not fit. Later in the day, Martin watched as a passing car stopped; three people got out and lifted the couch, set it on the roof of the car, and shamelessly drove away. They stretched their arms out the open windows to hang on.

No new family moved in, and on some days he crossed his yard, went around the fence, and in through the side door of his neighbors' house. He walked through its abandoned rooms. Amid the tattered curtains, the prints of mice in the dust along the counters, he felt strong, a hybrid of sorts, as his voice and his footsteps echoed. He found long strands of hair which he be-

lieved were Grace's, dirty fingerprints around a bedroom doorknob, marks on a wall where she might have been counting
down days. Expansive, he felt his wife above, watching him, and
she listened as he told her there were always new emotions,
unforeseen excitements. He knew she already knew everything
he told her, for she shared the emotions. She learned them as he
did.

And sometimes he would drive, to sort out his thoughts, for
hours and hours, south to St. George or north to Salt Lake City.
One day he even returned to the zoo and watched the animals
there, visited Shasta in her glass case. He found that Eddie
Polenka had been right, for the cages in the ape house were now
only rooms of thick glass, so a person was able to get up close.

He leaned against one pane, and a chimpanzee sat, its back
turned, far away by the other wall. Bored, it fiddled with a stick,
ignoring him. Martin tapped along the wall, tired, thinking, and
then—so quickly he didn't see it turn—the chimp came flying
straight at him, hands slapping the glass, body slamming into
the thick pane. They were pressed close together for an instant,
only an inch between them, eyes staring in some recognition;
then they were separate, both recoiling. As the chimpanzee
hopped and clapped, celebrating, Martin stumbled outside, under
the trees and the sky, into the wind. His heart was racing.

THE SILVER STATE AND
THE GOLDEN STATE

RUNAWAY SWISS TRAIN

Harrison wasn't much taller than Carlos, but probably weighed twice as much. He was constantly stretching his muscles, pulling one leg up, bent, behind him, or pushing against a wall as if he might move it. Carlos watched Harrison's chimpanzee, Rufus, lift a whole barbell with one foot, absentmindedly. Carlos tried sign language on him. I love you was the only sign he really knew. The chimp just stared at Carlos, right through his hands.

"What are you trying to do?" Harrison said. "Hypnotize him?"

"Nothing," Carlos said. "Forget it."

"We had a hypnotist in here once. What a joke! The people he took in—good God. And the rest of the time, when he wasn't onstage, whenever he'd talk to you, he'd always look off to the side, saying he had to be careful. Why don't you look into my eyes, I asked him, but he didn't dare. Of course, he lied about that, too. Rufus! Cut that shit out!" Harrison waved the electric cattle prod and Rufus rolled onto his back, his feet in the air, clasping and clapping like two hands. Carlos had been watching as the chimp poked his fingers through the cages at the rabbits, jabbing at them, as he found a spray bottle and squirted the tigers.

"Hey," Harrison said. "Pretty much everyone is hypnotized, anyway, somehow or other, and the rest are actors."

"What do you mean?" Carlos said.

"Don't worry about that," said Harrison. "Can't you tell what's important here? Concentrate on that, man, and don't get hung up on every little thing I say. Most of this stuff I deal around the casinos, but some of it's for my personal use, which is another reason you don't want to cross me."

Harrison always set the money down and then stepped back from it before Carlos picked it up. That's how it started this morning, like any other time, and Carlos had taken the empty duffel bag and gone out to catch the bus south to Los Angeles. The bag was large enough to hold a child; the two straps were so long he could get his arms through them. When it was full, half the bag rode up over his head—he walked top-heavy, unbalanced.

The bus rides down were not so bad. He had done nothing wrong, not yet, and he tried to relax, to pretend he was traveling for some other reason. Visiting relatives, taking a vacation. For two years he had worked in the kitchen of the buffet at the Tropicana, as a prep cook. This new work he did on the side.

The men he met with in Los Angeles—they were boys, really, hands covered in tattoos, speaking a kind of Spanish he could not always understand or recognize—never lived in the same place. He carried their new address on a piece of paper, in Harrison's handwriting.

"¿Todavía vives?" they asked him. You're still alive?

He gave them the money, wondering if they had any reason not to rip him off, and then they told him where to go next, when to be there.

For a few hours, then, he was unburdened. He took the bus down to the beach, watched a dog race the waves, men who glistened with baby oil and lifted weights. He bought an ice cream cone, soft-serve, the chocolate and vanilla swirled into a point. People on rollerskates shot by. He sat on the wall of the boardwalk in the sun, hoping someone would ask him the time or tell him it was a nice day. The waves broke out on the sandbar, then pulled themselves together in time to unfold again along the shore; this calmed him—without the ocean he could not make these trips.

The boys had been expecting him at the house. First they showed him the cocaine, then they packed it. Carlos dipped a finger in the bag they held out. It did not taste like sugar, salt, or baking soda; that's all he knew.

They laughed at him. "No tienes ni puta idea," they said.

He just smiled, wondering if he would be like them if he lived in Los Angeles. Their pet iguana sat motionless on a tree branch, resting under a heatlamp, its wattle under its chin and its neck that never stopped swallowing. A door opened and Carlos saw a picture of the Virgin with triangles cut in the palms of her hands. Melted wax surrounded unlit candles on the table. Some of the windows were painted black.

"It's not like we want to fuck with your boss man," they told him. "Quizás nos eche los animales!" They packed the baggies in metal canisters, coffee all around them in case there were dogs. These canisters they stacked into the duffel bag.

"You've met Harrison?" Carlos said. They did not answer.

On the way out, they gave him a bag of weed.

"Un regalo," they said. A gift.

Two younger boys passed him in the yard. One had green hands; the other's were blue. Their shoes had been spray-painted all different colors.

The duffel bag was heavy on his shoulders, not so much the drugs as all that was needed to hold and disguise them. This was the time when everything frightened Carlos. He crossed town, then settled down to wait for the bus. The straps cut into his shoulders; squatting, he leaned against the wall of a building.

"Looking for work?" a man said, hardly slowing down as he passed on a bicycle, and then the bus arrived. The driver opened the great doors along the side and people began to slide their luggage into the belly of the bus.

"Can't take that on," the driver said.

"Have to," Carlos said.

"Not unless you buy two tickets."

"Man."

"That's how it is," the driver said.

Carlos argued a little, pointing out that the bus would not be full, but he didn't push it. In the end, he bought two tickets. That was how it always worked.

Inside, he set the bag against the window, then sat down himself. He felt better once the bus started moving. At least being inside cut down on the number of people who might attack him, he thought, as they rolled through the city. He picked out people on the sidewalk; he wondered—if that man came after the bus, if he ran, could he catch us at the stoplight, could he force his way in before the red light turned green?

Finally they were out on the highway, where even the birds could not keep pace. The children who had been singing songs in rounds had all fallen asleep. Here, in the space between Los Angeles and Las Vegas, the angels and the meadows, Carlos felt much safer than he did in either city.

A young woman came down the aisle and stood facing him, her body swaying as she held on to the handrail over her head. He did not look up at her.

"There's plenty of seats," he said.

"What?"

"You can have two to yourself. Stretch out."

"I know that," she said, "but then anyone can sit down next to you."

"I'm learning about that one," he said.

She waited as he forced the duffel bag onto the floor, halfway under the seat; he put his feet through the straps so no one would be able to pull it away from behind him. Turning his head in the darkness, he could only see that she was thin and had short blond hair.

"I'm Miriam," she said.

He told her his name. He said he hadn't noticed where she got on. She didn't tell him.

"Where you from?" she said.

"Las Vegas," he said. "I'm returning to there."

"I'm staying with a friend in Vegas," she said. "Then I'm

going to visit my little brother—he's in a kind of summer camp."

It would be midnight before they got to Las Vegas. They rode in silence. He spoke once he was sure she was sleeping.

"You chose me."

"Didn't look too desperate," she said, and then she really fell asleep. Her head rested against his shoulder. Both her hands held on to one of his. Carlos did not allow himself to sleep.

Miriam awakened an hour later, when the air brakes hissed. The bus pulled into a truck stop outside Barstow.

"I'm hungry," she said, straightening up.

"Get something to eat, then."

"Don't want to go in there alone," she said.

"What?" he said.

"I see I have no choice," he said.

When he stood, she only reached his shoulder, and Carlos was by no means tall. He heaved the bag onto his back and they crossed the parking lot and went inside. He set the duffel against the window and sat down next to it. Miriam settled across the booth from him; under the lights it was obvious that her hair was peroxided. The two sides of her face did not match very closely. Her eyes were a thick blue, and one seemed larger than the other, more widely open. She rearranged the salt and pepper shakers, the sugar.

"Petroleum product," she said, holding up a packet of powdered creamer. She ordered the turkey dinner with cranberry sauce.

"The coffee is enough," Carlos said.

The other passengers from the bus were all sitting along the counter. Some of them were also starting new friendships.

"So," Miriam said. "What do you want to talk about?"

Carlos just watched the two men come into the restaurant. They walked straight in without looking at him, crossing right to the table; one had a moustache and wore jeans, a chain running from a beltloop to his wallet, and the other man was bald and wore a suit. They were older than Carlos, and white.

"Estamos tan contentos verte aquí," said the man with the moustache.

The men sat on the ends of the booth, blocking Carlos and Miriam in. The man who had spoken sat next to Carlos.

"No estés tan triste."

"No Spanish," Carlos said. "What would I be sad about?" He thought it might help him somehow if the men had to speak English, if they knew Miriam could understand every word.

"Whatever you're comfortable with," the man said.

"Do you know them?" Miriam said.

"It's all right," Carlos said. "Don't be frightened." He was calm, relieved; this did not surprise him at all. Under the table, he rested his leg against hers, to reassure her. This was all so perfect, he thought. So simple and stupid. Could he stand up and shout that these men were going to take his cocaine? Out the window, headlights slid up and down the highway. Carlos saw that the bald man across the table was also watching the lights. His face was sad, like he was thinking of something else and had his own problems somewhere. Carlos knew it was not these men's fault.

"You're not touching that turkey," the other man said.

"Leave me alone," Miriam said.

The waitress walked by with a tray in each hand.

"Everything all right?" she said.

"Perfect," Carlos said.

"That's right, my friend," the man next to him said. He

began to talk about a baseball game, then earthquakes. He asked if they knew about a boxing match, what had happened, and then the bus driver began calling.

The two men stood to let Carlos and Miriam out.

"Don't worry about the tab," the man said. He handed Carlos a twenty-dollar bill.

"You're forgetting your bag," Miriam said.

"Trust me," Carlos said. "There's nothing we can do here."

"So true," the man said. "Very wise."

It was suddenly much colder than it had been, as they came out of the truck stop. The other passengers were already lined up, yawning, smoking cigarettes. In the lighted window, Carlos saw the two men. The one who had done all the talking was laughing. The bald man was eating Miriam's turkey dinner.

She did not speak. She had the kindness to wait for him to say something. The bus started up, leaving the truck stop behind. The windows inside were all steamed up and the children who weren't asleep were now drawing on them with their fingers, writing their names. Carlos rubbed the steam away and tried to look out. On the other side of Barstow, they passed through the area called the Devil's Playground, past dried-out lakes and into the mountains. The sky was full of stars, hanging them out over the desert.

"Troubles," he said.

"What was in the bag?"

"Nothing legal."

Someone had been in the bathroom in the rear of the bus too long and people were angry.

"She's doing something in there," a man said.

"All I can tell you," the driver was saying, shouting over his shoulder, "is I have no doubt at all that I'm doing my job. Every single one of you's getting to Vegas in one piece, and once you're there I could care less. Just don't cross that white line. I could not care less."

"I'll tell you," Miriam said, "if you want to know, what I do to cheer up when I'm in Vegas."

"I'm in trouble," Carlos said. "I don't need to cheer up."

"Over at the Excalibur," she said. "The runaway Swiss train ride. You know, all the rows of chairs in the theater are on a separate suspension and the screen curves around you, close; I don't know how they did it, I guess they attached a camera up on front of a train in the Alps and they ran the film all the way down—but when they show it they speed it up about ten times and it's all matched with the seats so they jump and slide on the curves, you know, and there's all the sounds, the whistle and the wind and there are fans in there, I think, there must be, blowing cold air in your face and you're hanging on as it all goes dark, through a tunnel, and you rush out and hit a turn that is almost a spiral and you look over the edge—it drops straight off and there are houses miles and miles below—and you just don't stop, there are more and more corners like that, over and over, and sometimes you rush out of a tunnel and for a split second there's a little Swiss boy in a red cap, waving at the train, and he's gone so fast it's not clear if you ran him over, if you're dragging him under the train, because there are worse corners coming and you have to hang on so you won't get thrown right out of your seat into the aisle."

Carlos watched the desert unroll. They descended into the flats on the Nevada side, spooky and desolate, threatening to stretch five hundred miles north, all the way to Idaho. A cactus passed, then a Joshua tree. Only telephone poles could sustain themselves.

"It does the trick," Miriam said. "I always feel like I've survived something after that runaway train. I feel lucky. Once I'm
back out in the sun, it all seems so slow and easy. Are you even
listening?"

"I'll try to keep all that in mind," Carlos said.

"I'm trying to help you," she said.

He didn't answer, and she looked away from him. They rode
in silence until she spoke again.

"My brother's in a special camp," she said. "Out in the wilderness. For troubled youth, they say, but I don't think he's so
troubled. I think he'll be fine; I think he is fine."

The lights of Vegas could be seen twenty miles away. People
began taking things out of the overhead racks, waking their
children. Carlos and Miriam did not talk as the bus moved on
into the lights downtown.

"Glitter Gulch," the driver said, sounding like he could not
drive another block.

Carlos reached down and spun the dusty brass rings at the
ankles of his boots, and then he stood. He felt heavier even than
if he still had the duffel bag on his back. His shoulders hurt and
his mouth was dry. He could feel Miriam close behind him in
the aisle, getting ready to say something.

Outside, they stood and watched people pull their luggage
from the side of the bus and drag it away, off to their lives.

"The lights," Carlos said.

"You coming with me?" she said.

"There are some things I have to do."

"Why am I worried about you?" she said.

"That I don't know."

She wrote a phone number on a scrap of paper and handed it
to Carlos. He put it in his pocket.

"If you need a place to stay," she said. "Or whatever."

"Or whatever," Carlos said. "Thank you." He watched Miriam go—she did not turn around and look back—and then he went straight through the closest doors and found himself inside the Palomino.

Everywhere he turned, there were mirrors. He straightened his collar and turned around again. His hair was sticking up on one side, from resting his head against the window in the bus. Through the darkened glass doors behind him, all he could see were the red lights reflecting on the street, cars coming and going.

When the doors opened, he heard the men calling: "Totally free, totally nude, totally free, hey guy, hey friend, totally nude—"

Carlos wondered if when the men talked in their sleep, this was what they said.

"Take your time," a woman's voice said. "Take a little time to get comfortable." He could not tell where she was hiding.

Words in red and blue neon rested atop doorways further back. TABLE DANCING. FANTASY BOOTHS. There were posters set behind glass, cartoon stars and firecrackers covering the women's nipples, between their legs. They were kissing each other, snarls on their faces, licking brass poles. He walked a little farther inside, looking for a phone. Behind curtains he heard cries and panting, blurred voices in a language he did not know, all these sounds over a high-pitched buzzing. Blue light flickered along the edges of the curtains, onto the ceiling.

He sat down in a booth, trying to get his bearings. The folds of a black curtain pressed against the other side of the glass screen. He leaned his ear against the glass—it was plastic, really, covered in tiny scratches—and could hear nothing. Men's shoes passed beneath the curtains, outside the booth. If there was a real girl behind the screen, as it promised outside the booth, she would have realized something was wrong by now. She would have checked. Carlos felt a little cheated, though mostly he was happy to know there was not a woman who spent her nights waiting to take her clothes off a quarter at a time.

He sat there until his feet had fallen asleep. He was still not sure what to do. Now someone was waiting for the booth. He did not try to look the man in the eyes as he stepped back into the lobby.

"Take a little time to get comfortable," the woman's voice told him.

"Another satisfied customer!" the hawkers said, pointing to him as he came outside.

All the colors were at odds, trying to overpower each other. Down the street, a thirty-foot lighted showgirl kicked her leg. Carlos knew it would be smart to run, but he wanted to show Harrison that he did not have the cocaine, that it was he, Carlos, who had been taken. He tried a pay phone, but there was no answer. All he wanted was to tell the truth. Halfway across the street, a man reached out and took hold of his arm.

"I need your help for something," he said.

"No," said Carlos. He kept walking. At the bus stop, he searched for a schedule.

"Ride?" a cabdriver said.

"I need the shuttle to the strip."

"No winners ride the bus. I can promise you that."

In his pocket, Carlos felt the two bus tickets, the twenty-dollar bill, Miriam's phone number. He opened the door of the cab and sat in the back.

"It'll be a great night," the driver said. "There's still plenty left."

They went up a ramp, onto the freeway, in and out between other cars and the people inside them.

"You're not a talker," the driver said, back out on the freeway.

Carlos looked at the square photograph on the license stuck to the windshield. It did not seem like the same man, though now he was turned around and it was hard to remember his face in the red lights outside the Palomino. Carlos slid across the backseat to get a better angle. No, it was not the same man at all.

"Here," he said, climbing out of the cab without waiting for his change.

Outside Circus Circus, he passed the line of plaster figures, pale and white—a lion, a seal with its ball, a man balancing on one hand—and above them the neon clown, over a hundred feet tall, his lollipop as big as a car and spinning its circles, the center aimed right at Carlos.

He kept moving, through the doors, through the rows of slot and keno machines, past the gambling pit, the blackjack dealers in their pink vests and the sound of money, jackpots and the change-counting machines that would not stop. Above, there were children's voices. That was the difference between downtown and here on the strip. Carlos found the stairs.

"No, none of this is rigged," one of the game operators was saying to a parent. "Yes I could do it, but I don't want to give anything away. It's just a game, after all. Three tickets!"

Cheap music rose from the stage. The organist was half asleep and the drummer had nothing but a snare and a high hat. The show was just starting.

There was no room for horses, elephants, or giraffes. All the animals moved as if they were familiar with the whip; the flaming hoops were huge, held only a foot off the floor, and the tigers—bending their hind legs, haunches low in anticipation—just walked through them. They seemed too small to be real tigers, but perhaps that was only in comparison to Harrison.

Now that he saw Harrison, Carlos realized it might have been better to run, after all, but he knew Harrison had seen him and it was much too late. There weren't many people in the crowd, no one else between the ages of fifteen and fifty. Above the circus music, there was always the sound of coins falling, everywhere, as if it were recorded and played from hidden speakers.

The catch of the act was that Harrison—or Renard, as he was known—was supposed to be able to understand the animals and to speak to them. His barks and growls all sounded like threats to Carlos.

The whole time, Rufus was capering around the perimeter, wearing a tuxedo and a top hat tied around his chin. Circling faster and faster, the chimpanzee suddenly flew off the stage, careened down the aisle on all fours, turned, and reversed his flight. People stood, then sat back down when they saw he was safely on the stage again.

At the end of the show, Carlos walked down the aisle. Harrison waited for him, getting impatient as an elderly couple tried to talk to him, wanting to compliment the show.

"You may not believe this," he told them, "but I do it for the money. They actually pay me."

Two men were putting covers over the cages. Rufus, noticing Carlos, pulled back his lips to show his teeth in a kind of smile.

"Whatever it is," Harrison said to Carlos. "You know we're not going to talk about it here." He held a finger to his lips. "I got another show yet, so you have a little time to consider what you're going to tell me."

"I didn't do anything wrong," Carlos said.

"Wait downstairs."

Carlos turned and saw the security guard was standing close behind him, reaching out an arm.

"I'm coming," Carlos said. "You don't have to hold me."

They walked to the elevator. The guard put a key in the door, turned it, and they waited. The guard was still watching Harrison, Carlos noticed, for signals.

"Tranquilo," he said.

"I'm not doing anything," Carlos said. "Nada."

The door opened and the guard pushed Carlos into the elevator. He did not follow. A clown with yarn for hair stepped out of the way. They began to descend.

"Mind your own business," the clown said. When the door opened, he pushed Carlos out. Two little girls, pale like they'd never seen the sun, got into the elevator. The door closed and they were gone.

Sweating pipes snaked overhead, through holes in the walls, above doors that opened everywhere, into long hallways that were full of more doors. Carlos walked past a target with five knives sticking from the bull's-eye. Voices echoed, words coming apart, knives or swords being sharpened. The heels of his boots reverberated in all directions.

In a corner, Carlos saw an acrobat, a young man, peel off his costume and stand shivering for a moment before pulling on a dirty t-shirt and a pair of jeans.

"Hello," Carlos said.

"How you doing?" the young man said. "What are you doing down here?"

"Waiting for the animal trainer."

"Don't know him." The acrobat hung his costume on a rolling rack and pushed the whole thing against the wall. "Beautiful night out there, I bet. Going out in the desert with some friends, wait for the sunrise."

"Nice to meet you," Carlos said.

"You bet. Take care now."

Around the corner, Carlos found Harrison's space. A few small animals that hadn't been in the show slept in their cages; one tiger lay flat, asleep or dead. Carlos sat down on a weight bench held together by duct tape. The weights were cylinders of concrete, their red plastic shells cracking and peeling away. He tried to pick up a dumbbell and couldn't get it off the floor.

Standing, he put his hands in his pockets. If he got to Miriam, he thought, he could sleep safe and warm and no one would know how to find him. Maybe he would not go to work at the Tropicana in the morning; maybe he never would again. There was no reason he couldn't try something new. Then he remembered it had been Miriam who had convinced him to get out of the bus at Barstow. The number she gave him could be false, but she had said she was worried for him. She had told him about the runaway train.

He had not heard footsteps, no voices, yet suddenly the animals went wild, running back and forth, shaking the wire mesh of their cages. Too late he smelled the rotten vegetables and sour milk. He could not move, his ankles held firm, fingers around them; unable to keep his balance, he fell slowly backward, sitting down on the concrete floor. Rufus wheeled around to face him, on all fours, at the same level. In one of his long, primate hands he held Carlos's wrists together, useless; the prehensile feet were once again locked on to his ankles. The chimpanzee leaned closer, their eyes on each other's. Then, with his free hand, he reached out to touch Carlos's face.

WILDERNESS

Something was not right and there was nothing Marinda could do to find out what it was or to change it. Outside in the darkness the cats wailed, crying and answering each other. She leaned against the wall, listening. The cats might be playing, fighting or mating—all she knew was she liked the sound. Knots had been knocked from the planks in the wall behind her head, and corks plugged the holes; she wondered if a gust of wind might shoot them like bullets across the room. The opposite wall was pockmarked, as if this had happened before, and strips of wallpaper hung away, revealing pieces of a mural someone had once painted there. Dune buggies and motorcycles, girls in bikinis.

The cats cried out, an arching call. Marinda took a dried fish from the bag—Randy had bought them in bulk, thousands and thousands. The fish was thin and sharp; it slowly softened in her mouth. She did not know what they did with the bones, the Orientals who packaged these things. She listened to the cats. Pigs' dicks were like corkscrews, whales' were nine feet long, and cats' had barbs on them. If that was true, it was a wonder there were so many kittens in the world.

It was possible the cats were being tortured by the girls, but there was no way the girls could escape. Marinda looked at the door that led into the long room of bunks where they slept. There were only three of them now, and there was no place for them to go even if they did escape. Daniel sometimes talked about the delinquent triad: slow learning, love of fire, animal torture. Most every child she'd ever met was guilty of the latter two, and Marinda suspected the quick learners would only be more sophisticated with the fire and the animals.

She watched the girls and Daniel had the boys. They worked for Randy, trying to straighten out children whose parents believed or suspected they had gone astray. The children were sent out into the slickrock for three weeks, into the desert, after a week here with her and Daniel. Any disobedience and they started over; there was no hope of being sent home. On the trips the children were not allowed to talk to each other. Fighting was not tolerated. They were blindfolded if they fought, hands duct-taped behind them, and forced to hike like that. Even touching anyone else was not permitted. It was easy enough to get out of the habit.

Halfway through they were allowed to start talking to each other, but they were never allowed to touch. In those silent early days they were forced to eat alone, also, encouraged to believe some might get more or better food than the others. Randy liked to get them thinking. Out in the slickrock, she had been told, the children ate lizards, any plant, litters of baby mice.

Marinda could do nothing but wait. She touched the hook and eye lock on the door, thin as a wishbone. Everywhere out in the darkness was the desert, the scrub and sage and slickrock, the plateaus, ghost towns and reservations, the Grand Canyon and all that foolishness. Nothing out there for you, Randy told her when she first arrived. White thing like you won't last, and believe me those braves aren't after your scalp. She'd come from Utah, escaping a marriage that had gone very wrong. While she had been childless, she was making up for it now—the girls arrived fully born, and with real problems, ripe for her to help them if she could only figure out how.

Marinda stood and looked across at the lighted window in the house fifty yards away. Helen stood washing dishes, looking out. Marinda waved from her own lighted window, but Helen must have been watching something else. Theirs were the only houses for miles.

Marinda wondered where Daniel and Randy were, if they were having any luck. Squinting, she could just make out the dark shape of the barn, the top rail of the fence, the corral where the three of them had met that morning.

She had gotten there first. Randy's van was back; he'd returned in the middle of the night and tacked a note to her door, calling the meeting. He'd been halfway to Reno when he turned around, on his way to pick up some terrified shoplifter, some misunderstood child. That boy would have to be left for another time.

The van had green numbers painted on the sides, backward across the hood, even on the roof; they meant nothing, but they looked impressive and official. Randy used it to go get the children. He snatched them from their beds without warning, as their parents watched. A couple times the poor children of rich parents had been delivered by helicopter, set down in the sage. Randy loved that. He jumped out and stayed low under the blade, pretending he was back in Korea.

The corral was all broken down. Waiting, Marinda had looked across at the wall of her house, the side where all the paint had been whipped away. Daniel came up behind and put his arm around her. She smiled at him; they didn't need to say anything. The sun burned mist from the ridge, thawed snakes and warmed the back of her jacket. Her three girls were sitting separately, in a triangle fifty feet apart from each other. They had each found their own patch of sunlight and were writing in their journals, all dressed in army surplus and combat boots. The clothes they came in were washed and taken away, sold to a secondhand store.

"You look worried," she said to Daniel.

"Ever have the feeling something's going to happen?"

"I'm not surprised when things happen," she said. "If that's what you mean."

Randy came over the ridge, caught by the sun, walking toward them. He lived in a tent up there, somewhere; Marinda had never seen it, though he'd offered to show her. He took his time down the slope, stopping to say something to each of the girls—no doubt some sort of warning or threat. My hands are not tied, he'd say. Your parents are paying us to straighten you out. They are paying me, believe it or not, to do whatever I see fit.

He climbed into the corral, turned up the earflaps of his cap. He wore a full suit of long underwear and the legs hung outside his pants behind him, atrophied and forgotten. Randy prided himself on dressing the same, regardless of where he was or where he was going; he acted the same, as well—all strut and warning, all challenge—and there was something admirable in the consistency.

"Well," he said. "What we got here on our hands is a potential situation."

"Sorry to call," Daniel said. "Your guys leading the trip wouldn't talk to me. Had to be you. I wasn't sure what to do."

"Did the right thing," said Randy.

"Hope I'm overreacting."

"Well, I'm here now," Randy said. "We can't let this slow us down."

"What slow us down?" Marinda said.

"That," Randy said. He tore a splinter from the fence and used it as a toothpick. "That we don't know yet, but we will. Just a little, I don't know, dissension on this trip."

He trusted everything to the leaders of the trips into the slickrock, two Navajos in their twenties. Contingencies, Randy often said. Those guys, those Indians can handle it all. He had taught them to have no sympathy, to disbelieve everything the children said—the children were great manipulators, talents at getting their way. After all, that's why they were here.

"Something's gone wrong," Marinda said.

"Didn't say that," said Randy.

Marinda leaned into Daniel's shoulder. She nodded as Randy

went into a rave about how they welcomed a test, a chance to show they weren't just a hoods-in-the-woods program. He stood squinting into the sun, talking to the sky, all confidence. She thought of the brochure, the promises they made, how they stopped just shy of claiming the program was run by Mormons, which it was not. There were no photographs of Randy in the brochure, but there was a horse, here in the corral, borrowed just for that day. She had never seen the cats. Randy had had a dog, but it was gone now. Run away, most likely, or taken by coyotes.

"Other people," he was saying. "Anytime I deal with other people things get screwed up. Not you two; not this time, anyway."

"Probably it's nothing," Marinda said.

"Either way," Randy said. "I reckon sooner or later me and Daniel are going to have to go out and mop this one up. I'll try once more, at noon, and then we'll see."

They had just sent this last trip out, so Daniel did not have any new boys. That was why Marinda had only three. The girls looked up, in her direction, then back down at their journals.

"Listen to this," Randy said. "Heard it on the radio while I was driving. Some disagreement over something, some drug deal gone wrong, and an animal trainer—I don't know why this was, really—set his chimpanzee on some poor guy. Like an attack dog, you know."

"Jesus," Daniel said.

"Those things are fucking strong," said Randy. "This was in Vegas. That chimp broke both the guy's arms, tried to bite through his skull. No one could figure it out at first, because no one saw it happen. Somewhere around Circus Circus. No one

could understand what this guy was talking about, once he came
to, and the wounds were so strange. Arms were broken in about
ten places."

"What happened then?" Daniel said.

"With what?"

"The chimpanzee. How did they figure it out?"

"Oh," said Randy. "That's all I know." He smiled. "They
figured it out, though." He squatted down, took hold of the legs
of his long underwear as if surprised, and tied them around his
waist. "I like meeting outside like this," he said. "Don't tell me
you don't feel the walls closing in sometimes."

"Like 'The Murders in the Rue Morgue,' " Daniel said.
"Poe."

"What?"

"Nothing. Just reminded me of a story, that chimpanzee."

"Listen," Randy said. "I have a feeling that while you're
thinking about all this I'll be getting to the action part, as usual,
so why don't you go get your stuff together? We might be gone
overnight. We might not be gone at all, but I want you ready."

When Daniel had left the corral, Randy looked at Marinda,
standing close. He paused, as if deciding what to tell her.

"What would you think if I grew a beard?" he finally said.

"Go ahead and grow a beard," she said.

Once, only days after Marinda came to work for Randy, he had
turned to her and asked, Like to get laid? and she said, If that's a
question, yes; if it's an offer, no. Since then they had mostly
gotten along. She remembered all the moves he taught her—

how to use someone's strength against them, how to take a wrist and bend an arm back, how to take someone to the floor. Marinda was strong, but he had her down in an instant, his knee in the small of her back. Now you try, he'd said. That seemed like a long time ago.

She checked the lighted window again, but now it was empty. Helen had moved farther back, somewhere in the house. She would not have gone anywhere; she had to be near the walkie-talkie and the phone, in case there was any news.

Marinda had no phone. The dust was thick in her house. Up above, a fan was nailed so it stuck out sideways, but she had never turned it on. She did not care about the dust and she did not fear the hanta virus. Only one beam was dusted, and the joists clear above; she'd taken a broom to the small place where her head rose when she did pull-ups, to keep the spiderwebs from her hair. Now she jumped up and did a few, then changed her grip and did another set. She dropped gently to the floor, careful not to wake the girls. Standing still, the blood going in her ears, she looked down at the scuffed toes of her boots. She'd seen the girls drag their feet while hiking, to try to get their boots to look the same. She was careful what she showed them of herself.

Now she leaned close to the door where they were sleeping. These girls had been here only a couple days. Ever go three weeks without a shower? she'd asked them. I am not your mother. I'm going to break you down, take you apart and put you back together. I can tell when you lie. Always. I can tell when you're afraid. Always. I can hear you talk at night.

She'd heard the girls trying to outdo each other. How many men they'd done it with, and how old, and how closely related. How little self-respect, she told them. That's what you're talking about. Yes, she loved them, in her way. She believed she could help them, show them a better direction.

Marinda pulled herself up again, hanging with her chin hooked over the beam. In her kitchen, below, the linoleum was torn and the plywood floor showed through. She did not know what plywood was, exactly, or where the water dripping in the sink came from, anything about the pipes underground or whatever it was that served to keep up the pressure. She did not understand how the water heater worked but she knew it had coils; perhaps it was the same as the refrigerator, only backward. She let herself down to the floor again.

There were five books in the house, left here by Randy, and she had read them all. Other than the reproductive anatomy textbook, there was one about a man who sailed his raft around the world, one recounting an arctic expedition, another about a plane crash. The last one concerned a balloon trip gone awry. Sea spray and sharks, frostbite and sled dogs and vapor lock. They all made her shiver. Man overcoming long odds, she thought. Yes, yes.

She did not know how to shoot the gun they'd left her, nor did she have any shells, nor could she load them if she did. Randy had finally gotten through on the walkie-talkie, after lunch, but then the voices did not seem right to him. He was suspicious that he was not talking to one of his leaders, that one of the boys had control of the radio. If that was so, Marinda did not envy the boy. Today Randy had been worried. He'd raved about how his guides had passed the drug test. He'd kicked dirt around the corral, the walkie-talkie in his hand. When he got his hands on them—both the children and the guides—he promised they'd wish he was a fucking chimpanzee.

Now he was out there, after them; by now he'd probably

discovered what had happened and was straightening it all out. Marinda stood still, listening. Chances were, she knew, Helen had a better idea of what was going on.

Marinda looked across the space between the two houses once more, to the lighted window, then crossed the room and opened the door. She closed it softly behind her, as she did not want the girls to know she was out. Her breath rose before her, visible. She'd forgotten her flashlight, but she did not go back. Halfway to Helen's, she stood still. There was no sound, only the path the light made through the window. As Randy said, this was one of those places where you could go hundreds of miles, in any direction, without crossing a person who knew what they were talking about.

"I'm so happy to see you," Helen said, serious and smiling as she took hold of Marinda's arm, leading her into the warmth. "Wanted to come and tell you, but I didn't want to leave here in case—"

The walkie-talkie was sitting in its base, the red light on. Randy's voice barked out from the speaker: "Son of a bitch! Like we couldn't!" Daniel was shouting something in the background, and then it all went to static.

Helen turned away, toward the kitchen, and began making coffee. She did not finish what she'd been saying, and Marinda did not say anything. She sat down at the table, which was covered in paperwork from the program. There was no dust here. The curtains looked like someone had sewn them; there were magnets on the refrigerator; Daniel's books stood in unsteady towers, leaning for the walls. Letters and postcards were tacked here and there, from the reformed children, out in the world, thanking everyone for helping them, turning them around.

"It's a boy and a girl," Helen said. "They can't find them. Ran away together."

"I see," Marinda said.

"Randy said, before, that they were somewhere between twenty and a hundred miles out."

"He know which way they went?"

"More or less, he said."

"More or less."

"Yes." Helen poured a cup of coffee and then set it down and looked at it. "The last thing I need in the world," she said.

Marinda crossed the room and sat down on the couch. Records leaned against the phonograph. Most likely they were in alphabetical order. She imagined Daniel and Helen sitting together, close, listening to music late at night with the lights turned off. She knew that behind the cupboards the plates were neatly stacked, clean, that they matched each other and they matched the cups and saucers and bowls. The phone rang.

"Let it go," Helen said.

The machine answered it and they listened to a woman leave her name and number, the name and age of her wayward daughter, the reasons they needed help. She hung up and it was silent again.

"Hear the cats?" Marinda said.

"What?"

"Earlier, they were crying out."

Marinda watched the red light on the walkie-talkie. She wondered about Daniel and Randy, driving the jeep back and forth in the cold, across the dark slickrock, and the children somewhere out ahead, trying to stay out of the headlights' reach.

"Caterwaul," Helen said. "I always liked that word."

"I should check on my girls," said Marinda.

"I almost forgot them."

"Only three right now."

"Come back over," Helen said.

It really wasn't that cold. No one would freeze to death out there, at least. She wondered how long she could keep walking if she did not stop. She went around the boys' empty bunkhouse. Daniel said they were getting more boys out of the tribal courts now, that they came in with gang tattoos on their hands and wrists. These were fourteen-year-olds. He told her he could feel things slipping—he said Randy had never admitted how much they didn't understand, how little they could control, that Randy was the only one who couldn't see that trouble was coming, sooner or later.

The darkness was complete when she turned the corner, away from the light of Helen's window. Something shifted, some animal under the building. She held her breath and waited, then swung the door open.

The shed smelled like turpentine. With the light, mice disappeared from every surface. What she wanted was kept in a locked metal box, safe from their sharp teeth and everything else. She unlocked the box, almost expecting the whip to be gone, but it lay there, coiled and cool to the touch. They had gone through four since she had the idea; this one was braided black and white, twenty feet long, the tip already frayed and coming undone. This was all from cracking it against the wall of her house, which she had the girls do sometimes. It calmed them—you didn't need a college degree to figure that out, it was plain common sense.

Somehow she had worried that the whip had something to do with what had gone wrong. She was relieved to find it here; she felt absolved. Looking around one last time, she turned off the light and locked the door on the outside. The whip was coiled so she could hold it in one hand, its whole long taper. The girls from last week—she tried not to remember them, to avoid guessing at who it might be. It would be a quiet one who'd try something like this, and now the girl was out there, cold and scared and weak and thirsty. Had they thought to take water? They must have been huddling together for warmth, trying to dig a lizard from its hole, their noses running in the darkness, the moon behind clouds as they shivered, whispering, as they held on to each other and cried and fucked, trying to get warm, not knowing what else to do.

Marinda was surprised to find she had been walking away from the buildings, farther into the darkness. Some found this area beautiful, but she came from here. She knew better. There would be no more wildflowers this year. Somewhere there were prairie dogs, those little weasels. Coyotes. She kept walking.

The tents were only slightly darker than the sky. She almost missed them, almost walked right past. Closer, she took the rough canvas in her fingers, then pulled open the fly. When she let it go behind her, everything closed down into blackness. She smelled Randy in there.

Sweeping her hand, she knocked unknown things off shelves; finally, she found a candle. She always had matches in her pockets. She lit another candle once the first was going, then held her cold fingers to the flame. Randy had a generator out here, but that was a whole other level of things she didn't understand, noise she did not need. She wondered if the candles lit up the tent so it could be seen from miles away. Like a paper lantern, glowing.

Everything in the tent had its place. There was a weight

bench, heavy discs stacked around it. Wooden boxes said AMMUNI-
TION, but she did not look inside. A samurai sword hung point
down from a rope tied to supports above. The blade spun in
some unfelt wind. She wondered if he kept his money here, or
where he did—he must have plenty by now. Randy did not
seem a person to believe in banks.

Behind a Coleman stove, cans of beef stew rose in a pyramid,
a teakettle balanced on top. Marinda did not know how altitude
changed the boiling point of water or why hot air rose. She could
not even say for certain why the sky was blue, and she found it
difficult to believe that every star was a distant sun. Randy
would know these things or say he did; it was reassuring that he
had an answer for everything, even if he wasn't always right.
Every story he told turned on the moment he took charge of a
situation. So, he'd say, I was like, Bend over, I'll drive—then
things started to come around.

Marinda blew out one candle and took the other with her,
back outside, following the short path to the other tent. This was
where he slept. A stool sat before a low table; hand grenades
lined the edge. Cheap-looking medals hung from the mirror, and
its frame held a letter from the governor and a few shots of
Randy, shirtless, holding weapons, smiling with a bandanna
around his neck.

Marinda sat down on the cot. She blew out the candle, then
swung up her legs. There were no sheets, only rough wool blankets. She pulled one over her. Did he dream in this bed? Yes, this
was where he wanted her. Did he toss and turn? No, Randy was
not plagued by his conscience. He fell asleep as soon as he closed
his eyes. It was silent, only her breathing. Not even the mirror
could find any light. She lay there hoping they had water or

they'd find some, that they weren't stumbling now, leaning against each other, deciding whether to stay together or separate. She hoped they would make it, find a maze in the slickrock where no one could follow, survive for years and emerge as adults. She hated to think what Randy would do when he caught them. She knew he would.

Reaching her hand down in the darkness, she was startled by touching the whip where it lay coiled and forgotten along her thigh. Her eyes were closed, but she kept herself from going under. She was not sure if she wanted to be discovered here.

Did she leave any traces? Probably, Randy measured his candles each time he returned; most likely she had broken threads without noticing, spiderwebs. Now she let the whip drag slithering behind her. She flipped it forward, then caught up and passed it, swung it ahead again. From the ridge, descending, she saw the lights in Helen's house. Something in her wanted to take the whip to Helen and something else wanted Helen to take it to her. She could already feel the stripes.

At the edge of her own house, she tipped over a loose cinderblock, so she could look through the window at the girls. It was hard to see, but she studied the whiteness of the sheets. Two of the beds were empty. Her forehead rested against the cold glass. She closed her eyes, thinking. Of course, all the girls were in the same bed together; she saw that when she looked again. That was not unusual, and this time she believed she would let it go. She would not wake them.

So many of them sucked their thumbs as they slept, or their mouths nursed at invisible breasts. She had watched them. She knew how afraid they were, how confused, because she read their journals. They took the journals on the last day, though they'd promised they wouldn't—another sore point between Daniel and Randy—and she turned over the pages to read the words the girls scratched out when they learned of this double-cross. Bitch, they called her. Cunt. How ungrateful they were. Perhaps the gratitude would come later, like the letters and postcards tacked on the wall. Marinda did not know.

The phone rang, behind her, in Helen's house, far away. She did not understand voices in phone lines, satellites, electricity. She climbed down from the cinderblock. She knew calendars started with the sun, but she did not know why an hour was an hour or a minute was a minute.

She laid down the whip, coiled, next to the door of Helen's house, where it would be easy to get hold of. She did not knock, but just walked in. The coffeepot was broken on the floor and there was coffee everywhere, on the walls, even up on the ceiling. Helen was sitting on the couch. She had been crying. Marinda sat down next to her.

"How far did they get?" she said.

The phone hung twisting, off its hook. There was an operator's recorded voice, then a busy signal, then the operator again. The red light on the walkie-talkie was not shining.

"They airlifted the boy out," Helen said. "To Phoenix or Vegas. He lost a lot of blood."

"And the girl is dead," said Marinda. She looked at the broken glass of the coffeepot, sharp triangles and slivers. Well, now she had lost one, now that was done. She felt Helen's soft fingers on the back of her neck, the warmth of her body where they touched.

"Sunrise soon," Helen said.

Marinda did not respond. Helen was talking, but Marinda was not listening. The names would not help her, for she had felt it all coming. Now she had lost one. When she hiked with the girls, preparing them for the slickrock, she did not let them talk and she did not speak to them. Only at the outset would she turn, stare into their scared faces, and say these words: Tarantula, scorpion, black widow, rattlesnake.

HORSES AND WOLVES

Outside the Tropicana, I passed by the tiki heads carved of fake lava, taller than those on Easter Island. I walked into the casino in my coveralls, my hands scrubbed pink, my fingernails black crescents. My work boots' greaseproof soles were worn down so the nails showed silver, circling the edge, snagging on the carpet. I was thinking, joking with myself, that perhaps I could rub magnets along those nails, call the steel ball that hopped numbers in the roulette wheel—I would win every time, and perhaps then my feet would lead me straight, right to what I needed.

I walked through the casino, into the oasis at the Tropicana's center. A waterfall circulated the blue of the pool; people
splashed each other, drank frozen drinks at the underwater bar.
A girl waved, and I was sure she had mistaken me for someone
else. She sat in a beach chair, wearing an old-lady bathing suit,
with a skirt, and white socks on her feet. When she waved again,
I was certain she'd ask me if I worked there or if I knew the
time. Birdcalls and other jungle noises played from speakers hidden in the trees. I moved closer.

Her eyes were light blue with darker flecks, and one was
smaller than the other, as if her face was caught halfway
through an expression it would never finish. I walked around to
the other side of her, to escape the glare. The two sides of her
face did not match, I saw; they were different sizes, and if she
wore makeup she accentuated rather than disguised the discrep-
ancy.

Alan Johnson, she said. Looks like you've been industrious
today.

What? I said, then looked down at my coveralls, my name
right there on the patch over the pocket.

I'm Miriam, she said. That's something no one else around
this pool can say.

Pardon me? I said.

That they've been industrious.

Oh, I said. Thank you.

She drew me in like that, treating me as if I was interesting,
holding me there until I began to believe it. Bending at the
waist, she took off her socks. Lines circled her ankles and her
feet were pale white. She wore rings on all ten of her toes.

Sit down, she told me. Take off those boots. You obviously
have some time to spare.

She was right; my bus was not leaving for two hours. I work as a mechanic for a bus line that runs back and forth between Vegas and Los Angeles—they only send me up to Vegas if a bus has broken down and can't make it back. I sort out the problem, look around a little, then catch the next bus back. I sat down next to Miriam, explaining this, moving closer, telling her stories of New York, of Montana, trying to impress her.

You want me to invite you to my room? she said.

No, I said, being careful. I feared I would not know what to do if I had her there, if she whipped her arms through the straps of her suit and I held those straps like handles and pulled the whole thing inside out. I did want to see if the halves of her body matched, if she was marked by scars or stitched together.

Well, she said. I don't have a room here.

Four months later, I am in Los Angeles, sitting in the parking lot of the taco place, taking my break, thinking of her. The sun hurts me where it lights the little sores, the welding burns on my arms. A bus swings off the street, parks over by the shop, and people climb out; I turn my back to it.

In my hand I hold a note:

ALAN—YOU HAD A VISITR—
WILL RE TURN LATR—.

It is grimy, like everything I touch. Cars choke along the drive-through, radios singing out open windows. I worry the note, folding and unfolding it again. Since I met her, I have seen

Miriam five times; she is traveling, she says, and each time she returns things change a little. We start over, then over again.

I go back into the garage, through the front and out into the shop. Posters of girls in bikinis hang everywhere; they hold pipe threaders and impact wrenches as if they know exactly how to use them and take pleasure in doing so. Someone has written my name under one of them, as some kind of joke. Hooks and ghostly white outlines mark the pegboard; greasy tools tangle on the table and the floor.

My first month in L.A., I spent all day in a pit, cars rolling in to park over me—a mindless job where I drained oil and replaced filters. Few of my jobs have required my mind; the job with the bus line is at least an improvement, and improvement is what I'm after.

I put on my leather chaps, my visor still tilted up on my head. Wheeling out the tanks, I adjust the oxyacetylene mixture, then light the torch. My visor snaps down, and I squint through the narrow, rectangular window, ready.

Not even new engines can handle these summers. Radiators burst slow seams, unable to hold. I turn metal to liquid, bounce sparks along the floor, fill the seam, the new metal going dull as it cools and solidifies. The flame hisses and spits.

The metal splinters and coils red around itself, abandoning its edges. All I can see is the hot metal, the sparks leaping to prick my arms; because of my visor, I do not realize right away that the light in the shop has changed, that a shadow falls across the floor. A figure stands in the doorway, just an outline, not moving. I close down the torch and the flame goes out with a snap.

Miriam? I say, but there is no answer.

I pull off my visor, my helmet, and see him standing there—
binoculars around his neck, his red face beneath a bent baseball
cap, gray hair sticking out the sides and back.

Don't tell me I look good, he says.

It has been almost a year since I have seen Eddie Polenka,
and then it was far from California. Now he is a little more
stooped—he is twice as old as I am, after all—and in one hand
he holds a thick book.

Anatomy, he says. Aren't you surprised to see me?

It's been a while, I say. From where I sit I can smell the hint
of orange peels and newspaper, formaldehyde and leather. I'm
not ashamed to say I've learned from Eddie Polenka. Not, perhaps, in the projects we shared, back in his workshop, but
through the experience of being that cold, in a new place where
I knew no one—and in seeing what that isolation would make
me liable to do, who I'd be drawn to and who would be drawn
to me.

I thought maybe we could rekindle our friendship, he says.

No, I say. I don't need you.

There was a time.

Maybe so. I stand up, the torch still in my hand.

Working at a museum, he says. I remember you saying you
did that once.

You working security? I say.

Not exactly, he says. Was thinking we could, the two of us,
take in a couple races this afternoon.

What? I say.

Look who's here, he says, and I hear the door open, in the
other room. Beautiful, Eddie says.

Fanning her face with her hands, Miriam comes rushing

in, smiling, right around Eddie. She leans to kiss me with her hands at her sides, careful not to touch my coveralls. Her face is flushed, as if she's been running. I kiss her, then kiss her again.

Your girl? Eddie says.

Miriam, she says, standing there, looking from him to me, then to him again.

You can call me Edward, he says.

I've never heard that before. Edward. I look around the shop for a reason he should leave.

I got your note, I say to Miriam. I'm glad you're back in town. Missed you.

What? Miriam says.

That was mine, Eddie says, moving closer to Miriam. We're old friends, he says. Alan and me. Very old friends. Wisconsin. We really had some times up there.

I listen to him talk, watch him work; I recognize his charm, for I've been its object. It frustrates me—these are not two people I'd ever wanted to bring together.

Haven't seen him for all this time, Eddie is saying, and I don't ask much of him, but still he turns me down. Track's so close and everything.

How's that? Miriam says.

I'd hoped we could go to the races.

The ponies? she says.

You're welcome to accompany us, Eddie says.

Maybe I will, she says.

Miriam, I say.

You can take the rest of the afternoon, she says. You've certainly done it before.

I unbuckle my chaps, then drop my helmet so it bounces along the concrete floor. Miriam is stubborn; I know she will go unless I provide an explanation, one I cannot give without a scene—in front of her, I don't want to expose myself like that.

Outside, the ground is parched and all the plants are thirsty. The trunks of the palm trees look like they've been hacked with knives, machetes. We pass two cars that bounce on their front wheels, trunks full of batteries, stopped at an intersection. I kick a can off the sidewalk, into the gutter, and both Eddie and Miriam glance back as if to reproach me.

Alan said you've been away? Eddie asks her.

Over by Arizona, she says. My little brother's in a camp out there. She laughs. For wayward youths or something.

Children, Eddie says.

He's fourteen years old, she says. My brother. They wouldn't let me see him. No visitors and all that.

You never know with children, he says. They can be a little wild, but that's nice, too. I see them at the museum, every day.

Museum? Miriam says.

I set up exhibits, Eddie says. Working on a whole flock of emperor penguins. The big ones, you know, for an arctic diorama. Hollow out their bodies, slap in a balsa wood core—you just lift them up by their feet and shake them and their feathers fold right back into place. Of course, I'm just an assistant, an apprentice of sorts. Eddie looks over at me. My work's undergone some refinement, he says.

Miriam walks close to him, listening to every word, the backs of her shoes riding up over her sore heels. She wears shiny black shoes, a short red skirt, a white blouse like lace. Eddie shuffles along, hardly lifting his feet, his pants riding low, and I am thinking how strange it is that they arrived so close together, as if they'd planned it, as if they'd known each other.

When I knew Eddie in Wisconsin, all he cared about was taxidermy, working on cats and dogs, raccoons. Some he found and some he trapped or poisoned, though he'd never admit to that. He'd stretch their skin over half-deflated basketballs, skeletons of broken chairs and wire, the bones of other animals. He had cats with five legs, dogs with tails all up their spines, deer with baby mice climbing out their ears and eye sockets, badgers with butcher-knife legs and teeth of bent forks. He called this taxidermy, and it satisfied him, as far as it went; what his animals lacked was movement.

They were marionettes, at best, ropes running to pulleys up in the rafters. He wanted to put some of them on wheels, others jerking out from walls, dancing and fighting with each other, mating—all sorts of lewd acts. He'd tried to get them hooked to his tractor, even taken the springs from alarm clocks, but he had no mechanical clue; that's why he curried my friendship. I needed company then, but still I was reluctant to get involved. I admit I tried, I explained things to him, drew diagrams on napkins as we sat close on bar stools. I even went out there and worked with him, built the motors and fit them in— took toy remote controls and slid them inside the skins of rabbits and cats, fit lawnmower engines with hydraulics, bicycle chains that jerked deer on metal wheels, neon in their antlers. Sometimes, working together, the pleasure of it, made it easy to forget what I was doing with Eddie; other times I knew exactly what I

was doing, my hands in an animal that had once been alive, and
I gave myself over to it.

Have to know how they're built, animals, Eddie is saying,
slapping the anatomy book. How they move. His mouth is un-
stoppable, now that he has an audience.

Fascinating, Miriam says.

He goes on, a cold shadow from my life before, cast both over
and between us.

You can cut the leg tendons and reattach them later, he says.
All the muscles get replaced by wire and cotton. You take the
cartilage from the ears, then use it as a guide when you replace
it with leather. I had a whole barnful in Wisconsin. Life's work.
Of course, he says, Alan's plenty familiar with all that—he could
tell you how we brought them to life.

Oh, yes? Miriam says.

Not really, I say, trying to laugh. I see that Eddie is not going
to embarrass me, implicate me, not yet. He wants to leave that
possibility hanging, wants me to know he could tell her things
that might change her opinion of me. He has that power and he
holds it over me, delicately, to see if I can be provoked.

It's not that I don't want Miriam to hear those stories, about
those times, I just want to be the one to tell her. I want to tell
her what I know—that I've seen people hurt each other, that
sometimes I've been one of them, that the way she goes about
everything is beautiful, only always too trusting. I want to say
that I try to maintain my wonder and keep it from lapsing into
astonishment at the world, straying too close to fear. I reach out
to touch her shoulder, and she does not feel my hand. Eddie
keeps talking. Why would he be in Los Angeles if he had not
followed me?

So you've known Alan for a long time, she says to him.

Oh yes, he says. That Alan's full of surprises.

They go on, as if I'm not there, still talking loudly enough to be sure I overhear.

The bandannas worn by the young men across the street mean all sorts of things, I know; I fear I might dress a way that means something, by mistake, or that my hands might accidentally make a sign someone doesn't like. I keep my hands in my pockets. Letters are spray painted on the buildings, words leaping alleys—YOUA REMYB ROT HER. Across the street, the letters read s LAMIN AM. Manimals.

Eddie and Miriam walk ahead, side by side; suddenly, he stops, looks at me, then past me, as if searching for something.

Where's your dog? he says.

What dog? Miriam says.

Ran away, I say.

He always had a spotted one, Eddie says. Pretty little dalmatian.

Ran away? Miriam says.

Surprising, Eddie says. You always kept such a close eye on it.

Around you, I say.

Alan, Miriam says, taking Eddie's elbow. Let's get to the track before all the races are over.

We walk across the parking lot, toward the tall round building that hides the track. Other people funnel toward the entrance, as well, and I look sideways and try to figure which distant people will arrive at the same time, who might brush against me. The number of children surprises me, and the women—I suppose I expected only old men like Eddie. As we all come together, bottlenecked, I struggle forward, anxious not to lose sight of him and Miriam.

Inside, betting slips lie on the floor, blown by fans into thick, matted piles. People eat foot-long hot dogs, drink beer from plastic cups. Paintings of horses line the walls, flowered wreaths around their necks or stretching for the line, in mid-air. The jockeys crouch in their bright silks, whips like tails out behind them. On television screens, horses run races on the other side of the world, and people are betting on those, too. I hear the announcer's voice faintly, outside. High on the wall, a board like those in train stations adjusts itself. Instead of destinations there are the names of horses, odds instead of times. The odds change without warning, new numbers snapping down, and then each letter spins and settles and a whole new list of names rises up, as if the letters have been shuffled and fallen that way by chance.

Come on, Eddie says, taking my arm and leading me outside. He has Miriam's arm in his other hand.

They are bringing the horses, parading them in a circle, Eddie explaining that this is to show that there is no trickery, no underhanded last-minute substitutions, that these are not only horses, but the horses promised. He reads their names from the program—Niagara, Born to Be Blue, Spectacular Brian, Alicia's Secret, Maui Candi Lei, Burning Ambition.

The jockeys come out in silk triangles and checkerboards, moving with a disdain that makes all around them seem too large, clumsy. Trainers whisper calming words to the horses, who are taut, gaunt, far from relaxed. Some wear blinders and some do not; I put my hands up flat to the sides of my face. When I take them down, Miriam is gone.

Went to place a bet, Eddie says. You know, I've been thinking of you.

Oh? I say.

I skipped town when we were in the middle of some projects, he says. Figured you'd forgive me.

Didn't notice, I say. I was moving along myself.

Well, he says. Got some things over at the museum. Things you might like. Birds to fly, cats to climb. Dinosaur skeletons.

You should let those dead things rest, I say. It's like keeping someone awake when all they want to do is sleep. Let them rest.

Who? he says. You've been in California too long. Brain's going soft.

I am awake, I say. I don't like this.

Relax, he says, pointing to the horses, watching them, and I watch him, I look into his eyes and see his mind turning. The skin of a large animal must be rolled in salt, flesh side in, and left for a night—that's what he is thinking. He's told me enough of his methods that I know. I can anticipate. Horses whinny to each other and people shout at the jockeys, calling them by name. In his mind, Eddie fashions a manikin, a clay model. He covers it in plaster of Paris, to make a mold, then builds a hollow burlap horse that will be light and strong, that will wear the skin like its own.

There she is, he says, touching my arm. Look at that beautiful face.

The bleachers are mostly empty. We climb halfway up, Eddie careful to sit between me and Miriam. She has bet on the race, all kinds of combinations—Trifectas, Quinellas, nothing simple. Mostly she bets on the names, on guesses and coincidences.

That's the way, Eddie says. Nothing like it for losing money.

The race starts with a gunshot, the horses disappearing around the first corner, tailing out, and behind them the gates fold back against the rail, out of the way. We watch in silence, Miriam with Eddie's binoculars to her eyes so the strap connects her to him. People around us mutter to themselves—others shout to the horses as if they'll be heard and understood. I have never seen a race before; I expect the horses to move like the tiny ones in the Vegas casinos, jerking slow circles, disappointing the bettors who hover above. These are fast and smooth, powerful, barely in control. We are forty feet from the rail and still I wince when they pass.

Nothing, Miriam says when the winners are announced. She looks over at me and smiles, then past me, down to the track where two horses are being helped out a side gate. They have pulled up lame.

Right now, Eddie says, a hundred people are making jokes about how great it would be to be put out to stud. He spits on the boards between his feet. Nothing's fun when you have to do it— that I can tell you.

Pretty cynical, Miriam says.

It's like how professional gamblers get no thrill, he says. It's a job to them, like any other. Same as anything, you have to deviate to keep things fresh.

Lend me twenty, she says to me, then takes the bill he holds out. Folding the losing betting slips, she hands them to me without saying why. I put them in my pocket.

Arctic Gift, Vatan, Shasta's Pride, she says, reading the program aloud. Knifemaker, Yalostme, Carnival Wolf.

Pretty good, Eddie says. Danger tied down in shackles, brought out for entertainment, you know—animals half tamed are people run wild.

What are you saying? Miriam says, and I see how she is intrigued by Eddie; sometimes, I know, she is drawn to people who don't know what they're talking about.

You better place your bets, he says, then chuckles, watching her go.

Twenty feet away, Miriam stops and turns to where a group of boys is sitting. One is saying something, pulling at the side of his face with one hand, pointing at Miriam with the other. The rest of the boys are laughing.

Then Miriam's voice rises, high and calm.

I walked through a glass door and they sewed me back together, she says. Juggled with sharp knives and they cut me coming down. Got caught in a tornado.

The boys are silent. She continues on down the bleachers.

You're in good hands there, Eddie says to me.

True, I say, keeping him in the corner of my eye—the spidery blood vessels in his cheeks, the liver spots on the backs of his hands.

Lend me one of those slips, he says, then takes it, scratching on it with the stub of a pencil. Don't always trust the odds, he says. Like to do my own figuring sometimes. He looks out over the horses, then behind us, then at me, out to the horses, back to me. He writes a little more before handing the paper over.

I fold the slip again, put it in my pocket. Down below, a new group of horses is being paraded around.

Took me sixty years to get out of the Midwest, Eddie says. I'd only seen oceans on maps.

I just nod, trying to act as if this is expected, seeing him here.

Sitting next to him feels almost familiar, and I don't want it to, I hold it off, nothing I want to rekindle.

You know, he says, my biggest dream would be to work on some people.

What? I say.

Prehistoric stuff, he says. For the dioramas with the cavemen and everything. The taxidermists do all that sort of thing, you know, because we know how to do the modeling. That would be even better—showing something that doesn't even exist—that gets right to your heart, keeps your blood circling.

I've heard this before, I say.

To put people together so they looked right, he says. That would really be something. There she is.

Miriam takes the steps two at a time. She waves to the boys and a few wave back, self-conscious, won over.

Got some of it back, she says, money in her hand. Races in Hong Kong and Australia. Didn't even watch them.

That's the way, Eddie says.

What's the matter with you? she says.

Nothing, I say. I turn my head and watch an airplane fly between us and the sun. I close my eyes and see my dog—a zipper down her back, marbles in her eye sockets, razorblades on the end of her tail. She walks like a machine, as if she's been wound up; she lifts one hind leg high, then the other. Sparks spit between her teeth. She is no longer herself.

Shadows lengthen, reaching for us as I open my eyes. They claim a row of bleachers at a time. A group of young men behind us, their shirts off, sunburned, have been hollering all afternoon, even louder between the races, and only now I understand why.

Down below, between us and the track, the young boys are running their own races, back and forth. The drunks in the

stands cheer the winners, booing and throwing trash at the bigger boys who try to enter the race in the middle. Perhaps the
boys have come with their parents, though it seems more likely
they are the children of the trainers or the jockeys.

Look at him move, Eddie says.

The shortest boy, the one who made fun of Miriam, is the
fastest; the only chance he'll lose is if his pants fall down, a
distinct possibility—he pulls them up with one hand, his other
arm jerking through the air, his sharp elbows out behind.

I wonder if they're betting, Miriam says.

There's an idea, Eddie says. He turns his head, slowly, watching the boys run, then he stands and heads down the bleachers.

You all right? Miriam says.

Fine, he says, fine, descending down the aisle, then going
over the side, his head finally dropping out of sight.

We watch him go, then turn our heads to look at each other.
Miriam moves the anatomy book and slides to where Eddie had
been sitting, closing the space between us.

Why didn't you tell me about your brother? I say. I never
even knew you had one.

Well, she says. I just got back. And you never told me about
your dog.

That's different, I say. I look down at her shoes and imagine
her toes, the hidden rings.

Why are you so afraid of him? she says.

Who?

Edward.

I'm not afraid of him, I say, but that doesn't mean I have to
spend time with him.

He's a lonely old man, that's all.

He's a bad influence, I say.

On you?

Yes.

Miriam laughs. Are you so easily influenced?

That's when I see him, down by the track, surrounded by the boys, talking to them.

Why didn't you just say you don't like him? she says.

Because he's likable, I say. That's one thing he is.

Miriam reaches out her hand and puts it in mine. She scrapes a fingernail down my arm and holds it up.

You didn't give me a chance to wash, I say. If I had, I'd put my arm around you.

Go ahead, she says.

I don't trust him down there, I say.

That says more about you than it does about him, she says. Did you ever think maybe you're a little paranoid?

Both yes and no would trap me there, I say.

Avoiding the question's more incriminating, she says.

Maybe so, I say, but I look up from the hairs above her knee just in time to see Eddie, the boys all around him, disappear under the bleachers.

Hold on, I say. Stay here.

People shout at me to sit down, that they can't see, and I don't turn to argue with them. I go after him, over the side, hands slipping on the rusty, rickety bleachers.

Down on the ground, I look underneath, but it is dim and I am not certain what I see. People shout above me, stamp their feet close to my head. I have to go deeper for my eyes to adjust; I feel my way between the supports. When I am close enough, I do not make a sound or a move. The boys are dancing, jumping in the air, and Eddie is nowhere around.

I realize, then, that he is beneath them, on the ground. They are kicking him, bending over to strike out with their fists. No sound escapes down there.

Eddie curls his legs, he rolls over, he tries to protect his face. They leap in, one by one, clustering, then disentangle to watch each other before leaping back into the fray. Eddie cannot escape. He crawls on all fours, flails with his arms, kicks his legs. The boys are all around him, everywhere, light filtering down, the cheers of the crowd covering everything.

They do not hear me. They do not stop until I take hold of one, the shortest one, the fastest one, the one with the mouth—he wriggles away, turning his head as if to bite me—and then, realizing I am there, they disperse. They look back at me with faces full of shadows that make them look older, that steal their eyes. They stumble and slow when they see I'm not following, but they keep moving away.

Eddie crawls around until he finds his hat, then rakes at his hair and clamps the hat back down.

Hell, he says.

Take it easy, I say, holding out a hand to help him up, to steady him. What happened? I say.

Someone started something, he says, still catching his breath.

I do not question him further. For some reason, then, as I'm watching him gasp and recover, I recall how he was the only person in Wisconsin who showed me anything more than common courtesy—true, he had his reasons to befriend me, but on winter afternoons we'd drink beer with a dash of Tabasco, to cut the chill and scare off hangovers, and we turned away the cold. Those days he subsisted on Pabst Blue Ribbon and the pickled eggs and turkey gizzards he bought at the bar. He drove his tractor, back and forth on the highway, between the bar and the house.

Under the bleachers, this silence expands. I stand so close to Eddie I can hear nothing but his breathing, rasping in and out. He shakes off my hand and we stand there, the lines of light cut by people's shoes and ankles. Candy wrappers, ashes, cigarette butts rain down. The horses come closer, I feel them under my feet again, then away again, down the backstretch, and the announcer's voice still circles, pulling them around. We walk out into the sunlight.

Miriam's already halfway down the bleachers.

What happened? she says.

Nothing, Eddie says. It looks a little like he's been bitten on the neck; blood slips down from behind his ear. Miriam tries to wipe it away with the cuff of her shirt.

Those boys ran out of there like they'd done something wrong, she says, like something was happening.

Well, Eddie says, almost smiling. Whenever someone says they want to show you something—unless you know them well, and that can be even worse—it's always a bad idea.

Are you all right? she says.

Enough of this, Eddie says. What's up with the races?

I'm even, she says, and you came out a little bit ahead.

I won't ask questions, he says, taking the money she holds out. But I've had enough for one day.

His pants are torn at one knee, and he holds his shirt together where buttons are missing. We walk on either side of him, back inside, then out toward the parking lot.

I can catch my bus here, he says, and the three of us sit on the bench, waiting, all different colored cars around us, resting on their shadows. The silence I'd felt under the bleachers still holds me in thrall, though I hear the announcer's voice; perhaps the boys, also, have resumed their races.

When the bus comes, it lowers itself with a hiss, the hydraulics relieved, the doors slapping open. Eddie stands slowly. He nods to us, then climbs on. We watch his head in the window of the bus, looking forward, his profile pulling away.

Later that night—after the races, after Eddie is gone—I wait as Miriam takes a shower in the bathroom of my apartment. I sit on my bed, unfolding betting slips from my pockets; I remember the names of the horses and I laugh at our losses. I think of Eddie Polenka.

Many times I listened as he spoke of his obsession—so smooth and seductive, he almost made sense—yet he could never really admit what was behind it all. Perhaps he didn't know. I believe he was afraid, that his creatures were born of fear; taxidermy is an attempt to control something dangerous, to bring it into our homes. We want to tame and hold what is most frightening, to show we can, to ease our fears. Yet these attempts never satisfy—they deny the fascinating claws, the danger that first excited us. This is why Eddie was always tinkering, why he desired movement and unnatural variations for his animals. It is also why I must try to recollect and tell how I came to be here.

Sometimes memories are like taxidermy. Pieces of the past won't settle; they demand recall; they prick me at night and I drag them out like carnival wolves, half tamed into the present. The retelling promises me another chance, but it's impossible to hold, to domesticate what won't sit still—tendrils are always loose, in pursuit. This is how the past animates itself, how it provokes me.

As I listen to Miriam sing with the water in the shower, I unfold the last slip and see that Eddie had not been figuring odds. He had left me a note:

YES I TOOK YR DOG—YOUD LIKE TO TRY
SME THING RIGHT? YOUD LIKE TO HURT ME—

It does me so much good to know that somewhere I have turned a corner and proven him wrong, that I was the one under the bleachers, the one who did not join in, the one who saved him. In the shower, the water stops running and Miriam begins to hum. I am sitting on the bed when she steps out, combing her hair, one side, then the other. Her skin is smooth and her body is rounded and perfect and whole. She is so close the water flicks cold onto my skin.

What? she says, pointing one hip. What are you smiling about?

You, I say.

She turns a slow circle, so I can see her better—the vertebrae in her spine, her smooth shoulders, her pale soft belly and the lengths of her thighs, her bare arms. I am going to fall asleep tonight with her skin against mine. In the morning I'll wake and I'll know we have been touching for all those hours.

ACKNOWLEDGMENTS

Everyone helped me. Thanks to the Rocks and to the Vinings; to Tina Pohlman, my editor, for her mind and advocacy; to Leigh Feldman, my agent, for wherewithal and fortitude; to the many at the Stanford Creative Writing Program, for their insight and sweet abuse. A debt to Susan Messer, for her story; also to Deirdre and Sam Straight, for the clown's strange vehicle.

ABOUT THE AUTHOR

Peter Rock was born in Salt Lake City, Utah. He completed a Wallace Stegner Fellowship in fiction at Stanford University in 1997 and is the recipient of a 1996 Henfield Award. His most recent novel is *The Ambidextrist.*